T0339887

HIDE AND SEEK

alyssa brooks

HEAT | NEW YORK

THE BERKLEY PUBLISHING GROUP
Published by the Penguin Group
Penguin Group (USA) Inc.
375 Hudson Street, New York, New York 10014, USA
Penguin Group (Canada), 90 Eglinton Avenue East, Suite 700, Toronto, Ontario M4P 2Y3, Canada
(a division of Pearson Penguin Canada Inc.)
Penguin Books Ltd., 80 Strand, London WC2R 0RL, England
Penguin Group Ireland, 25 St. Stephen's Green, Dublin 2, Ireland (a division of Penguin Books Ltd.)
Penguin Group (Australia), 250 Camberwell Road, Camberwell, Victoria 3124, Australia
(a division of Pearson Australia Group Pty. Ltd.)
Penguin Books India Pvt. Ltd., 11 Community Centre, Panchsheel Park, New Delhi—110 017, India
Penguin Group (NZ), 67 Apollo Drive, Rosedale, North Shore 0632, New Zealand
(a division of Pearson New Zealand Ltd.)
Penguin Books (South Africa) (Pty.) Ltd., 24 Sturdee Avenue, Rosebank, Johannesburg 2196, South
Africa

Penguin Books Ltd., Registered Offices: 80 Strand, London WC2R 0RL, England

This is an original publication of The Berkley Publishing Group.

This is a work of fiction. Names, characters, places, and incidents either are the product of the author's imagination or are used fictitiously, and any resemblance to actual persons, living or dead, business establishments, events, or locales is entirely coincidental. The publisher does not have any control over and does not assume any responsibility for author or third-party websites or their content.

HIDE AND SEEK

First edition: December 2007

Library of Congress Cataloging-in-Publication Data

Brooks, Alyssa.
    Hide and seek / Alyssa Brooks.
       p.   cm.
    ISBN 978-0-425-21875-4
    1. Aspen (Colo.)—Fiction.   I. Title.
    PS3602.R645H53 2007
    813'.6—dc22
                                2007021400

147204767

I want to thank all who helped with *Hide and Seek*, especially my husband, whose increasing support at home permitted me endless hours of writing bliss; my critique partner, Larissa Lyons, who steadfastly found all my silly mistakes; and, of course, my editors and agent, who pulled it all together.

Finally, a huge thanks to my fans, who make it all worthwhile!

prologue

"Go out with me." Maxim held a lit match over the beaker he held in his hand, the flame slowly burning toward his fingertips. "Tonight."

His commanding voice heated Elisa—both in arousal and anger. It seemed he would never give up and she was too damn close to giving in.

And failing chemistry. She, a normally straight-A student. Which also meant—no thanks to him—she wouldn't be able to move onto Solid Waste Management and Recycling next year, not unless she enrolled in a summer class. She'd planned to volunteer in the Peace Corps.

"Come on. Knock it off!" she hissed under her breath, unconsciously reading the label on the glass container. ETHYLBEN-ZENE?

"Maxim!" Emitting a small squeak, Elisa took a step back. "That's very flammable!" What was he thinking? This was *Harvard!*

How had he even gotten in? As hard as she'd worked . . . He winked at her. The asshole. "Come on, baby. Go out with me."

"If I've told you *no* once, I've told you a hundred times. Now blow that match out before you blow up the lab."

A shiver ran down her spine, tingles pooling in her loins. *Jesus!* This was *not* turning her on.

But it was. Why was she letting this playboy affect her so much? Because of his antics, they'd gotten a D on their last project.

Yet she stayed his lab partner. She told herself it was to please Professor Hobbs, but that was a lie. She was pleasing herself.

"I promise to show you the time of your life," he insisted.

I bet, she thought.

"Now," she ordered, whispering so the professor wouldn't notice them. "Do it! Or I'll never go out with you!"

If she wasn't afraid of an explosion, she'd smack him.

Elisa's breath shortened as she stared at him. Go out with him? Why did he keep asking? She'd have to be nuts.

Though he did look rather sexy in those safety glasses, with his wispy, unruly hair sticking out where they hooked on his ears. And the way he left his lab coat half-unbuttoned, as well as his shirt, so just a hint of golden chest hair peeked through, driving her nuts.

With his hard tan body, long golden hair, and deep, soul-searching eyes, he was the sexiest guy on campus. Somehow, he always looked like he'd just rolled out of bed . . . and like he could easily hop right back in it. *All* the girls appreciated his looks . . . and weren't ashamed to show it.

Except her. She was far too busy for the likes of him. They were complete opposites and she'd made it totally clear how she felt about him. So why did he even want her?

More importantly, *why* did she want him?

"So you will?"

"I didn't say that!"

Despite how short the match was getting, Maxim lowered his hand another inch. He raised his brows.

Elisa opened her mouth, then clamped it shut.

Damn it! Maxim's request was hardly a new one; her considering saying yes was. Ever since Professor Hobbs had forced them together as lab partners three months ago, Maxim had been sniffing at her skirts like a hungry dog. No surprise, a man-slut like him wanted to conquer *every* female . . . apparently even one as nerdy as her.

"Ouch!" The flame reached his fingers and Maxim shook his hand, blowing out the fire.

He was so not her type.

But he was so damn cute. And every time their hands brushed, she swore *she* was going to explode.

After all, this *was* college. Wasn't she supposed to be having fun?

What could one date really hurt?

One might even say she owed it to her femininity.

Maxim relit another match. "Elisa, what d'ya say?"

Maybe she didn't approve of his philandering ways, maybe he didn't "get" her, but somehow, they'd become friends. He was fun to work with. He made her laugh—when he wasn't making her get bad grades and endangering her life.

She wouldn't have sex with him on the first date, she promised herself. Not even by the third. Not even if he begged. If she wasn't going to do it with him, what would a couple of dates hurt?

"Okay, I—"

The classroom door slammed open, drawing their attention. In walked Jenny, one of Maxim's many ex's, the head cheerleader who'd been absent the past week or so. One look revealed why: boob job. Her yellow knit shirt was strung so snug across her bulging chest it was a miracle she hadn't toppled forward.

Elisa's heart lodged in her throat as her gaze dashed to Maxim. He was staring, practically drooling. Jenny looked his way and winked.

Maxim's jaw dropped. The match dropped.

Kaboom!

o n e

Holy shit! Could his eyes be fooling him?

Snatching the American tabloid, *Shine,* from the rack, Maxim stared in disbelief at the candid snapshot splashed all over the front cover.

Elisa? Elisa Cross from college? Women's rights activist, hippy wannabe, environmental science brainiac Elisa, who'd refused his every advance? Advances he would normally never have made toward such a difficult female, except that there had always been something about her . . . something intriguing . . . despite the fact that she'd so accurately dubbed him a man-slut.

The beautiful woman caught on camera, sandwiched between two men, passion gleaming in her sea blue eyes, her dark, wavy hair curtaining her upper body from public exposure, made his cock twitch. Instantly, he longed to wrap his fingers in her incredible mane and ride her like a stallion.

Maxim caressed the glossy cover, tracing his fingers along the outline of her lips. Damn, he couldn't believe it. It *was* her, though she appeared quite different from the girl he remembered. She looked like a woman now, fully bloomed, ripe . . .

His cock swelled, reminding him how much he'd wanted her then. How much he still wanted her now. No matter how many women he fucked, it was Elisa who haunted his dreams, torturing him with what had never been.

Lab partners back at Harvard, he'd become infatuated with her, and had blatantly flirted, asking her out time and again. But her answer had remained the same: *no, not a chance.*

Until that one time. He'd almost had her. Then he'd blown it. Literally.

He touched the magazine cover, remembering. She'd had all of five friends, while he'd been downright popular. She'd gotten straight A's; he'd bribed his best friend into doing his homework. She'd been convinced she'd save the world one day; he just wanted to sweet-talk the next female into his bed. What had attracted him to her so deeply was beyond him, but it was different than what he'd felt for any woman, any time in his life. Something about her made him feel *real*, like life was meant to be more than the simple existence he lived, like happily ever after could exist. He liked being around her.

He read the tabloid's headline. *Lance Cross's daughter CAUGHT! The mega soap star disowns her and adopts monkey to inherit his fortune.*

Sure, he believed that.

But there was no denying the picture. It didn't appear doctored, not in the least.

Disappointment and anticipation simultaneously filled him. Elisa had despised him for enjoying sex so openly—and frequently—and often with more than one woman. In fact, it had been her main reason for refusing him so many times. Now, here she was, publicly exposed with two men?

He didn't like it. Not one bit.

He should be one of those men. He should be *both* those men.

Maybe now he could be. Elisa must have loosened up—a lot—to be caught in such a situation. The possibility intrigued him to no end.

But he certainly didn't want this article intriguing anyone else. A twinge of jealousy twisted through him. He grabbed the remaining copies from the vendor's display and pulled out his wallet. "I'll take them all."

After paying the grinning merchant, Maxim rushed through the Khan, the outdoor marketplace in Cairo, in the direction of his convertible Jaguar.

He flipped open the tabloid to her article, speed-reading. *Porn star Elisa Cross denies her sexy new career despite downloads and DVDs now available worldwide . . . her famous father publicly refutes her . . . her legal firm says "You're fired!"*

Jeez. Poor Elisa. He didn't believe the porn star claim for a minute, but the rest of the scandal? What the hell had happened?

Getting out his cell phone, he highlighted Dylan's phone number and called his old dorm buddy, a man who was practically a brother to him.

Dylan picked up after only one ring. "Hello?"

"Have you seen *Shine?*"

Dylan grunted in amusement. "*Shine?* The tabloid? Not my cup of tea, Maxim. What are you doing up so early, anyway? It must be six a.m. in Egypt."

Having reached his car, Maxim hopped in the open top, and started the engine. "Seven. I haven't turned in yet—had a glorious night with two redheads who wanted a *thorough* tour of Cairo and all its finer points, if you catch my drift. Besides, I'm avoiding the hotel. The opening of the newest resort in Africa went well, life is running smoothly again, which means my mother is bored. She's taken up residence in the room next to mine and has been making a daily effort to shove *proper* females off on me. She's got it in her head that I couldn't possibly run the hotel efficiently, not until I marry a nice girl and quiet down."

"When *do* you plan to settle down?"

"Why would I?" Maxim scoffed, not liking the turn of conversation already. Not now, not after the past few hours. Why was it that everyone felt the need to get on his case lately? He was fine! *Happy.* "I've got everything a man could want—plenty of sex, fast cars, and money to burn. The hotel is booming, I've hired plenty of goons in suits to do the boring work, and I spend every day loving life. I live abroad. I travel when I please and where I please. No female badgering me to change my plans, no kids, or potential kids, to worry about. It's a wonderful, incredible way to live, I swear. I'll never understand why you settled down and—"

"You sound like your trying to sell bachelorism to me," Dylan jested. "Is someone getting slightly bored?"

Maxim gripped his steering wheel, feeling like slamming down on the pedal and speeding away from the truth. Losing interest, he'd actually shortened his evening with the twins last night and had spent the early morning hours roaming the dirty streets of Cairo, thinking about the *future*. He kept telling himself he must be getting a cold, but in truth, lately every single day, every single woman, seemed the same.

Releasing a pent-up breath, Maxim answered, "Maybe."

He'd never admit that to another damn soul, but Dylan he could trust with his feelings, corny as that sounded.

Dylan came through with a sympathetic response. "Don't sweat it so much. Every man gives up his wild ways eventually."

Exactly what he was terrified of! Maxim decided it was time to drop the subject. Bored or not, he wasn't settling down. He couldn't. "Speaking of which, how is married life treating you?"

"Sadie is amazing. You know that."

"Good, good. Now about that tabloid." Maxim returned to the purpose of his call. "Elisa Cross is splashed all over the front of it."

"Elisa from college? The sexy, smart chick you lab-partnered with and almost blew up?" Dylan chuckled. "She wouldn't give you the time of day. I think she was one of the most intelligent girls at school, avoiding you as she did."

Maxim chose to ignore Dylan's jest. "That's the one."

"What about her? Still pining?"

"Well, according to the picture, she's changed her stance on man-sluts. Now, it appears she's quite into threesomes."

Dylan grunted. "No shit."

"No shit." Maxim retrieved a magazine, again studying the photo, particularly the look in her eyes, the way her pupils were glazed over, making him question her sobriety. She'd either been really turned on, or really, really inebriated. He hoped the latter.

"Dylan, I think I'm a little bit pissed."

It wasn't like him to get jealous. He shared women with his good buddies all the time, and until now, had never wanted a female to himself more than he wanted to pluck Elisa from the magazine cover and take her home.

"I think you still have the hots for her. I think you've always felt different about her."

"I never kept it a secret. You know I'm not the type to mince words."

"So find her," Dylan suggested, as if the answer were so simple. Was it?

"Really? Find her? That's weird."

"Hey, you're the one who said you're free to travel anywhere you please. If you want her, go after her, and this time, don't take no for an answer, because I'll tell you right now, Elisa *did* harbor an attraction to you, she was just too smart to admit it."

Maxim scoffed. "She almost did. Until Miss Tits walked in and made me blow the lab up."

"Elisa was hurt. Can you blame her?"

"I did apologize." Over, over, and over.

"You scarred her!"

"So now you're on her side?"

"Hey, Elisa was a nice girl and my friend. What with the way you carried on, I didn't want to see you date her. She had big career plans, was going to save the world, and you were returning to Egypt right after graduation to work for your parents. It couldn't have worked out. You would have hurt her and I wasn't prepared to allow that."

Dylan was right. Elisa had always been better off without him, hence his willingness to stay away despite how he ached for her. Looking at this photo, he suddenly begged to differ. "And she's not too good for me now?" he asked, more to himself than Dylan.

The way he saw it, Elisa *needed* him around. Look where she'd ended up on her own—publicly embarrassed, disinherited, and unemployed.

Dylan laughed. "Now that you're all grown up and ready to settle down, and—"

"I never said that."

"Oh, sure. Maxim, she's still on your mind, after all this time. Go after her."

Maxim nodded, dropping the magazine. "You're right. Thanks, Dylan."

Why shouldn't he go after Elisa? Get her out of his system once and for all? If he went home like this, he wouldn't sleep for days. He'd be up every night, thinking about her, imagining her in his arms, looking at him the way she looked at the men in that damn photo, and meanwhile, he'd have to suffer his mother and her string of fortune-sniffing females dubbed suitable to marry. Besides, with Mother in town, she could look after the hotel.

He just wanted his life to stay the way it was—with women and parties aplenty. He sure wasn't settling down, not ever, but as far as he was concerned, the doors were open to finally sample Elisa Cross. He wasn't stopping until he was *well* satisfied.

"Don't forget to visit your old bud while you're in the States."

"Will do," Maxim promised and then hung up, pressing down hard on the gas pedal as he sped in the direction of the airport.

Could she really use this thing? What's more, could having a piece of rubber shoved up her cunt really compare to a man's cock?

Elisa wiggled the nine-inch hunk of see-through purple rubber shaped at an odd angle. Nope. She tossed it back in the container. "So not me," she muttered to herself.

Filled with various sex toys, all dusty from neglect, the Rubbermaid box held what her sister Lizzy called the *solution* to all her relationship problems.

"Men are for using, and losing, but never trusting," Elisa recited to herself.

Crap! Why hadn't she listened to Lizzy half a year ago?

Lizzy had been asserting her stance on the male sex to Elisa since she'd met Derrick—as well as presenting Elisa with sex toy gag gifts as encouragement to dump the jerk. Lizzy wasn't weird . . . well . . . not in the perverted sense. The night club owner was just as kooky as a woman could be, perhaps even a little over the edge, and she did not care for men. At all.

"She's got a real fine point." Elisa's eyebrows rose as she retrieved a massive-sized vibrator from the collection. "No man is this well-endowed."

Sighing, Elisa tossed the toy back. Too much for her first test-drive with a fake dick.

With a frown, she continued to sift through the extensive selection. If she'd just listened to Lizzy once, maybe she wouldn't be in this awful situation. Deep down, Elisa had always known Derrick was an ass, but the days had turned into months, and somehow, he'd gained her affection, her confidence. She hadn't even loved the jerk . . . she'd just lusted for him and her desire had put blinders on her. She'd let him connive her into doing things she'd otherwise never do—clueless that each encounter had been caught on video. Posted on the Internet. Sold on DVD. *The bastard.*

Her soap star father and his fame already shoved her into the limelight she despised. Now she'd been turned into a porn star without ever having a clue. What a fool she'd been and now she was paying the price. After *Shine* had exposed her less lucrative "career" in filmmaking, her world had crashed to pieces. She'd lost her father's esteem, her peers' respect. The gossip had been too much to take and her boss had taken over her case, giving her some "time off" to let things blow over, which likely meant she'd be fired. Hell, even her dog had left her, choosing to remain with her slimeball ex.

Unable to bear the weird looks and double-edged comments, she'd begged her father, who was barely speaking to her, for permission to use his hunting cabin in Aspen. Thankfully, he'd obliged her, though grudgingly, and only because he wanted her out of the public eye.

Her life as she'd known it was over. No one would ever respect her now, if she even had the nerve to show her face to the world once more, which she doubted. This cabin was the best place for her. She loved the quiet and Lizzy lived nearby. What else did she have anyway, besides a now-useless degree in environmental law and a string of failed relationships?

One thing was for sure, she'd never, ever, not on her life, trust a man again. If only she could have learned that lesson back in college, the first time around. Clearly she was alone in this world, and she'd learn to survive alone. It was better this way. She was done being sweet and innocent, done playing by society's rules. She was too damn smart for that. From this day forth, she'd be bold, brassy, even bitchy. Lizzy would look like a damn angel by comparison.

Elisa refused to be hurt again. The walls she'd built around her heart were ten-inch thick cement, strong, unbreakable, and she intended to keep them that way.

She'd start her change by learning to be in charge of her body. No man would command her physically, not ever again. Her desire was hers and hers alone. She needed to learn to own it.

Fetching a more natural-looking imitation cock from the box, she shoved the remaining toys under the bed and stood. A glass of wine waited by the burning fireplace in the great room, and she intended to enjoy the bittersweet drink as well as her body.

She wagged the dildo. Thank God this place was secluded.

In an instant, Maxim's cock hardened and the whole damn pain-in-the-ass, *cold* trip to find Elisa became worth it.

Hot damn! She had a freaking dildo!

Maxim's breath fogged the window and he wiped it away, staring in wonder at the incredible sight before him. Elisa lay with her legs spread on a bearskin rug, in front of a blazing stone fireplace, readying her glistening, pink pussy with two fingers. Never had he seen a more glorious sight.

Elisa pressed her clit, taking the nub between her long, graceful fingers, stroking up and down. With her other hand, she deeply massaged her left breast, working the creamy mound as she took her peaked, rose-colored nipple between her fingers. Squeezing the bud, she drew it upward, coaxing it into a tight bead.

His throat tightened. His face burned. His cock pulsed with rash, demanding need. His coldness and runny nose vanished, every feeling in his body forgotten but his raging arousal. Sweeping his eyes over her body, he drank in the sight of her from head to toe. Over the years, her already long-ass hair had grown to an impossible length, and the silk mass of chocolate brown curls reached past her delectable derrière. Womanhood had matured her curves, making them lusher, more voluptuous.

Shit. He'd wanted her back in college, but not like this. Just the sight of her made him feel like he'd die if he didn't get to touch her. Hold her. Love her. He couldn't even breathe.

Oh God. The ridiculous search he'd put himself through looking for her had so been worth it. With every second he had the privilege of watching her masturbate, every mile he'd traveled became more inconsequential. If he never laid a hand on her, never so much as spoke to her, he'd still feel like the luckiest man on earth.

Lifting her hips, Elisa slowly inserted the dildo into her pussy, an inch at a time, until she reached the base. Her hips lifted higher and she moaned aloud. Slowly, she withdrew the rubber rod, and then plunged it deeper, assuming a constant rhythm as she moved it in and out of her wet sheath.

Oh, fuck yeah! The blasted skis, the freezing cold, even his chapped lips . . . none of it seemed like such a bother now. When he'd paid a visit to her apartment and discovered she'd vanished, he hadn't been prepared to give up so easily. Why, he didn't know . . . but almost a thousand dollars worth of convincing later, he'd finally bribed her location from a neighbor, a woman who hadn't seemed like much of a friend to Elisa, only greedy, especially after she'd gotten a look at his rented BMW.

Learning she was in Aspen had been the simple part.

Her cabin was ski-in, ski-out, and since he hadn't stepped in snow, much less experienced cold weather, since college, his trip down the trail had been pure misery. But he'd made it and apparently just in time.

Too bad he was out here instead of in there, but at least he wasn't cold anymore. No, he was hot. He was sweating.

His thigh muscles tightened and his cock strained in the confines of its taut skin, the vein along the underside thumping as blood surged to the area. About to explode from the sheer pleasure of watching her, his thoughts became blurry.

He could knock. *No.* That would be stupid. He was too built-up. And she'd stop. An intelligent conversation would be impossible, and from the way she handled that toy, she was skilled in the art of pleasing herself, which meant she may not have any use for him. The last thing he needed was to make a jackass of himself. Elisa Cross wasn't the type of woman that had a problem with rejecting him.

Blood pulsed through his body, making his heart race. This was, by far, the most incredible thing he'd ever seen. His cock twitched again, his desire for Elisa becoming unbearable. Damn it! He had no other choice. Reaching under the elastic band of his ski pants, he wrapped his hand around his stiff prick and began vigorously jerking himself off.

Stumbling, he pumped his cock hard and fast, furiously seeking relief. Closing his eyes, he stepped away from the window, unable to watch anymore if he wanted to maintain his sanity. He just needed to relieve the pressure, then he'd knock. Ask her assistance with this *hard* problem of his . . .

Taking another step, he leaned against the wall and pumped his dick, tuning out everything but visions of fucking Elisa, her long hair tangled in his hands, her bottom lifting to his demanding thrusts, her . . .

"You fuckers! Can't you leave me alone?" Elisa unexpectantly screamed from behind him. "Who are you? And what the hell do you think you're doing?"

Maxim's eyes flew open and he yanked his hand free, whirling around. He found himself face-to-face with a pistol, wielded by a fuming Elisa wrapped in a throw blanket. Her hair billowed around her, her Blue Nile eyes wild. With anger.

"Maxim?" Her gaze widened, startled, confused by his presence. "Maxim Cox? What are you *doing* here? Oh my God. You're jacking off on my porch? You asshole."

He glanced with unease at her weapon. "Maxim Cox, none other. You remembered my name."

"Who could ever forget a name like that?"

"My parents named me well," he joked, trying to ease the tension. By now, she'd caught onto the fact that he was no bear or sick window creeper. Why was she still holding him at gunpoint? "Still determined to get back at me for ruining your last lab?"

She didn't laugh at his jest. She didn't even crack a smile. And she didn't lower the pistol. "Ruining the lab? You just about killed me. I failed chemistry so you could get a good look at a pair of fake tits."

Had he been fooling himself to think maybe, just maybe, she'd be happy to see him again?

Maxim glared at the firearm in his face. Want her he might, but he didn't take kindly to having a weapon of any kind directed at him. "Get that thing out of my face."

Her head tilted to the side, her grip on the blanket tightening as she hiked it up. "What in the hell are you doing?" Her narrowed, angry gaze drifted downward, settling on the tent in his pants. For a split second, he swore he saw a glimmer in her eyes. *Need.* Then, just as quickly, disappointment and disgust contorted her features. "I shouldn't be surprised. I shouldn't."

"What's that mean? You're the one in there with a damn dildo!"

"That's none of your business!"

He grabbed his cock. "Well, then neither is this!"

Heat rushed to his face, making him feel like a damned teenager caught doing something dirty. God help him, he was even freaking blushing. Something he didn't think he'd ever done before. Maxim didn't normally get embarrassed. He also didn't normally jerk off; he didn't have to. But Elisa made him crazy. She always had and he had a terrible feeling she always would.

She shook her head, her demeanor turning to ice as she stepped back. "Get lost. Now."

There it was again. That look. The same as in college. Elisa Cross wanted everything to do with him and nothing to do with him. Clearly, she was a sensual being, one who craved sexual fulfillment, who needed a man, not a dildo. So why did she continue to refuse him? What about him turned her off?

He was good-looking enough. He had money. He had fast cars. Charm. Skills. He knew how to talk to a woman, how to make her scream from an orgasm. He had a lot to offer a lady . . . intelligence, fun, pleasure.

She should be crawling all over him, damn it!

"Leave? Not a chance, sweetie," he proclaimed.

This time, Elisa was giving him a chance, if nothing more. If she still didn't want him after that, then fine. But he wouldn't leave until he had a fair opportunity to show her how compatible they really were. He wanted that date he'd lost, damn it.

She scoffed, lowering the gun. "Don't think you're coming in."

She whirled around and darted inside, slamming the door in his face with a reverberating bang.

two

The very first man to break her heart.

Why him? Damn it, *why?* She'd rather be facing the devil himself than Maxim Cox, man-slut extraordinaire.

Backed into the corner of the door and against the wall, Elisa
clenched the blanket covering her naked body, feeling exposed.
Embarrassed. *Worried.*

Forget the fact that he'd just caught her masturbating, that
she'd just caught *him* masturbating, a discomforting event to say
the least. Maxim was trouble. Big. Fat. Trouble. And not the kind
she needed right now.

But oh God, he'd looked so good. Not quite what one would
expect from a rich boy, he was fashionably scruffy, his wheat-
colored hair wispy and intentionally disheveled, with expertly de-
signed sideburns fading into three-day stubble shadowing his jaw.

His eyes reminded her of a wolf's, golden brown, striking, intense, and always on the lookout for prey. Standing well over six feet, his body was tanned, muscular. He beamed sexuality . . . and one look from him heated her up all over again.

He'd almost fooled her once. She wouldn't be duped again.

He knocked on the door once more. "Elisa, I refuse to leave until you talk to me. Give me a chance." An unusual mix of well-spoken English influenced by Arabic undertones, Maxim's already seductive tone lowered a notch, becoming more persuasive, making her feel like his words were wrenching her heart from her chest. "Come on, sweetie, no harm's been done. You're horny, I'm horny . . . it's natural. Let's be natural together . . ."

Not on her life. She needed to close the curtains, hide. Avoid Maxim at all costs. The last thing she should do was remain standing here, listening to his convincing demands to open the door.

So why wasn't she moving? Damn her feet!

"Get lost, Maxim!" she yelled, her lower lip shaking as she sunk to the floor. She hugged her knees and tears of frustration threatened her eyes. Given her recent circumstances, she was already raw and vulnerable . . . hurting. After what happened with Derrick, she didn't want to be around any male, and Maxim Cox was the last man she needed. Seductive as he could be, he was the epitome of danger. All he wanted was one thing: *sex*.

Sex, sex, and more sex.

He'd seen that damned tabloid and he'd come here for *sex*, thinking she was an easy target to finally sink his claws into.

He didn't stand a chance in hell. He might've back in college, but he didn't now, and he never would. She was sticking to her guns. She didn't need a man. She had her dildos.

Maxim needed to leave.

"Elisa, sweetie, let's talk. I want to hold you. We'll talk. Nothing more. Come on, what do you say?"

Despite her hard feelings, his words poured over her like honey, warming her, coaxing her . . . grating on her nerves. Heaven help her, maybe she wanted him to leave, but she also wanted to oblige him . . . to invite him in, to fall victim to his advances, to spread her legs.

Something was seriously wrong with her.

Hence her desire to be secluded and alone! Why, *how*, was he here? "No one even knew where I was located but my father. Did he send you?" she questioned.

"Your neighbor knew."

Valerie! Damn that woman, always in her business! She never should have trusted her with her emergency key. The witch must have snooped through her apartment. "No doubt, Valerie made a pretty penny off you."

"Your location cost me a big one."

Why was Maxim going through all this effort, just to screw her? Such behavior wasn't like him. He made no sense!

"Wasted money."

"Come on, Elisa, just talk to me."

"No. Get lost now, or I swear I'll shoot your dick off!" she shouted, making every effort to sound like the world's biggest bitch. Why wouldn't he take a hint?

She didn't want to deal with him. With herself.

She wasn't sure she could handle it.

"Why?" he demanded, pounding on the door.

"I'm done with men, Maxim, particularly your type."

"What's that supposed to mean?" His strong tone faltered and she could almost think he sounded hurt. Yeah, right.

"You came here for sex, Maxim. You aren't getting any, so hit the trail."

"That's not true. I don't care about sex. I want—" His sentence dropped off and he swore under his breath.

"No?" Elisa scoffed. She didn't buy his bullshit for a minute. He was just trying to steal her heart so he could use her body. "Then why are you here? Specifics, please."

"I came for you. I want *you*, Elisa. Always have."

Her stomach flip-flopped and excitement flitted through her. Adrenaline rushed her veins, making her heart race.

Damn it! She hated when he did that. She knew his ways well from college. She'd witnessed him seducing more than his share of females into bed, felt the effect of his words more than once as he'd tried to score with her. He could have broken her heart with some of the things he'd said . . . if she'd fallen for his crap and slept with him. After all, that's clearly what he'd wanted from her. Had his supposed feelings been true, he would have had eyes only for her.

She looked down at the two-inch burn scar that marred her left hand from the explosion. She'd almost agreed to date him. What would have happened if Miss Big Boobs hadn't walked in?

Would he have changed?

Yeah right.

If he was going to be such an ass, why pretend to be sweet? Couldn't he just be an ass? God, she hated men like him.

God, she just hated men.

"You can't have me," she told him, anxious for his response despite all her reasoning.

Her old, unfed desire for him was rising—and fast—to the surface, which was still tender from her last relationship. Her yearning for him stung like saltwater on a wound, because she knew he was nothing but poison.

Maxim Cox was dangerous. She needed to stop playing the fool and accept that. So he was hot. So what? He was also the biggest man-slut on this side of the universe.

"Don't tell me I can't have you. Do you know how many years I've wanted you? How I've dreamt of you? Thought about you?" he asked. "No, Elisa, I'll admit, I'm a man. Of course I want to score. But I didn't come here for sex. I came here for you. *You.*"

Mush, mush, mush. She was turning into a puddle of liquid lust. Where was her hard shell? Her rock wall?

Her freaking common sense?

"Yeah right," she snapped, the tears coming again. Why did she want to open the door and her legs so badly? He'd just hurt her! Just like Derrick!

Maxim grunted, pounding three steady knocks against the door in frustration. "Elisa, do you think I'd go to all this trouble just for sex? I've got plenty of women at home and I don't have to freeze my freaking balls off to get them."

She cracked a half smile, sniffling. She swore she could hear his teeth chattering through the door. The moron. Just like Maxim—no clue when it came to anything—anything but sex. "You should have worn a better coat."

"I don't even know how to ski *downhill*, Elisa, much less cross-country ski through the mountains on these damn awkward things, but here I am. *Here I am*. For you," he reiterated. "It's not *just* about sex. Open the door. Please."

"Horseshit!" Elisa rose to her feet, clutching her blanket and taking several steps away from the door. "Go! Away!"

There was a loud bang, followed by a steady stream of cursing about snow and ice and difficult women, followed by another loud bang, and, "I'm cold!"

"What you are, Maxim Cox, is spoiled and selfish and self-centered and sex-focused and I am finished with men like you," Elisa cried out. "I am through with men, period. You aren't coming in my cabin! *Ever!*"

Maxim's lips were turning blue. The tip of his tongue felt frozen. His teeth hurt. His nipples ached. His balls were ice cubes.

He was fucking *cold*.

Worse, it would be dark soon.

Shivering, Maxim rubbed his arms to create friction and paced between the pine trees stationed a few feet in front of Elisa's single-story cabin. Smoke rose from her chimney into the evening sky, the only sign that the dark cabin was occupied.

What now? He had no clue how to get to Elisa. He never had, not from the moment they'd met. She was smarter than him. Better than him. Prettier than he deserved. He accepted that. But he still wanted her.

Elisa wouldn't be seduced, she wouldn't be sweet-talked, and she sure wasn't falling for his charm. He'd even tried honesty and clearly that hadn't gotten him far with her. He needed a plan, because otherwise, he'd freeze to death before she let him in.

Pausing, he looked at the cabin. A curtain moved in the shadowy window. Ah, so she was watching him. Interested in him. But still not budging. What would it take?

He didn't have the slightest idea.

"Oh, come on, Elisa! Cut me a break!" he hollered, his words echoing back at him. He shook his head, muttering to himself. "She's probably enjoying this. Hell, she's probably recording it. I'm making a fool of myself. I must have lost my damned mind."

Maybe that was it. Perhaps he just needed to drive her crazy. Get on her nerves until she gave in. Walking to the cabin, he explored the perimeter, stepping in her frozen flower beds to peer in her windows. Finally, the subtle glow of a fire revealed her location.

She was huddled in her bedroom. Now wearing a warm and cozy-looking flannel nightgown, her knees tucked under her chin, and her hair wrapped around her like a shield, she cuddled on the loveseat, a fuzzy blanket warming her legs. She dabbed her huge eyes with a handkerchief and bit her lush lower lip. In her shaky left hand, she held a magazine. He guessed it was the treacherous tabloid that had driven her to seclude herself here in the mountains.

She looked so tiny, so helpless and pitiful. He hadn't realized the scandal had hurt her so deeply.

The urge to wrap her in his arms and squeeze her until she smiled pulled at him. Stepping closer, he pressed his face against the window. He followed his instinct and knocked softly.

Elisa jumped, her body literally lifting an inch off the seat. Her gaze flew to where he stood. She leapt to her feet, everything pathetic about her instantly transforming into anger.

"What, haven't you seen enough, you perv?"

Her insult stung, but not as much as seeing her cry. She was hurting and she needed to lean on someone's shoulder. His shoulder. "I want to talk to you."

She stormed to the window, her eyes narrowed. "Well, I *don't* want to talk to you."

"Elisa, just give me a chance. You need—"

"You to leave!"

Whoosh! She flung the curtain across the window, shutting him out. He took a step back, lost. What had he ever done to her? Why wouldn't she just talk to him? He realized he'd given himself a bad rap, but he'd never hurt her. He'd never even come close.

Momentarily, he considered going to other windows, then realized maybe he was being a bit of a creep.

He stalked back to his trees and resumed pacing. No wonder she wouldn't give him the time of day. Maybe it wasn't personal. The scandal with the tabloids was making her an emotional basket case. The world has seen her at her naughtiest. For someone like him, it wasn't that big of a deal. For someone like her . . .

As he'd suspected, she was in misery.

Why did that make him feel like dirt? He hadn't taken the pictures.

But he had almost killed her all those years ago.

A fluffy white snowflake flitted from the darkening sky, falling to the already dusted-white ground. Another followed, and another, and another. In less than a minute, dime-sized flakes poured down on him.

Great. Maxim kicked at the snow and shuddered. He'd never gone through so much trouble for a woman in his life. His mind told him to give up, to hike his way into Aspen and find a willing female to warm his cold body. But his heart, his soul, begged to differ. It wasn't about sex, not with Elisa.

The more she pushed him away, the more he desired her. He wanted to comfort her, to prove himself, to show her men weren't all bad, as she currently thought. Granted, he wasn't exactly the man for the job, but that made him want to do it even more.

He'd probably turn into an ice statue before she wavered, but he wouldn't return to Aspen. Nope, he'd made up his mind, and he was a stubborn man at best. He refused to leave, refused to give up.

As he paced, the snow continued to dump from the sky. Maxim hated the weather in Colorado, but, for once, maybe the cold wasn't such a bad thing.

He plopped down in the snow, well aware of the fact that he didn't have on the ugly, puffy pants the ski shop had insisted he needed, or the coat. He rolled around, covering himself in wet, cold snow.

Elisa might have a heart of stone when it came to men, but not when it came to the human race. Always out to save the world, she wasn't a murderer by any stretch. He knew damn good and well the sweet woman wouldn't leave him out here to freeze to death, especially not soaking wet in what appeared to be a blizzard.

Lying down, he yanked off his hat and thrashed around in the snow. She could hate and deny him all she wanted, because damn it, he was going to make her feel sorry for him. Make her feel guilty. A couple more hours like this, and not only would she be opening the door, she'd be warming him up.

Done with crying, past being vulnerable, Elisa tossed a chunk of wood in the hearth, hugging herself as she enjoyed the heat radiating from the blazing fire. She *really* shouldn't feel sorry for Maxim. It was his fault he was freezing. His fault he was here in the first place. He hadn't dressed properly. Hadn't brought food. He didn't even know how to ski. How was she responsible for that? For the weather?

Oh no, she had no reason to feel guilty at all. Except here she was, warm, toasty, and he looked like he was turning into an Eskimo.

The sky had dumped snow on them for a good hour; it had quickly amounted to several inches. The weather station was calling it a nasty storm, predicting two feet of accumulation before the blizzard moved on in the morning.

Maxim should've listened to her and returned to Aspen. He would have, if he were smart. But he hadn't budged. Instead, he'd curled in a pathetic ball of red skin and shivers on her front porch.

Occasionally he knocked, pleading that he couldn't ski in the snow, the dumbest thing she'd ever heard.

Maxim was determined to stay; she was just as determined to see him go. Unfortunately, for all his whining, he had more spine than her. He was winning their little battle of wills.

She couldn't ignore him any longer. Mind you, Maxim wouldn't succeed in getting in her panties, but she would let him inside the cabin, let him warm up and feed him. For the night. That was it.

Crossing the great room decorated in earthy tones and hideous animal heads her father had collected over the years, she walked to the front door and placed her hand on the gold knob.

Unprepared to open her home to him just yet, she drew a deep breath and commanded herself to get bitchy; she'd need all the resistance she could muster to withstand his advances. She knocked once on the closed door to get his attention and then hollered through the wood, "Did you dress like a fool on purpose?"

"The puf-puff-puffy coat the ski ra-ra-rental company gave me w-w-was hideous" was Maxim's pathetic response. "N-n-not to m-m-mention uncomfortable."

He'd freeze to death rather than dress properly? For fashion? Yeah, she believed he was a changed man. *So grown up.* Her grip on the knob loosened. She should leave him out there just on principle.

"Maxim, not everything in life is about looking and feeling good, you know. One would think you'd have grown out of that juvenile idealism by now," Elisa mocked. "You've got money. If you didn't like the store's options, why not go somewhere else? Buy something fashionable and comfortable and expensive, if you were going to be this persistent? I mean, the more cash you spend, the more impressive of a guy you are, right?"

"W-we *aren't* in college anymore, Elisa and for your information, I was in a rush, and don't think I'm so shallow that I wouldn't have worn the coat had I expected it to get this cold or thought that I'd be outside this long. I'm from Egypt, for Christ sakes. I didn't know what to expect. The weather really wasn't all that cold at first, so I left the extra clothing behind. When I started for your cabin, I was moving around and the sunshine actually made it a little warm."

Elisa bit her lower lip. He was still a jackass, but he had a point. "Yes, Aspen is known for its warm sun. Doesn't make the air any less cold, though."

Guilt suffused her. Was she judging him too harshly? Maxim wasn't an outdoorsy man. While he was an American, his parents had raised, or rather, pampered him in Egypt, a much warmer climate. That didn't make him less of a man . . . or a slimeball, tracking her down like he had. But the fact that he'd braved the freezing wild and put on skis when he never slid his feet in a pair before, all for her, was more than masculine. It was remarkable. And sexy. *And stupid*, the rational part of her brain reminded her.

"Y-y-yeah, well, my take on things has changed. I didn't expect the shade from the pine trees would be so ch-chilling. I didn't expect it to snow. And I never imagined . . ."

She heard a scuffle as he stood and the sound of his hand resting on the outdoor knob. Elisa clenched the cold metal, imagining a connection between the two of them. "Never imagined what?"

"That you'd be this difficult."

"I must admit, you've impressed me, Maxim." She smiled. "You're going to an awful lot of trouble to screw me. It won't work . . . but your efforts are commendable. I never saw it coming, not from you."

"That's because you have the wrong idea about me." His teeth-chattering dissolved, and his voice lowered, became smoother, more seductive. Elisa immediately felt the change in herself. She could easily fall for his charm, if she let herself.

That couldn't happen!

Fortifying the rock wall around her heart, she turned her tone to ice. "I doubt that."

"I didn't come here to fuck you, Elisa. I came here because I still feel—because I want you. Because I always have. And from what I've seen from you today, you feel the same way about me."

Sure, she'd thought he was hot, back in college. *In college.* She'd also thought he was an asshole.

"Oh, Maxim, you always knew how to talk to a female," she said with contempt, rolling her eyes.

"Elisa, I saw you crying. I know you're hurting. Stop playing this hard-ass role and be real, sweetie," he drawled, his voice rich with persuasion and his foreign accent. "Let me comfort you. We'll talk. Nothing more."

Damn, she could fall, so hard, so fast. But she wouldn't.

"Oh, you're good."

"I'm not playing you, Elisa. I'm s-s-serious. Come on, it's cold and I want to speak to you face-to-face."

"Suddenly Mr. Sexpot has turned into Mr. Sappy? I don't buy it."

He jiggled the knob in response and she seized it in her grasp. "F-fine. M-m-mock me. Believe what you want. Christ, I must have lost my mind." His hand dropped from the door, his voice fading as he walked away, going into a fit of cursing she could barely hear. She pressed her ear against the door and listened. "Shit! Damn it! I go through all this freaking crap, and for what? Why? FUCK! Okay, get it together, Maxim. Ughh . . . !" Several moments passed, followed by, "Not interested. Damn. She's obviously not interested. S-shit, it's cold. I should get home."

His self-flagellation made her half smile, half agonize. Did she actually *want* him to stay? Crud! She was crazy too!

A minute or two stretched on and she worried he was leaving. Suddenly, he yelled, his scream echoing off the mountainside. "Fine! I'll just sit out here and freeze."

She chuckled, almost glad he was sticking it out. Almost believing he did want more than to screw her.

"You know I won't let you freeze," she hollered, her fingers toying with the lock.

"I'm still out here," he grunted, footsteps bringing his voice closer.

"I'm still thinking."

"Well, how long does it take?"

"I didn't exactly expect you to show up and interrupt me in the middle of . . ." The thought of him watching her as she fucked herself with that damned dildo made her face blaze. Just as quickly, visions of his hands commanding the piece of rubber flitted though her mind, instantly heating her loins. Her cunt quickened, desire gushing forth.

Again, his hand rested on the knob. "Is that why I'm still out here? You're embarrassed?"

"Wouldn't you be?"

"Elisa, I think you are so beautiful. Watching you was beautiful. I want to see more, I want to hold you—"

She swallowed, knowing he was so close. Much more sweet-talking and she'd melt into a pitiful, pathetic puddle, she'd let him in, let him fuck her, let herself be hurt. "Here we go again. Sap. Sap. Sap."

"Would you stop that? Damn." He wriggled the knob. "Just let me in and I'll prove myself."

Prove himself? Yeah right.

She was the one that needed to do the proving. Creamy need trickled down her inner thigh and she clenched her vaginal muscles. Talk about insane! How could she even be considering letting him in? If he touched her, she could never withstand his advances.

So much for being a bitch. In control.

One asshole was all she needed to make a fool of her in a lifetime and Derrick had filled that role. To the hilt. Yet, she wasn't one hundred percent sure Maxim was lying. Maybe he had come here for her and not just sex. *Maybe.*

Or maybe he was a damn good talker.

Yeah, but who crossed halfway around the globe just to get fucked?

Not Maxim, that was for sure. Yet, he had. For her. She

If a guy could get to her this easily, she was hopeless. Lizzy was so right. She needed to stop letting men control her desires. She needed to be in charge of her body. Her yearnings. She needed to be powerful, not only over her physical cravings, but over him. Over men in general. Reclaim her self-confidence, her shattered feminine power.

If she could do that, if she could be the stronger, more dominate partner, then surely no one, even the likes of Maxim, could hurt her.

She wasn't letting him in because she couldn't help herself. No, absolutely not. He was here, they might as well reminisce. She was strong enough to handle that. *That's* the way it should be.

She straightened her spine; standing taller made her feel bigger. "You really want me to believe you came here for more than sexual gratification?"

"Yes," he reiterated, trapping himself.

She smiled with satisfaction. "Then you can prove it."

"How?"

"You can come in, but don't touch me. One advance and I'll kick you out into the snow so fast you won't know what hit you."

To her surprise, he laughed. "Open the door."

"Swear it," she demanded.

"I swear."

Mentally fortifying herself, Elisa unlocked the door and stepped back.

three

Here goes nothing. Gingerly holding the door open, Elisa invited Maxim inside, feeling as if she were welcoming the devil himself into her home. "Remember, don't try anything."

I can do this. I'm in control, not Maxim, she promised herself.

Standing, Maxim brushed the snow from his clothes and granted her a lopsided, cocky smile. He shuddered, stomping the ice from his boots. "Thank God you've come to your senses."

His intense eyes devoured her and heat rose to her cheeks. Clutching the door, she thought about slamming it in his face.

How could she do this? How on earth could she be at ease around him after he'd caught her masturbating? She couldn't even look him in the eye.

"Yes, I *have* come to my senses," she replied, mentally reminding herself that if she wanted to be strong, she should start by being confident. "The last thing I need is a dead, frozen Mr. Cox on my front porch. The paparazzi would have a field day with me. Again."

"Ouch." He stepped inside, looking around before his eyes once again settled on her, making her feel exposed and raw. "I'm surprised—but damn glad—to find you have electricity this far out. Running water too?"

"Of course. My father paid a pretty penny to ensure this cabin was comfortable, but secluded, which was exactly why I chose to come here. I wanted to be *alone*."

"Yet you're allowing me to come in."

"You haven't exactly given me a choice, now have you?" She crossed her arms. "Now that you're here, and refusing to leave, it was either let you freeze or let you in."

Their eyes connected, and he stared so deeply into hers that she swore she could see something beyond the cockiness and sexual prowess he was known for. Haunting emotion. A hunger.

As if knowing he'd revealed too much, he ripped his gaze away, striding further into her temporary home.

"You must be cold." She followed behind him. "I'll stoke the fire. You need to take those wet clothes off."

"Here?" he chuckled. "In a rush to get to the goods, baby?"

"Yes," she joked. "Let's go. Now."

"Now?" he growled in a low voice. "In front of you?"

"Yes." She strived to keep her words even, to play it cool. "Don't so much as leave a sock on." *Good grief!* Had she really just said that? "But don't you dare think about touching me. Remember your promise."

"That's no fun."

"When have I ever been fun?"

"I don't know. I always thought you could be entertaining."

"Yeah, when you were making fun of me."

He looked taken aback. "What? I didn't—"

"Sure you did. When your eyes weren't roaming." Her tone dripped with sarcasm. "Come with me. I'll get you a robe."

A short while later, Maxim was wrapped in a warm, terry cloth robe that was entirely too small on him, and standing before the fire. The heat seared his chilled skin and his shaking calmed.

He'd never been so cold. Nor had he ever acted so crazy.

And he'd done some insane shit.

He knelt on the stone base of the hearth. Pulling back the screen, he picked up a log and laid it on top of the glowing embers. The movement caused the short robe to pull up, leaving his ass hanging out. Uselessly, he attempted to tug the fabric back in place, then gave up. He held out his hands, practically placing them in the fire in an attempt to ward of the chills possessing his body.

"Maxim?" Elisa walked from the kitchen holding a steaming cup.

Crap! Quickly, he scrambled to sit flat on his butt. He didn't need to expose himself to her so she could get the wrong idea. Again.

"Feeling better?" She handed him the cup and he wrapped his hands around it. He stared at the bag floating in the amber liquid. Tea. Not coffee, but good enough.

"Come sit next to me."

Casting him a hesitant look, she parked herself on the couch. "Oh, come on. I don't have cooties," he chuckled. But it wasn't funny. The woman was so indifferent to him, Maxim was certain the trip out here had been a waste. "You aren't going to make me shout across the room, are you?"

"Yes." Her voice was unnecessarily cool.

"Elisa." He tilted his head to the side, staring at her, analyzing her. "Please."

Finally, a smile . . . small, doubtful, but a smile all the same.

"When you put it that way." She blew out a frustrated puff of air. "But no funny business."

Standing, she moved to the bearskin rug laid out in front of the fireplace and sat cross-legged. "They say if the storm slows down, it could snow all through the night. Nearly two feet before it's all over."

"Mmmm . . ." He nodded. "I've no idea how I'm going to get out of here."

"I guess I'm stuck with you."

Maxim set the cup down and took her left hand in his. So soft, so small.

She tried to jerk free, but he held tight. "I won't bite."

"I'm not so sure about that," she ground out. "I said no funny business."

She was shaking, clearly scared of him. Or angry. He couldn't believe it. Didn't like it. He turned her hand to the side, torn inside as he took in the sight of the scar that maimed her beautiful skin. The scar that he'd created.

Damn his libido. His immaturity.

Fake tits.

"I'm sorry." He leaned down and softly kissed the old injury. He closed his eyes, relishing the fact that she was no longer pulling away. "I know I said it before, but I want you to know I really mean it. I was a dumb kid."

Something flashed in her eyes. Shock? Satisfaction?

"Okay," she responded quietly. "I won't argue with that."

He kissed her scar again, lingering this time. His tongue flicked out, tasting her. If only he could erase the pain of the past with his mouth, as children often believed injuries could be healed. But he couldn't.

He looked at her and she smiled, revealing pearly white teeth. Retrieving her quivering hand, she gazed up at him, and it took all his willpower not to kiss her senseless despite her dumb rule. "Stupid as I was, I sensed something wonderful in you."

Elisa raised a brow, looking doubtful. "Despite the absolute dork I was."

"My turn not to argue."

"Hey!" She play-slapped him, just like she had so many times while in the lab. Back then, she couldn't seem to keep her hands to herself. "Should have shot you when I had the chance."

"Yep, guess you should have. Glad you didn't though."

She grinned. Suddenly, the tension filling the air disappeared. Her laughter was playful, lighthearted. Dizzying.

She shook her head. "I really oughta beat some sense into you."

"I'd deserve it." Hell, he'd take her hands on him any way he could get them.

"I can't believe you just said I'm a dork! Don't you know a man should never agree with a lady when she puts herself down?"

"I should know that, given my experience with women."

"Yeah." Awkward silence took over. Her lips turned down in seriousness as she studied him. "I don't get you, Maxim. It's been a long, long time, and out of the blue you show up here, professing to want me."

"I know. It's weird." He picked up his tea, taking a sip of the minty herbal blend. The warm, soothing liquid poured down his throat as he debated what to say. Even he didn't fully understand *why* he was here. His growing lack of interest in the opposite sex had been bad enough, but after seeing that tabloid, something in him had flipped. "Let's just say I'm bored with life. Regretting certain decisions."

"So you came to me?"

Maxim shrugged. "I always feel differently when I'm around you."

"Differently?"

"I can't explain it." How could he, when he didn't understand it himself? All he knew was that he could no longer face a future filled with meaningless flings and parties. It seemed they just didn't do it for him anymore.

Whoa. Wait a sec. A *future*? What was going on in that head of his? He didn't come after Elisa to create some sort of future. He didn't intend to have a future with any woman.

He just needed a break from his normal lifestyle.

"My God. Maxim, it almost sounds like you're going to say you're in love with me." Elisa swallowed deeply. "But of course not. That's ridiculous."

Love?

"No!" He leapt to his feet and started pacing. "NO. Of course not."

"Then you are here for sex."

"Yes," he spat out without thinking. "No. I mean . . . crap. What am I saying? I thought maybe . . . maybe you could give me a second chance on that date I blew."

He'd be lucky if she didn't boot him back into the snow.

For a second, she looked pissed again. "Why?"

"Just to see. You know . . ." He stopped pacing and knelt down next to her. Taking her chin in his hand, he looked her in the eye. "I don't care about the sex, okay, Elisa?"

"No."

"No?"

No? What was she saying?

Elisa hesitated, not sure how to answer, not even positive what she'd meant. When Maxim had kissed her hand, he'd done her in. He hadn't been here an hour, but all of the old feelings she'd had for him had come rushing back. The desire. The interest. The way she tingled when they touched.

The way she wanted to smack some damn sense into him.

What now? Did she take her "no" back? Pretend she'd made a mistake?

Or stick with her initial, gut reaction?

What *did* she want from Maxim?

She'd promised herself she'd be strong, bitchy even, and strong, bitchy women didn't run. They faced their weaknesses. Smashed them down.

Even when their weaknesses were currently wearing a robe half his size and they didn't know how to cross their legs.

God, he had a big dick.

Maxim's fingers moved along her jaw, making her shiver with white hot need. "No, Elisa?"

Oh yeah, her flame had been relit. Fire sparked between them, combustible. After seeing that cock, her dildo seemed like a joke.

Elisa nodded slowly. "No."

"What do you mean, no? You want to have sex with me?"

Yeah, she wanted him. And why shouldn't she have him?

Wasn't it weaker to avoid men, to avoid her feelings, to run and hide away? Screw those sex toys. She needed to learn to control her feelings, to control men. Most importantly, to control *them* without letting them control *her*.

What better victim to practice on?

She pulled his hand away, moving onto her knees. Her chest brushed against his and sensations shot through her nipples. She exhaled deeply and squeezed her eyes shut.

Her interest in him was too piqued to turn back now. She wanted, needed, to know what Maxim had to offer. What she'd missed out on all those years ago.

"I meant *no*, no sex between us, but I do want you to touch me, pleasure me, *just* me." She felt as if someone else was speaking the words, feeling incapable of following through with them, but knowing it was do or die; play or be played. "Make me climax. Any way I ask for it."

"Pleasure you?" His face lit up as he reached around her and seized her ass, squeezing as he pulled her tight against him. "Happily."

A nervous shudder shook her. She was so in over her head, but she refused to sink. Not this time. Not with this man. Not again.

Nope, this time she wasn't the fool.

He was.

She grabbed his hands and yanked them from her ass. Rising to her feet, she stood and looked down at him. "But if you really, truly want to prove yourself to me, then you give me orgasms without having any yourself. You cannot fuck me. You cannot attempt to relieve yourself. You obey my rules, or —"

"What?" The look on his face said it all. "Rules? Are you kidding?"

"Absolutely not. Men are pigs. Selfish, greedy, betraying swine, and I'm through with them. Think you can convince me otherwise?"

"I know I can." He stood, nodding. "If that's what you truly want, I will."

"You'll be my guinea pig, Maxim," she said coldly. "If I'm going to resist being taken advantage of, I need to learn to use 'em and lose 'em myself."

He moved closer, too close. Their bodies pressed together. "So you're going to use me?"

"Like a gigolo."

"I won't argue with that. Use away," he flipped off, sounding satisfied.

Somehow, she didn't believe him.

Suddenly Maxim seized her by the shoulders, his hands still cold, even through the warmth of her flannel nightgown. He pressed against her, forcing her to feel the effects of his long wait outside; the hard-on he had for her. He drove her backward, up against the wall. "Let's go."

"The rules," she protested. "You agreed to—"

"I recall an agreement to give you a climax and not to take pleasure of my own." Moving his hands from her shoulders to her spine, he tangled his fingers in her long waves, wrapping her hair around his wrists and binding her to him. "I don't recall you saying anything about kissing or touching. Ergo, I touch." He brushed his lips against her cheek. "And I kiss . . ."

His lips feathered along her jawbone, and she lifted her chin, fighting the racing need running through her. "I—" Despite herself, Elisa thawed into his fierce embrace, wanting him more than she had a right to. Cupping her face, he drew her lips to his, and his mouth crushed hers, sweeping her into a kiss so ferocious, so carnal, she was knocked senseless.

"You said nothing about sucking either," he said, his mouth capturing her tongue, his lips smashing hers, bruising and hard. She reciprocated his attack, kissing him more wildly than she'd ever kissed any man.

"Or fondling." Releasing her hair, his hands grabbed her ass, squeezing. "I'm afraid your rules weren't very clear at all, and you know me, Elisa, I'm not one to behave."

He's commanding your body, your desires, Elisa. No, no, no! Get it together!

But it felt so damned good!

No!

Elisa tore free, trying to shove his heavy body off her. "Rule number one. You don't touch me unless you're told to." She gave him another shove.

A dark look flashed in his gaze and he stepped back, giving her a few inches of space. "Sorry, darling." Shaking his head at himself, he flashed a lopsided smile, making her heart kick in her chest. "Not quite my intent." He winked. "I want you so hot, you're combustible."

"I'm not kidding, Maxim. If you—"

"Okay, okay, I get it." His cock stood long, hard, proud under the strained fabric. "So tell me to touch you."

Elisa swallowed. "Rule number two, you can only touch me the way I command."

"Come on now, that's no fun." He sandwiched her against the wall and pressed his erection to her cunt. Cradling the back of her head, he pulled her forward, kissing her again. His lips, his tongue were everywhere on her face, her mouth . . . devouring her. "Don't you like the way I touch you?"

A jolt of arousal shot straight to her loins, heating the area. Hell yes, she liked it! Too damn much! All Elisa could feel was his cock lying against her pussy, long, hard, threatening. Her will was close to shattering, breaking to bits like a busted piece of fine porcelain.

No! It wasn't supposed to happen like this. Why was she letting Maxim have his way with her? Why was *she* permitting herself to be seduced?

Where was her damned control? Was she so weak?

No!

She was powerful, strong, dominant, and she'd prove it to him. She'd prove it to herself!

Wrenching away, she pushed him, harder than she meant to. Maxim fell backward, stumbling to the rough-hewn oak floor with an ass-breaking thump.

"What the hell?" Clutching his rear in pain, he looked at her like she was a nut job.

And she was. God, why had she done that?

"I'm sorry, I—"

"Really?" He raised a brow, quickly standing, and becoming formidable once again. "You're going to have to make that up to me, I think."

Her eyes drifted to his cock and her insides quivered.

Stepping closer, he reached for her breasts.

"NO!" She put her hand up, halting his advance. "It isn't happening this way."

He smirked. "Then what way is it happening? I'll try any position with you, baby."

"We have an agreement, Maxim," she reminded him firmly. "I don't know what your deal is, but keep it or get out."

Chuckling, he snatched a piece of her long hair and wound it around his pinky finger. "Shall I kiss your feet, my queen?"

"Don't mock me." Lifting her chin, she pulled her hair from his grasp. She studied his every feature, now weathered and matured from the boy she knew in college. Maybe he was different; maybe he wasn't. The old Maxim could never have withstood what she was about to ask of him; she doubted he could now. But if he did, she might believe he'd changed. Might. "Rule number three, don't challenge me, or otherwise try to usurp my position. You want something, *anything*, you ask. Politely. Your next attack, sensual or otherwise, you're done." She paused a moment. "Now, if you think you can play by those rules, come please me."

She waited with baited breath for his answer . . . one he thought twice about this time around. Studying her, he hardened his jaw, and the look in his eyes turned dark. "Jesus. He really hurt you, didn't he?"

His question stung and she looked away. "Like the rest of the world, you saw the pictures. What do you think?"

"I don't know."

"Then why did you come here? Search me out, like a dog in heat? Wait outside my home in a blizzard and all but kill yourself to get inside? *Why?*"

"Not to hurt you, I promise that." He started to reach for her, then dropped his hand. "I'm sorry I attacked you."

His apology caused a surge of emotion to storm through her, forcing her to erect a dam of hardness to keep it in. With a silent nod, Elisa stood in awkward silence, not sure what to say or do first. Not sure if she should allow this to progress. Not sure *how*. After all, she'd never been the one in charge before.

Moments passed as she contemplated Maxim and his sudden, strange appearance. He was the last person she'd ever expected to see, yet here she was, about to have him pleasure her. For the most part, he seemed like the same old sex-charged, superficial, cocky Maxim, but there was something different about him, something lonely, desperate, heartfelt . . .

Not to mention his presence was so weird. Unexplained.

Yet a piece of her she wanted to deny welcomed Maxim's company.

He cleared his throat, jarring her, and she had to say something.

"Well, do you agree, or not?"

"To what?"

"My terms."

"Oh those." He winked at her. The devil. "How could I say no?"

"Take the robe off," she told him, amazed when the words she spoke came out successfully. "I want to see you naked."

After all, she'd waited more than half a decade to see what all the hype was about.

"Yes, ma'am." Grinning, Maxim proudly dropped the garment to the floor, revealing his cock. A dark patch of thick pubic hair shadowed the area around the thick, meaty shaft, which stood swollen and ready for her. *Too bad*. His cock would surely be disappointed.

"Call me *queen*. I liked that better. 'Ma'am' makes you sound like a cowboy and me sound old." Walking around him, she inspected him thoroughly. From his six-pack and built pectoral muscles, to his broad, muscled back and arms, to his chiseled ass, she soaked in his every masculine feature. If she hadn't known him, she'd have thought Maxim was in construction or some other blue-collar job, at least until she took note of his trimmed, well-kept nails. He was so built, so tanned, but Elisa knew that was simply from hours of indulgent efforts at the gym, not working hard. Maxim had never lifted a finger out of necessity his whole life. Then again, neither had she; her father was rich and she had a huge trust fund. But unlike him, she chose not to take advantage of the fact.

If you asked her, what Maxim needed was a woman to put him in his place. Someone to jar him from his comfort zone. Maybe he'd never change, but she hoped he'd never forget her.

Maxim shifted his stance. "Enjoying yourself?"

"I will be." She smiled smartly, and traced a finger over his wide shoulders, walking around to face him. "I think, Maxim, I'd like you to kiss my breasts first."

Wetting his lips, he nodded confidently. "Not a problem. I love—"

Elisa put up her finger, quieting him. "Remember, you can't touch any other part of me. Not until I say."

He smiled, probably because he didn't get it, and then held out his hand. "Come here."

"Patience." Elisa removed her nightgown, throwing it in a heap to the floor. She wore no bra—she rarely did—but she'd always made a point of ensuring her panties were sexy. Lace and silk made her feel feminine.

Standing before him in only a pair of black thongs, confident in her role, her remaining anxiety dissipated. She felt powerful, womanly, and invincible. She loved it.

Pressing a finger to his chest, she slowly trailed the digit downward, over his navel, to his cock. Her thumb rested on its wide head, flicking back and forth, and making him groan. "And you can't touch yourself."

"Not a habit of mine," he answered stiffly, his control already clearly in danger.

Smiling, she bent down and kissed his tip gently, knowing damn well she was teasing him unmercifully and enjoying every second of it. "Not from what I've seen."

"That was your doing."

"Oh? How is that?" she asked, bringing her body closer to his, so that their thighs met. "Did watching me with a dildo turn you on?"

"Like you wouldn't believe."

A whoosh of relief flooded through her, transforming her embarrassment over the earlier scene into raw feminine power. Sexiness radiated through her body, making her glow.

"Then I wonder how pleasuring me with one will make you feel." She ground her cunt against his cock. "Especially when you can't touch yourself for relief. Hmmmm . . . an interesting concept. I wonder, Maxim, if your desire for me will keep you here or drive you away."

His Adam's apple bobbed up and down and she grabbed his head, pulling his mouth to her breasts. Digging her fingers in his short hair, she smothered him with the lush flesh, adoring the feel of his face buried in her chest.

Maxim gathered her breasts in his palms, lifting them, and bringing the mounds together. Gently, he kissed her left nipple, then her right, and slowly licked circles around her areolas. His tongue flicked over her nipples, coaxing the buds into tight peaks.

Loving it, she mashed his face into her. "More! Harder!"

Taking one of her hardened, sensation-infused nipples with his teeth, Maxim licked his tongue across its center, then suckled sharply, drawing arousal from her. With his free hand, he pinched and tweaked her opposite nipple, his attentions intense, not soft, not kind, and just the way she wanted. The way she needed. The way she commanded.

Pleasure bolted through her pussy, her labia and clit becoming swollen and wet. Already she ached to take him inside of her . . . something she would not, *could not*, do.

She pushed him south, forcing him on his knees. Abandoning her breasts, he kissed his way along her torso as his hands spread open her thighs. When his mouth reached the juncture between her legs, he parted her folds. He planted a soft kiss directly on her pulsing nub.

"What shall I do now, my queen?" he asked, breathing against her pussy.

Fuck me, fuck me, fuck me!

Elisa swallowed, hardly able to control herself. "You know."

"No, no, I'm afraid I don't." Maxim continued to hold her cunt wide open, his hot breath blowing across the tender area.

"You'll have to tell me, and in thorough detail, or I might miss something."

"Lick me."

His tongue darted out, barely making contact with her mons. "My queen, I must follow your rules. Please tell me how."

Her pussy shuddered, needing him so badly, she could hardly think. "Slowly. All the way."

"All the way?" Again, his tongue teased her, but naught more. Her knees became weak, threatening to give out on her. She could cry from the agony of wanting him.

Elisa grasped his hair and yanked his head, forcing his face in her cunt. "Lick all of me, not just one spot, but slowly, smoothly."

"Better, Elisa, better." His tongue followed her instructions, laving her pussy in measured, long movements. Elisa told herself to enjoy it. Every second. Every stroke. She was leading and he'd stop when she was ready for him to stop; she was nowhere near prepared for that.

Throwing her head back, she moaned aloud, savoring his oral pleasuring. He licked her like she'd lick a soft chocolate ice cream, swirling his tongue, smearing his lips against her, delighting in every tasteful inch of her pussy.

Her legs were turning to Jell-O. His tongue strokes weren't enough. She needed something to brace herself with. She needed more.

"Oh God. Wait," she commanded, halting his tongue movements. "I want to lie down."

She walked to the bearskin rug and lay down on it, propping up both of her legs and spreading herself wide. "Suck my clit."

"Your wish," he obliged her, his tone punctuated by his accent. "Is my every desire."

Elisa could hardly believe it was true.

Maxim crawled between her legs and claimed the dripping bead with his teeth, suctioning hard. Working it in and out of his mouth, he drove her into a frenzy from the pressure.

"Damn," she ground out. "You're good."

He sucked harder, so hard, it almost hurt, but in such a glorious way. Her body lifted off the floor as she moaned aloud, her fingers grasping desperately at the fur beneath her.

Christ, she couldn't take this sexual agony. Maxim had her ready to burst. She needed him to fuck her. Now.

No! That was what the dildo was for!

"Get me ready. Put . . . put your fingers in me," she told him, lifting her hips slightly. "Hurry."

Releasing her clit, he promptly drove two fingers into her slick sheath. Pumping them in and out of her, he licked all around her hole, pressing his tongue alongside the digits. She arched and pushed her lower half against him, needing more. So much more.

He slid another finger into her depths, then another. Her pussy opened for him, stretching and accepting the width of his hand eagerly, but needing more length. Needing him.

Elisa grasped for the dildo, her hands searching the bearskin rug until she found it lying next to her head. Picking up the sex toy, she handed it to him. "Here."

His eyes lit, connecting with hers. "You're serious?"

Unease curled through her, but she pushed the self-guessing away. "Yes. Now." She was being strong, not embarrassed, and she wanted this. "And hurry."

"Wow."

"What?"

"I've never had the privilege before." He grasped the fake cock at the base, and without preamble, drove it into her with one forceful thrust. Her pussy contracted with delight at the invasion, her arousal instantly driven to a pinnacle.

Maxim chuckled with delight. "This is going to be fun."

Maxim fucked her with the dildo in driving thrusts, pushing the rubber deep inside her, then ripping it out all too quickly. The toy reached her womb, it plunged so far within her, and she arched, screaming out with ecstasy.

Holding her hips at an angle, she met his pumping with vigorous bucking, positioning her lower half so that the dildo angled upward and stroked her G-spot time and again.

She thrashed and moaned so much, she began to get worn-out, despite the wave of rapture she rode on. Slowing her movements, she let him take sole control of the pleasuring.

Maxim drove the shaft in as far it would go, then stilled, slowly, torturously grinding it into her in wide circles that stretched her tunnel.

The movements were too much . . . too damn wonderful . . . and she found herself teetering at the brink. Her loins turned to fire, every inch of her mons and her cunt fiery hot with built up need. She was ready to detonate, all she needed was . . .

"Stop, Maxim. Fuck me!" What was she saying? *No!* Quickly she corrected herself, "Fuck me harder with the dildo. Faster. More, I need more!"

He slid his arm under her bottom, lifting her lower half and supporting her. Softly, he kissed her mons. "Are you sure you don't want *me?*"

"Please just do as I say!"

"Fine. As you wish, my queen." His voice was hollow with disappointment. "Harder, faster, it is."

He rammed into her and her body and her teetering release lurched. Again, he thrust into her, and this time, she lost it, spiraling into a violent orgasm that had her whole body convulsing.

She moaned in finality, and then went still, panting as her body recovered from the intense moment. Worn-out, she felt like a wet noodle, lying there limp, about to pass out from the physical and mental exhaustion, though she needed to maintain control.

Leaving the dildo buried deep inside her pulsing hot vagina, Maxim crawled over her. His legs straddled her and he leaned forward, nuzzling her face. To her surprise, tears slid down her cheeks . . . tears of pleasure, emotion, but not sadness.

Maxim kissed and licked the droplets away. "Are you all right? Was it too much?"

"No," she whispered. "It wasn't enough."

"Do you want . . . ?" He pushed his cock against her upper thigh, the movement applying pressure to the already inserted dildo. "We could use both."

"No," she said in a harsh voice. "You haven't proven your-self yet."

What? What would it take?

First he'd half frozen to death for Elisa, now his dick was so hard, so ready for her, he was in pain. And she said *no?* He still had to *prove* himself?

Damn! He was a man, not a superhero!

His jaw shook with frustration and he fought to steady him-self, to calm his nerves. *Fine.* If this was what she wanted, this was what she would get. He needed to show her he was serious more than he needed to get off.

It didn't matter anyway. Soon she'd be begging for him. Plead-ing to have his cock. Maybe then he'd turn Elisa's little game around on her and she'd see how being left in such agony felt.

For now, he'd oblige her. What choice did he have? He wanted, no needed, to be successful in proving himself to her, for his own sake as much as hers. He couldn't stand to see her tears. Whatever it took to make them disappear, he'd do. He kissed her salty cheeks, licking away the trails of moisture and tangling his hands in her lengthy tresses. How long he'd waited to feel the silky strands wrapped around his fingers. At one point, he won-dered if even touching Elisa was possible. Fucking her with a dildo wasn't quite what he'd had in mind, but nonetheless, Elisa was naked and underneath him. Getting inside her was only a matter of time . . . and effort.

He brought her hair to his nose, inhaling her scent, a spicy, woodsy perfume he'd never smelled before. Everything about Elisa was so different, so foreign from the spoiled females he knew. "God, you smell wonderful," he told her. "You are, by far, the most incredible woman I know."

She smiled sweetly at him, cuddling in his arms. "The answer is still no."

"When will it be yes?"

"When I'm ready."

He stroked her cheek and kissed her dewy lashes. "Then I guess I'll just have to make you ready."

She laughed, as if he'd just said something ridiculous. "Do your best."

four

I think I'd ski down Mount Everest for you." His hand gripping her lush ass, Maxim held Elisa flush against his torso. The dildo was still inserted deep in her pussy and the scent of her arousal floated through the air, mingling with her exotic scent.

Nuzzling her neck, he inhaled deeply, feeling like the luckiest man on earth, even if he did currently sport a raging erection which—if she was to be believed—wouldn't be satisfied anytime soon.

For now. She was a woman after all. She couldn't resist him forever. He could wait a little bit—he was quite confident he'd be well rewarded for his patience in more ways than one.

Leaning in, he planted his lips to hers, but she did not respond. Her mouth remained pressed shut. Despite how close to an embarrassing, premature explosion it brought him, he rotated his hips, rubbing his cock against her mons. "Come on, angel. I'm hurting. What's a man got to do to please you?"

"Nothing you can manage." Elisa turned her head, sighing. "Ski down Mount Everest? You'd break your neck. You barely made it here and we both know you couldn't make it home." The lack of emotion in her voice surprised him. He heard no humor, no teasing, just a blank statement.

Maxim hid his smile. Apparently it wasn't a good time to inform her he'd faked his helplessness. He'd just have to keep that little secret to himself. The last thing he wanted was to be booted back into the snow . . . the weather here in Colorado was god-awful miserable.

Ah, but thoughts of getting inside Elisa made it all seem so much warmer.

He'd just have to up his seduction efforts—before he exploded.

Maxim nuzzled against her, soaking up her body heat. His fingers found her nipples, tracing the outer rims of the tight circles. "You are truly the most beautiful female I've ever laid eyes on. Do you know that?"

"Until your next conquest." Smirking, she rolled her eyes. "I wonder what the hundred women before me would think about being booted from their status as 'the most beautiful female.' "

Ignoring her sarcasm, he stroked her soft bottom. "No, Elisa. Do you have any idea how long I've fantasized about this? How much I've dreamt about you?" He was determined to get through to her. To get *in* her. Whatever it took. "When I look into your eyes, your soul sparkles like diamonds. I feel richer than—"

"*What?*" Elisa sighed and rolled over, shaking her head. "Don't try to sweet-talk me, Maxim. It won't work."

Okay, maybe he'd gone a bit far ... even he had trouble believing that.

Except oddly, the statement hadn't been total bullshit.

She shook her head. "You know, I don't know what I was thinking. That may be you could be sincere?"

"You—" The protest on the tip of his tongue fell away. Damn it, he must be fooling himself to believe Elisa would ever been anything but a frigid—

He stopped himself, knowing damn good and well Elisa might be too smart for her own good, but she was far too sweet to be called a bitch, even if it was only in his mind.

"I don't know why you keep trying to pull that crap on me, but like I said, I'm not stupid enough to fall for your lines." Elisa removed herself from his arms, reaching down to pull the cum-coated dildo from her feminine depths. She tossed it on the blanket and rolled away from him. "You know, Maxim, you can't prove yourself in the time span of a half hour. It's going to take more than pleasuring me with a dildo once to make me trust you."

In one swift movement, she grabbed her nightgown, leapt to her feet, and quickly brought the flannel down, hiding her curves.

He gulped, realizing she was right. *Could* he manage?

He had to. For once, pleasing a woman meant something to him.

"I'm sure you must need a cold shower." Her tone was firm, her shoulders squared, and her back turned to him as she pointed down the long dark hall behind them, and then quickly folded her hands. "If you'd like, the bathroom is the last room on the left."

Though she was clearly trying to hide how she felt with a strong voice and tall stance, when she'd gestured, he'd noticed her fingers shaking slightly. He didn't know why she had to make such a big deal of this. So they desired each other, so she'd acted upon her needs . . . so a dildo had been involved. What was so wrong with that? She wasn't married, wasn't obligated in any way. They were two consenting adults.

Over-thinking seemed to be a real issue for Elisa.

But not him.

He was still horny as hell.

Maxim stepped forward, cradling her hips in his palms and pressing his rigid cock against the crack of her ass. "Come shower with me."

"Whatever." Her feet sped into motion and she stalked toward the kitchen. "I'm going to go fix you something to eat, then find out when this blizzard is going to end."

"So I can go?" he ground out, every fiber of his being yearning to catch her, throw her over his knee, and spank her until she wanted to be bad; Elisa was too damn good to be mentally healthy. He was going to lose his mind trying to woo her.

"Yes," she hissed, her words barely audible. "So you can go."

His cock melted, his massive erection turning into shriveled disappointment. Really? That was *it*? Elisa was done with him? Back to being—yeah, he was going to say it—bitchy? To rejecting him? *That* fast?

After what had just happened between them, he wasn't in the mood to be pushed away. Cast off. Discarded like some dildo worker without a union during layoff time. He didn't understand how she could change so swiftly, but he sure wasn't going to simply accept her mood swing.

Suddenly, he lost it. Going after her, he caught her by the shoulders, spun her around and pulled her flush against him. "Elisa, *please*." He gave her no time to protest, tangling his fingers in her hair and swept her mouth up with his. The kiss was hard and fast, needy and unrelenting.

He wanted her. She wanted him. No was not an option. Not anymore. Damn it, he was going to *prove* to her just how much she wanted him.

Elisa squeaked in his mouth, passionately returning his affections as he explored her moist depths with his tongue.

Together, they stumbled forward, until he had her backed against a wall. He pulled her head back, devouring her. She was so delicious.

He couldn't wait anymore. He needed her. He needed her to need him.

Cupping her breasts, he massaged them deeply. His thumbs flicked her nipples and felt the buds harden under the attention. Damn, he couldn't wait to suckle them, to—

Suddenly, she shoved him with all her might, wrenching her mouth free. "Stop!" She pushed him again, putting distance between them as she wiped her mouth free. Breathing heavily, she shook her head. "Go take a shower, Maxim."

Not again. "I must be in hell."

She slinked past him and headed toward the kitchen. He reached for her, but she jerked from his touch and stood with her back to him. "Hell is where the devil belongs."

"Ouch." He pulled back, clenching his jaw as he stepped away. "Okay, I'll give you some space and go take a shower."

"Good."

Much as Maxim wanted to be sweet and subservient and continue wooing her, her attitude plain ticked him off. Irritation squeezed at his heart, prickled at his nerves, and he couldn't bite back the words on the tip of his tongue. "Do me a favor," he called.

"Aren't I doing enough for you? I do believe I've saved you from freezing to death."

Maxim's lips pressed flat as he growled through them. "Well, I believe I did just 'pay' for my room and board, at least for tonight."

His pride roared at the truth and he fought to contain the thousand curses dancing on the tip of his tongue.

"Fine," Elisa huffed. "What do you want?"

Maxim ground his teeth and shoved down the urge to storm from the cabin. Jesus, did she have any idea how she was pushing him? With any other female, he'd be gone by now. He didn't even really know *why* he was going through all this trouble for her, except he'd wanted her, so badly, for so long.

After his brother, Keaton, had died in the car accident— murdered by his cheating wife, as far as Maxim was concerned— he'd sworn never to love. But from the day he'd met Elisa, he'd been tempted.

Elisa accused him of being a player, but here he was, being sincere, and she was driving him away. That hurt. He ought to take a hint.

"Pour some wine." Maxim headed down the hallway, toward the bathroom. "You need to loosen up."

Why hadn't he seen this coming? He wasn't playing with fire, he was holding a match to explosives just like he had back in college. Elisa had always had a talent for pushing his buttons. If he didn't get cooled down soon, he'd detonate. He definitely needed that cold shower.

What had she been thinking? She should've let him freeze. Hell, she should've shot him.

Elisa retrieved salad makings from the fridge and practically threw everything on the counter.

The bastard. If she had a bottle of wine, she'd shove it up his ass.

The last thing she intended to do was loosen up. Maxim wanted her *easy*, and easy was a surefire path straight to heartbreak, do not pass go, do not collect two hundred dollars.

Maybe she wasn't being nice, or easy, but she was handling him and all considering, she was doing it well. After foreplay like that, saying no hadn't been easy. The urge to let Maxim do anything and everything he wanted to her had been powerful, so maybe she'd been bitchy, but at least she'd been strong.

Strong. Right. So why did it feel like she was about to puke? Why was her heart beating a mile a minute? Why couldn't she breathe?

Damn him. Tacky and sluttish as he was, Maxim was too sexy, too damn conniving . . . too much for her to handle.

Elisa's hands shook violently as she tore the lettuce, letting the pieces fall into the salad bowl. She'd gone grocery shopping in town a few days ago, and she had plenty of fresh fruit and vegetables on hand. Good thing she had no appetite, because she was feeding him the healthiest, most anti-man meal she could pull off. One even she wouldn't care to stomach. Then he was going to pleasure her again. She wanted another orgasm and she deserved what she craved. Damn right.

Her hands shook so hard, she knocked the bowl on its side.

Oh God. She couldn't do this. She couldn't just use him and lose him.

She was crazy to think she could.

No! She *had* to and she would! If she could handle him, she could handle any man.

Yeah right.

She might as well chain herself to this cabin and throw in the towel. Seclude herself for the rest of her life and become a miserable, crazed hermit.

"You already vowed never to leave this cabin," she reminded herself out loud. "Several times in fact."

But after a few weeks here, she was lonely, bored, and wishing she were somewhere else, *anywhere*, making some sort of difference. She had too much to offer to just wallow in solitude for eternity. Surely, she could find a place in this world . . . it would just have to be one where no one knew about tabloids. Like a tribal village in South America. Or Antarctica.

"Oh, why does humid weather and bugs or miles of snow and ice sound so good right now?"

Because she'd already gone insane, hence her decision to allow Maxim in her house, and possibly even her body. Hence her new habit of talking to herself.

"You've really done yourself a favor this time, genius." Shaking, Elisa sliced the tofu she'd marinated earlier and slid it into a pan coated with olive oil. While the large white chunks cooked, she chopped some carrots and tomatoes.

She had to stop worrying. Guarding her heart from him would be easy. She just needed to distance herself from anything emotional. To stay aloof.

"Use him and lose him," she reminded herself, pouring cold, canned lentils over the salad. Several vibrated right out of the can and onto the floor. "Damn it!" She gathered the spilled beans, shaking her head. "I have to pull it together. Handling Maxim is not that hard. Not hard at all."

A deep chuckle sounded behind her. "But I am, Elisa."

Elisa practically jumped out of her skin, whirling around, beans flying in Maxim's direction. "What?"

Maxim leaned in the doorway, looking right at home, relaxed, except for his cock, which stood proud and tall, forming a tent in the painted-on grey jogging pants he'd apparently stolen from her dresser. Her body practically floated inside the leisure wear, but the sweats clung to his sturdy hips and thick thighs like a second skin. He wore no shirt, and little droplets of water still glistened on his tanned flesh, which was mottled with goose bumps. She could never have imagined such a hilarious sight would look so incredibly sexy, but it did. All. Too. Much.

Desire buzzed through her, gathering at her center. Clenching the handle of the spoon so tightly her fingers hurt, she stared at him, caught off guard by the instant, intense way she craved him.

"You're pretty damn cute when you talk to yourself." He flashed her a lopsided, dazzling smile that just about knocked her over. "I was enjoying that."

Elisa swallowed, working the muscles in her throat, but the knot lodged in her windpipe refused to abate. For the second time, her eyes darted to his cock, thinking of the immense width he'd had pressed against her pussy only a half hour ago. She could have taken him.

Why hadn't she?

Oh, right. Control.

She had to stop this! Get a grip . . . and not on a spoon!

Elisa lifted her chin high enough that she couldn't look down at his raging erection. "So you were spying on me?"

Maxim cocked a curious eye at her. "What was I supposed to do? Hang out in the bathroom until you called me for dinner?"

"You were supposed to take a shower."

"I did. I took a cold one." He gestured to his cock, a hand movement she absolutely refused to follow. "It didn't cool me off, as you can see, so I'm glad you've loosened up some. Where's the wine?"

"I didn't drink any." Elisa bent and picked up the rest of the scattered lentils. Maxim strode into the kitchen, kneeling next to her and aiding her efforts.

"Well, how about we pop open a bottle over dinner—" His hand paused in midair, palm out, a lentil lying in its center. Frowning, he glanced to her. "Are these cold beans?" His eyes darted to the smoke rising from the stove. "And God, what's that smell?"

"Oh no! The tofu!" Elisa leapt to her feet, knocking the pan off the gas flame with her bare hand. Heat seared her skin and she cried out in pain. "Ouch! Damn it!"

Grabbing a spatula, she quickly scooped the squares onto the kitchen counter. Thankfully, they were only somewhat black, but her hand sported a red, two-inch burn across her palm. She shook away the hurt, cursing under her breath.

Maxim pulled her into his arms and secured her wrist. She knew she should resist, but how could she? She was in pain.

Sorry excuse.

"Let's get that cooled off." He led her to the sink, holding her palm under a flow of freezing cold water. "Better?"

"Yes," she whispered, ready for her hand back. "I'm fine. It's not that bad."

"It's bad enough." Lifting her injury to his mouth, he kissed directly above the blistering mark, working the sensitized area with his tongue. A million pins pricked her skin as her body ignited hotter, her hungry pussy screaming to be filled and fast.

She should make him stop. Really, really, she should.

But she was in pain.

Maxim kissed up her arm, sending shivers over her skin. His mouth worked its way to her shoulder, then licked across her collarbone, and suckled up her neck, until he had her lower lip in his suction, drawing it between his teeth.

He nibbled at the plumped flesh, delicately biting the perimeter. "You taste like pure heaven," he murmured, licking her. Flutters twittered in her belly. Oh no, he didn't! His sentiment set off flares in Elisa, and she pushed him back, breaking the glorious kiss. "Stop, before the rest of the meal is ruined."

Wiping his mouth with the back of his hand, Maxim stepped away, his head bowed. "Determined to keep me at bay, aren't you?"

"Yes."

"You know Elisa, I—" His words fell, his solemn look lifting into a smile. "Never mind. What's to eat?"

"It's a new recipe. There it is, on the counter. Take a look."

He stared at the food, his eyes wide. "Dinner is burnt tofu and cold beans and salad?"

For the first time in quite a while, Elisa wanted to laugh. "Yup." The shock written all over his face was worth every penny she wasn't making off her porn career.

"Jesus." He blinked a few times, then shot her a look that screamed *you're crazy*. "You better have a brand new bottle of French dressing. I'm going to need the whole thing."

Elisa's smile broadened, but her emotionless voice hid her humor well. Remaining aloof, she spoke matter-of-factly, keeping Maxim at a safe distance. Maybe if she made him uncomfortable enough, he'd want to leave. "I'm sorry. I don't have any dressing. Nor do I have any wine."

She really didn't either, thanks to her deep appreciation for French dressing and more recently, French wine. What could she say? She'd been under a ton of stress lately.

"What?" A muscle in his cheek twitched. "I think I misheard you, 'cause I thought you said there's no wine."

"I did."

"You're telling me I have to eat salad with *no* dressing, *no* wine, and *no* sex afterward?"

"Yes." Hiding a smile, she met his gaze, daring him to argue with her. "If you don't like it, you're welcome to ski back to Aspen."

Silence hung heavy around them, thick and loaded with tension. She was playing with fire, dumping an unidentified substance over flames, not sure what the reaction would be, but well aware she could blow them both up. Maxim wasn't used to being tested, of having to work for a female's affection, rather than being slobbered all over by some drunk hussy desperate for his cock.

To her surprise, he flashed a dazzling smile and rubbed his hands together. "Leave? I think not. Your company alone will sustain me." He reached out, massaging her shoulder. "It's my fault I distracted you from your cooking anyway. Now, what can I help with?"

Elisa stared at him in shock. Maxim might not be used to having to make such an effort, but she certainly wasn't accustomed to having to fight so hard for composure . . . or to push a guy away. No matter how much she tried to give him a hint, Maxim just kept coming toward her. After all these years, he was just as relentless. Persuasive. Dangerous.

"There's milk in the fridge," she told him, shirking away from his touch. "Pour us each a glass."

"Ah, milk. Something I do enjoy."

She gave him an evil smile. "Oh really? On second thought, I may want to save the milk for when you leave."

"Don't be mean, Elisa. It doesn't become you." Swinging open her fridge, he grabbed the gallon container, unscrewed the cap, and drank straight from the jug—*her* jug—with his lushly plump lips. "So, tell me, what have you done since college?"

What did he think he was doing? The nerve of him! He was contaminating her milk! Who knows where his lips had been . . .

Actually, she knew exactly where his lips had been. And to her knowledge, he hadn't brushed his teeth, either.

Elisa tore her gaze away. So his lips were molded around the spout, exchanging her taste for milk. Watching him guzzle was not sexy. It wasn't. She wouldn't allow it to be.

Refusing to let his childish actions get to her, she retrieved some silverware and plates, motioning for him to get the glasses from the cupboard, then led him to the breakfast nook. "Let's see . . . what did I do with myself? You mean besides unknowingly become this country's biggest porn star overnight? You want to know about the sex, right? The guys?"

Sitting down at the table, she forked a bite of burnt tofu, and glared at Maxim as he planted his ass in the chair.

"No, actually." Maxim appeared startled as he situated his weight, looking huge in comparison to the tiny furniture. "I didn't mean that. I wanted to know what *you've* been accomplishing, not your asshole boyfriend."

Elisa rolled her eyes. When would he finish with this act? His constant bullshit was too much to tolerate. He didn't need to pretend to be interested in her. "Oh, please. Next you'll tell me you give a damn about the environment. Like back in college, remember?"

"College was a long time ago, Elisa." Staring down at his plate, he spoke quietly. "I've changed."

She didn't buy it. No way. Maxim just wanted her sympathy. Her fondness. So he could screw her.

She'd prove it. "Really? What have you done since then?"

He shoved his food around, his tongue lolling against the inside of his cheek. "Stuff."

"What kind of stuff?" she pressed. "Do you have a real job yet?"

"You know I work for my parents."

"No, Maxim, do you have a real job?"

His head snapped up, his eyes narrowed with irritation. "You know what, Elisa? I have my reasons for working for my parents and they aren't for you to judge. You're being mean, and I'm exasperated. No, I'm pissed, Elisa, and I give up."

Score. She'd known he'd never stick to his guns. Prove himself. Well, it was about time. She was tired of battling for composure.

Just like she'd thought, Maxim was the same as he'd always been. This was a game to him, *she* was a game, and currently not fun to play. Hence his surrender.

"Yes, I'm not being nice, and you know Maxim, *I* have my reasons, not for you to judge."

His lips twisted, flattening. "Yeah. I know exactly why."

"Oh, no surprise, since you know everything, almighty Max Cox."

Their gazes locked, hers defying his.

"The walls around your heart are a hundred feet high," he declared. "You say I'm afraid to live? At least I have fun. You're still as uptight and afraid to live as you were back in school. Maybe worse."

"Whatever."

"Seriously. You had me screw you with a dildo. Why won't you just give me a chance to talk to you? Am I really that bad?"

"Yes."

"Like I said, you're afraid to live. Scared to freaking death you might actually like me, aren't you? That maybe, just maybe, I am a decent guy, and you'd fall in love, and you'd have no reason to be such a . . . a . . ."

"A bitch?" Elisa offered. "Maxim, I'm not afraid to live and I'm not afraid of you. I'm just not a slut. Don't you get it? We're far too different!"

"A slut?" His brows rose sky high. "I'm not the one who ended up a porn queen!"

That took her down a peg or two, now didn't it? And lit her fire, straight into a burning inferno of rage.

"You deserve the crown, you *queen* of bullshit and bad lays!" she snapped in retaliation.

The moment she'd uttered the insult, she knew it was the wrong thing to say. She hadn't just called him a slut, but gay and bad in bed, which probably wasn't true.

Silence again fell around them as they glared at each other.

Finally, Maxim slammed down his fork and spoke again, his words a low growl, emitted from between ground teeth. "You know, maybe if you'd let loose a little, have some fun—"

"Be more like you? You mean I should sleep with everyone to cross my path? Throw away my future for parties and booze and babes?" Elisa drew in a deep breath, at her wit's end. "I'm sorry, Maxim. That was immature of me to—"

"I'll be all too happy to get out of here!" He leapt to his feet, knocking over the chair. "Don't bother to pack me a doggie bag, not that any animal would touch that crap!"

five

He'd stolen her jogging pants.

Maxim's thievery didn't elude him. Actually, he couldn't stop thinking that he should return the too-tight sweats and put his wet jeans back on. But he wasn't going back to her cabin. Not that he'd made it far—he currently stood between his two pine trees, pathetically unable to even stand on his skis in the knee-deep snow. But he'd rather freeze to death than ask Elisa for any favors.

After her final insulting comment, he'd gathered his coat and pathetic wet gear, and escaped from her house with a hot temper, bruised pride, and her pants . . . which she really wasn't getting back.

Guilt tugged at his heart, reminding him that they weren't his to keep. Telling him to go back inside and return them.

Crap. What was wrong with him? They were just Fruit of the Loom. Nothing special.

Maxim groaned and hoisted his body upward, finally on his feet *and* in his skis. "Fabulous!" he muttered to himself, gripping the poles. Now he could get out of here. He'd had enough of the cold and enough of Elisa's cold heart.

Again, his chest tightened, reminding him of the jogging pants he was stealing. Of the way she'd panted—*heated*—underneath him as he'd screwed her with the dildo. The way she'd come.

And then the way she'd laid into him over that pathetic, tofu-excuse for a meal.

Stupid guilt over the damn sweats or not, he was getting out of here. Gingerly, he slid one step, then another. He gave up on Elisa. Threw in the towel. He didn't want her *this* bad.

Liar!

Well, clearly she didn't want him. Or she'd be acting more . . . more . . . female. Nice. Human.

She asked you to pleasure her, asked you to prove yourself.

Suddenly, he lurched, his feet quickly sinking into the snow and making him tumble forward. Landing face-first in the icy white blanket covering the earth, Maxim hollered, his outburst muffled, his legs tangled. Pummeling the snow, he let Mother Earth know damn good and well how he felt about her right now. This wasn't fair!

He twisted and turned and fought to straighten out his legs without taking off the skis that kept locking together, making his life impossible. But he couldn't. He was all tied up in knots. Stuck.

Falling backward, Maxim melted into the snow. What the hell was he doing? The snow buffeting his body instantly cooled his anger, reminding him why he'd stayed. Why had Elisa behaved the way she did? She was clearly scared. Trying to push him away. And not only had he let her, he'd stolen her pants. He'd acted like a jerk . . . not a smart way to gain her trust and confidence.

He couldn't leave yet, because he didn't want to.

He really didn't care about the sex. He wanted to pleasure Elisa again, to convince her to give him a chance, if anything, to get her to *like* him. It couldn't really be that difficult, now could it? Certainly not as impossible as skiing back to town, then immediately back again, once he'd realized all too late the huge mistake he'd made, which he would.

Maxim rolled his head in the cold cushioning beneath him and closed his eyes, releasing a pent-up breath. Suddenly, his chest felt less constricted, his heart, lighter.

To his surprise, his legs easily untangled and he hefted himself up. Then, to his shock, he skied quite successfully up to her cabin, prepared to prove himself all over again.

Curled in front of the stone fireplace, Elisa hugged a steaming cup of hot cocoa in her grasp, staring at the licking flames. A blanket warmed her legs, but not her soul. She felt like a shell of a woman—one who'd just screwed up. Big time.

She kept telling herself she was doing the right thing, but every fiber of her being begged to differ. Her conscience told her she'd behaved badly. Her heart cried to have Maxim return. Her body, well, her body had some pretty lustful demands she could never fulfill on her own.

She needed Maxim, needed him for so many petty little reasons it was ridiculous, and yet the last thing she wanted was to *need* any man.

One thing was for certain—he'd been right: she was putting up walls, huge, stone defenses around herself. She was afraid of him . . . of losing herself to another player. Her physical desire wasn't the only thing she had to learn to control. If she couldn't manage her emotions, she'd always be an ant underneath some big man's boot. She—

The front door creaked open, then clicked quietly shut. Surprised, Elisa straightened. "Maxim?" she called, unable to imagine it was anyone else and hoping it wasn't . . . for a myriad of reasons.

"The one and only." His heavy ski boots clanked on the hardwood floors as he strode into the great room, looking cold and wet from head to toe. Icicles hung from his shaggy golden hair and clung to his stubble. "I sincerely hope you weren't expecting some other man."

"I thought you left." She smiled, actually appreciating the shivering sight of him as she clutched her cocoa nervously. "What's the matter? Couldn't make it back to Aspen?"

For a moment, he just stared at her, something haunting about his brown eyes. Sad.

She studied the truth evident on his face. Never before had she realized how fathomless his gaze was . . . the secrets it hid. The more he was around, looking at her with those deep eyes, the more she second guessed her assessment of him. Maybe he wasn't just some shallow male whore. Maybe he wasn't lazy and self-centered. Maybe he was troubled.

He shifted. "I realized I'd stolen your sweats. Thought I should return them." His tongue darted out and ran along his upper lip. "You know . . ."

Stolen jogging pants were a stupid reason to come back. He knew that, she knew that, but what she didn't get was the unspoken meaning behind his blithe words. *Why* was he here? Now? In the first place? She just didn't get him.

Elisa reminded herself to keep her distance . . . but nicely this time.

"Oh, well, thank you, I suppose." She raised her chin, looking him square in the face. She couldn't mince words or play games with Maxim, not now. She had to set him straight or this would never work. Things between them were too volatile. "I assume, if you're coming back, that you realize the rules have not changed."

"Of course." His smile was glassy. "Would you have me pleasure you again?"

Elisa swallowed. Oh, but she was playing a dangerous game with her own self, as well as Maxim.

Setting the mug aside, she firmed her tone, as well as her muscles, refusing to become Play-Doh in his hands. She'd take what she wanted, but she wouldn't be jerked by any man. "Maxim, clearly I'm not one of your easy girls. So don't walk back in here deluding yourself."

"You're not easy, Elisa. Precisely why I am here." He unzipped his coat, yanking it off.

Underneath, he wore no shirt and his skin was blistering red. The fool. If he kept freezing himself, soon he'd be sicker than a dog.

Her gaze wandered over his built pectoral muscles to his well-defined abdomen. Excitement flared in her loins.

"There's hot cocoa in the kitchen if you'd like," she suggested. "You should get out of those wet clothes. Get warmed up."

"Thanks." He disappeared from the room. A few minutes later, he returned in dry clothes, steaming mug in hand. He sat next to her, so that his cold body brushed her warm one in sharp contrast. "Why do we fight?"

She shivered at the truth. "It's easier than getting along, I suppose."

"Why is that?"

I want you, unreasonably.

Elisa shrugged. "We're so different."

"Are we?"

She didn't answer his question. She couldn't continue this conversation, not honestly. After a few moments of silence, she said, "I've never had a serious relationship. Derrick . . . I don't know. I really liked him, I did, but it wasn't love."

"Good thing," he grunted. "Let's just say I hope for his sake we never meet."

"I hope you do. Have at him." She chuckled. "What about you? Any girls manage to pin you down for more than a date?"

"No one's ever held my interest." He sat his mug on the floor in front of him and wrapped his arms around her, squeezing. "No one but you."

She looked up at him, smiling. "I'm flattered."

Maxim winked at her, his lips hovering dangerously close to hers. "You should be."

Suddenly, she wanted him to prove himself. Wanted to get past the hard part so she could believe him. Trust him.

Make love to him.

"Undress then and I'll be back." Elisa stood and walked down the hall to her room. Kneeling, she pulled a Rubbermaid container out from under her bed and popped open the lid, revealing sex toys galore.

Her fingers rimmed the edge, her mind still focused on Maxim's bare chest. His body.

She didn't just want any old dildo this time. She needed one so rock-your-world fantastic, she'd be satisfied—completely—with it. Not yearning for Max Cox.

But which one?

The choice wasn't easy, weighed down by the reality that she'd have to present whatever she chose to him. No matter how strong she made herself, no matter how much she wanted this, she couldn't stop feeling self-conscious.

Stalling, Elisa slowly sifted through the box of sexual goodies. What would Lizzy think if she knew Elisa was letting a man operate her toys? Would she be all for it? Or against it?

Likely the latter. Letting Maxim touch her was too risky. But no matter how hard she tried, Elisa couldn't be like Lizzy. She couldn't simply turn her back on men and never think twice about sex. So for her, learning to deal with them in a hardcore way was the next best thing.

Elisa retrieved a rather large, but floppy, imitation cock. Nah. She wanted something firmer. "Firm as Maxim's cock," she whispered under her breath.

"Perhaps I can be of assistance?"

Her heart kicked in her chest as she jerked around to find a very naked, very erect, Maxim watching her. "You've really got to stop doing that."

He granted her another one of his dubious, meant-to-charm smiles. "Why don't you let me chose, if I'm going to be the one conducting?"

Forget butterflies. Her stomach was being attacked by killer wasps, buzzing all around her insides, making her feel nauseous.

"Because . . ." Elisa hesitated. She couldn't really think of a good reason *why*, except that, somehow, letting him have control of which toy he'd be inserting in her was too intimate, too personal, which was probably ludicrous, given she was about to let him pleasure her.

She picked up a very plain, very straight, flesh-colored vibrator. "This one will do."

"Do? Not even close." Dropping to his knees next to her, Maxim claimed her hand, sending shivers down her spine. He peeled open her fingers, forcing her to drop the bland toy. "Come now, Elisa. If you won't play fair, you could at least share."

She swallowed deeply. Despite the protests raging in her mind, she couldn't seem to form a legitimate response. All she could think of was the biggest sex toy in the room—Maxim. Of making good use of him.

After closely examining his choices, Maxim selected the biggest, most complicated vibrator from her stash. Brilliant blue and waterproof, the head of the fake cock was curved like the head of a spoon, so it could easily reach, and press into, a woman's G-spot. It came complete with a clit stimulator, which was decorated with little bumps to provide stimulation.

Elisa gulped. She was so in over her head, drowning—hell, ready to swallow all the water in the world—if only he'd just shove the damn vibrator in her without preamble. She'd turned that specific one on once before, just out of curiosity, so she knew it had three functions—pulse, twist, and jack rabbit.

She blew out a nervous breath, reminding herself the best dildo and a mind-blowing orgasm was what she wanted anyway. "Looks great. That'll do." Her agreement came out pathetically shaky, reminding her of the man trap she was falling for already. Maxim might be good, but she was better . . . and in charge.

Lifting her chin, she commanded herself to be strong. Her wavering was allowing Maxim to control the game and that wouldn't do. He was at *her* mercy. Their gazes met, uniting in acute understanding.

She stood, her every nerve alive with need. The thrill of once again being the queen—of her body and his actions—electrified her from head to toe, her libido responding in earnest. Her clit pulsed for his touch and her pussy hungered to be filled, lining with liquid passion.

The temptation to rush into the heat of the moment, to throw aside her idealisms and let Maxim completely have his way with her, was powerful. She knew she had to take things slow. To be careful.

Sitting on the edge of the bed, she let her legs dangle off as she lay back and stretched her arms above her head. The position thrust her breasts upward, her sensation-infused nipples brushing the soft fabric of her nightgown. "Undress me, Maxim. With your teeth."

His hungry wolf eyes flashed over her form, his smile devilish and dimpled as he dropped the sex toy next to her. "All too eagerly, my queen."

Standing between her legs, he climbed over her, his rigid cock pressing against the inside of her thigh. He brought his mouth to the top button of her flannel nightgown, working the fastening free. Moving on, he undressed her one button at a time, his teeth and lips grazing across her bare skin. Shudders racked her body, running over her electrified flesh and straight to her pussy.

Trembling, she clutched his shoulders for support. As he worked the buttons between her breasts open, his tongue darted out, making contact with her chest. Her fingers dug into his muscles. Good lord. She was taking this slow because she wanted to maintain control . . . not lose it. How could his every slight touch feel so erotic? He hadn't even gotten to the good parts, and already, she could feel an orgasm building in her, threatening her very sanity.

She was afraid. What if she forgot herself, caught up in the throes of passion? Let herself—or Maxim—do things she'd regret? What if she lost her head, or worse, her heart?

What if she didn't?

Again, his mouth pressed and slid over the sensitized skin of her breasts and she clenched his shoulders so hard that her nails pierced his skin.

His eyes darted up, gleaming with passion. "Feeling wild?" Wild? That wasn't the half of it. Every fiber of her being wanted him to gobble her up, to lick and suck and bite her, to take her breasts and lather attention over them.

"Damn straight." She squeezed his shoulders tighter. "Don't stop."

By the time his mouth reached her waist, Elisa couldn't bear another second. His tongue darted into her belly button, shoving her over the edge. Fuck undressing her the rest of the way. She wanted him sucking her nipples. Now.

"Stop! Damn it, you're too slow!" Grasping him by the hair, she tugged him upward. "Kiss my breasts. My nipples."

A sigh of relief escaped Maxim as he climbed back over her. "Gladly," he whispered, his breath caressing her breasts. Not at all gentle, he claimed her left nipple, drawing it between his lips and sucking furiously. He pulled the achingly tight bud between his teeth, rolling it.

Lightning struck Elisa, ecstasy searing her body as he tormented the ever-hardening pebble. Pulling, he drew the bud outward, then suddenly freed it, allowing her nipple to pop back into place. His tongue darted out and he licked the tip, slowly drawing a circle around her areola.

"Oh, Maxim, yes," she panted, guiding his head to her right breast. "More."

Maxim rained kisses over the soft mound, then traced a path to her intensely erect nipple, claiming its center. Grabbing his head, she ground his mouth into her. "More. Suck more."

Maxim obeyed, nursing her like a babe feeding. Sparks shot through her pussy and she lifted, wanting to be filled.

To her disappointment, he pulled free. "God, Elisa, you're incredible. Beautiful." His words fluttered across her skin, the line making her flinch in disappointment. "You know, I could fall—"

In love? Hell no! She wasn't being prey to that line.

The moment had been so perfect, the ecstasy so glorious, and he'd ruined it. She wouldn't have any of his bullshit . . . not now . . . not as vulnerable as she currently was.

Stretching her arm, she smacked his bare ass and not lightly. "None of that now."

"Hey!" His muscles stiffened in protest, his cock driving upward, ramming against her mons, applying pressure to her nerve-laden clit.

She spanked him again, this time just for fun. "If I want to hear your sweet talking, I'll ask. Now . . ."

He glared at her defiantly, but the passion dancing in his confused gaze was undeniable.

His mouth smashed down upon her breasts, devouring the flesh. He suckled, nipped, and licked at her greedily, driving her to again deliver a warning to his rear.

"Nicely, Maxim," she demanded. "Your job is to please *me*, remember?"

"All too well," he murmured, slowing his vigorous actions and taking her nipple into his mouth. He licked around the bud, flicking the peak, then drawing it between his lips. She bloomed from deep within and arched into his attentions, enjoying his oral pleasuring so much, yet desperate for more . . . more than his mouth could ever give.

Cradling the weight of her breast in his palms, he drew on her harder. Meanwhile, his thumb flicked over her free nipple.

Pleasure shot straight to her clit. She swam in glorious, delirious desire until she could take no more. Half-drunk with lust, she pushed Maxim's head south. "Get this nightgown off of me. Fast."

He resumed the torturous task of unbuttoning her with his mouth, his lips hot and soft against her skin. She couldn't stand any more torture! "No, Maxim. Hurry!"

His hands slid along her sides as he dropped onto his knees between her legs, and cupped her bottom, still undressing her so slowly, she wanted to cry. "I can only go so fast."

"Rip it off."

"If you'd just be patient, I could please you." He squeezed her ass firmly. "As you truly wish."

Patient? That wasn't any easy thing to be when she was dying from need. But he was right. She was supposed to be taking things slow. Not getting caught up in the moment . . .

Or was it already too late?

The walls of her pussy flexed, demanding to be filled. Biting her lower lip, Elisa silenced her demands, and allowed him to continue his painstakingly slow undressing.

With every second that passed, she was certain she'd detonate. She could barely tolerate the tingle-invoking caresses of his mouth against her bare skin, but somehow, some way, she restrained the orgasm threatening her.

Finally, the last button released, Maxim opened her nightgown, fully exposing her to him.

"What would you have me do now, my queen?"

Elisa lifted her feet to the edge of the mattress, spreading and propping her legs wide. "Prepare me for the vibrator."

His fingers rested upon her mons, pulling her folds apart and diving in with his tongue. Swiping along her clit, he tasted her, then probed deep into her vagina.

Elisa's back arched as she held tightly to the comforter beneath her, almost unable to breathe.

His tongue dove in and out of her, licking along her labia, softly, slowly, sampling every inch of her pussy. She bucked against his face, fucking his mouth.

Inserting two fingers into her sheath, he spread them within her, forcing her inner muscles to stretch against him. He slid his other hand under her bottom, lifting her so that he could press his hand far inside her slick, welcoming cunt.

To her great physical appreciation, his fingers twisted and curled within her, searching around her pelvis bone and discovering her G-spot. The strongest wave of pleasure to ever rock her body slammed through her full force as he massaged the sensitive spot and his mouth returned to praising her pussy, licking and loving all over her clit.

"You like that, don't you?" he asked.

Not wanting him to stop, but desperately trying to hang onto her control, she whispered her reply. "Yes. Just like that."

"Good. I like it too," he told her. "I like the look on your face and being deep inside of you. You're so soft, so tight."

Any measure of restraint Elisa still possessed was wiped into oblivion as she went wild, thrashing against him, riding his mouth and fingers. "Maxim! God, that's so good!"

The threat of an orgasm strengthened, vibrating in her from head to toe, and she twisted away from him. She didn't want to come yet. Not like this. She wanted to experience her release all at once . . . and in a huge way. She wanted to walk away from this bed satisfied. Not still longing for Maxim.

"The vibrator," she told him. "Now."

"I thought you'd never ask." Maxim retrieved his fingers, licked her arousal from his lips, and took the toy.

Dipping back into her pussy with his forefinger, he retrieved some of her cream and spread the lubrication up and down the length of the toy, then positioned it at her entry.

"I know you're feeling needy right now, but I'm going to go slow. This is one big toy." Without turning it on, he pressed the fake cock an inch inside her, and no more, driving her insane. She pushed against him, writhing and trying to gain more length.

"No," she insisted. "Give it all to me. I can take it."

He lowered his head, gently kissing her mons and brushing his chin along her pubic hair. "Let me pleasure you, my queen. I promise you'll enjoy it."

Her heart squeezed tightly at the intimate action. Such consideration, such affection—from him—was not what she needed, not now, in this pinnacle moment; not ever.

But what she wanted was another story.

"Oh God . . ."

He inserted another fraction of the vibrator into her. Elisa was certain she'd go crazy, well aware that she was losing her grasp on her so-called dominance. Rapidly becoming putty in his hands.

No!

She had to, had to . . . do something . . .

Hooking her toes into the side of the mattress, she reacted with what came naturally at the moment, and bucked against the rubber shaft, impaling herself with the vibrator.

Her pussy stretched to accommodate the toy, her feminine muscles pulsing, drawing it deeper with every miniscule contraction. The ache in her womb, the need to be filled, was greater than she'd ever experienced.

But thank God, she was back in control. Of herself. Of her body. Of Maxim.

"Fuck me with it." She made her tone harsh, leaving no room for debate. "Or I'll do it myself and you can sit and watch."

Maxim sucked in a sharp breath and stared at her bared mons, at the vibrator wedged between her legs, hunger in his eyes. Lowering his head, he placed a gentle kiss to her clit. "If you want me—"

"Now!"

"Nope. I don't think so. I want you to beg me, Elisa. Plead. Scream." Shifting on his knees, he slowly rotated the handle in a circle, twisting the wide head in her tunnel. "Tell me what you need, and maybe I'll—"

"Don't play with me." Reaching down, she seized the handle from his grasp. "I don't need you, not at all."

Her threat was hollow. She couldn't bear for him to abandon her now. But he didn't know that.

"Okay, okay . . ." He placed another gentle kiss to her pussy. "I'll give you exactly what you want. If it's fucked you want"—he rammed the vibrator into her, hard, lurching her body—"it's fucked you'll get."

Ripping the toy from her pussy, he completely withdrew it, then plunged it in again, spearing her with quick, forceful thrusts that rocked her body.

Her desire already volatile, his forceful actions drove her into a fog of pleasure, and she was unable to think, much less control any damn thing, including herself. Or him.

Maxim pressed the scooped tip so that it continuously, in steady rhythm, made contact with her G-spot. Then, without warning, he turned the toy on high power, and it vibrated inside of her, shaking her from the inside out.

Slowing his plunges, he ground the toy deep, letting it rub and massage her G-spot as the clit stimulator worked the bundle of nerves, driving her to the brink so quickly, she almost wanted it to stop, though she couldn't stand the thought.

"Like that, my queen? Or do you require more?"

"That's good . . ." The words quivered from her throat, barely audible, even to herself. "Really good."

He continued to pump the pulsing shaft in and out of her, a tidal wave of pleasure within her swelling into a tsunami. Her limbs became unmovable, her mind useless against his sexual prowess; her strength had vanished, her will weak, her barricades fallen. She was at his mercy and he was driving her over a cliff.

"Elisa," he whispered, his hot breath blowing across her bared, swollen labia. "God, you're incredible. Say you want me . . . say you want my cock."

I want you. God, Maxim, I want you.

She couldn't deny him, didn't have the spirit to. But she didn't have the strength to ask for what she truly wanted.

All Elisa could do was hold tight to the bed, bracing herself as pure, unadulterated ecstasy literally shook her lower regions, her loins burning with an orgasm, yet refusing to release.

As much as she wanted to free the pent-up pleasure, the way he was fucking her was too incredible, too damned good, and she instinctually clamped her muscles tight, milking as much of the feeling as she could.

"Maxim . . . Maxim . . ." she whimpered and moaned, crying his name over and over.

What was she begging for? She didn't want to let go, but she couldn't take anymore.

"God, that's glorious." Maxim kissed along her ticklish upper thigh and prickles danced over her sensitive skin, doing the salsa straight to her heart. "Tell me if you like this."

He rotated the vibrator, so that the clit stimulator rested against her anus. Pressing the handle of the shaft downward, he drove the head against her G-spot, while the stimulator pressed into her bottom.

Elisa screamed out, shouting at the very top of her lungs as she convulsed and reared on the bed in a violent, earth-shattering climax. Her muscles seared from the manner in which she constringed them, her body slowly turning to mush.

Collapsing, she sunk into the mattress. With the toy still shaking within her, she lay limp, at his complete, utter mercy.

Maxim turned the vibrator off, slowly withdrawing it from her. Tossing it aside, he planted a kiss upon her mons, then took a slow lick along her pussy, swiping a taste of her cum.

The creamy liquid glistening on his lips, he stood. His eyes settled on her and he swallowed deeply. To her shock, he turned and walked from the room, earning more of her esteem and trust in that instant than she'd thought he'd gain in a lifetime.

He could have taken her. Had his way with her. She had no resistance left in her right now, no ability to restrain herself against his advances, and Elisa knew her weakness was obvious, especially to him. But rather than take advantage of her, he'd left. Respected her desire not to sleep with him yet. Respected her.

Such an act of decency for a man like him couldn't have been easy. Then again, she'd told him staying here wouldn't be. What she hadn't imagined was how very hard it would be on her; how very easy losing herself in his eyes, to his touch, could be. How very soft her heart was.

And that wouldn't do. Not at all.

s i x

Hardly able to walk, Maxim made a beeline to the bathroom. He was hornier than a sixteen-year-old on Viagra and needed to come so badly, he was pretty sure he'd do serious damage to his cock if he didn't.

He should have fucked her. Damn it. He *could* have fucked her.

Shoulda, woulda, coulda . . .

For once in his life, he was doing the right thing. And it sucked.

He threw open the heavy wooden door to the peach-tiled powder room and stumbled inside, falling to his knees. They smacked into the floor in a bruising collision, but Maxim ignored the pain, going straight for his cock.

Fisting it, he pumped his erection, blood rushing through his veins, and cum quickly filling his prick, rising in his shaft, prepared to erupt from his body. Release was so close he could taste it . . .

"Oh no, you don't!" Elisa burst into the bathroom, interrupting him a second from climax. "Put that cock down!"

His hand froze and he looked up at her, fighting the urge to keep going. Standing proudly naked, her arms crossed and shoulders squared, Elisa glared down at him. Her stern, militant gaze hardened her otherwise feminine features. "I said, put that cock down. Now."

Shit. Apparently, she was back to being her old self, which meant he was busted. His hand fell away, but his sexual desperation didn't fade. Not an iota. "Elisa, I have to relieve—"

"You agreed to my rules, and ergo, you cannot take pleasure of your own." Her unrelenting tone commanded obedience. Damn, she was being a hard-ass.

Right now, he didn't want to submit. Didn't want to play her stupid mind game. He only wanted, no *needed*, to get off, even if it was at his own hand.

What was so wrong with that?

He wasn't hurting her, or anyone else, damn it!

Again, he reached for his pulsing dick, prepared to do it right in front of her if he had to. "I need this, Elisa. Get over it."

"Then you quit," she said flatly, turning and walking from the room. Common sense—his freaking libido—told him to let her go. So why couldn't he?

Again ditching his needy cock, he jumped to his feet and went after her. In the hall, he caught her arm and whirled her around to face him.

"No, I don't quit," he ground out, wishing she'd play more fairly. Couldn't she sympathize with him just a little? "Jesus, Elisa, do you have any idea what you're doing to me? Any clue how hard it is to do those things to your body . . . how hard I am?"

Her stubborn emerald eyes glared at him, not showing the slightest sign of relenting. "Have you no sexual stamina? Aren't you capable of walking away? Aren't you a man?"

"That's exactly it, I am a *man*! Damn it, Elisa!"

"One who'd fuck any female who spread her legs. Exactly my point."

"No, I wouldn't. I wouldn't be doing this for any female. Just you."

For that matter, he'd never been this freaking turned on by any lay . . . not even the best. He hurt. Ached like he didn't think was possible. Hungered. All he wanted was to release some of the tension, so he could continue to pleasure her in any way she could imagine.

Why was that too much to ask?

"Oh, just me?" She chuckled, actually *laughed* at him, and unfolded her arms. "Please Maxim . . . you've never been with just *one* woman, not your whole life. We both know you're nothing but a slut. Give it up."

That stung.

Maybe he never went on more than one date with a girl, but he had damn good reason. He hadn't wanted to end up like this . . . pining over some woman, willing to lose everything for her, and eventually doing so.

Like his brother.

"I can't believe this." How he wished he could take her in his embrace and fuck away all the bullcrap between them. But he saw without a single doubt, Elisa was not going to alter her decision. He was stuck with this raging erection, likely for hours, and she was telling him not to touch it. He freakin' *hurt* and for her, for the sake of proving himself, he'd put up with the pain.

"Think what you want Elisa, but you're wrong about me," he told her. "You keeping acting like I'm inhuman. Like I haven't had my fair share of hard knocks and heartbreak . . . something you're all too familiar with. Take a good look at who you're purposefully *trying* to become."

"I'm becoming stronger, more resilient. There's nothing wrong with me learning to take what I want and—"

"Then ask yourself, how did I"—he waved along his torso—"become this?"

"I don't know."

"That's right. You don't, so don't pretend to understand me without ever giving me a chance." He walked past her. "If you'll excuse me, I'm going to go roll around in the snow and cool off."

"Maxim, I . . ."

"Don't worry. I'm not leaving," he called behind him. "I can wait you out longer than you'd ever imagine . . . actually, you and I both know I could have already fucked you. But *could have* isn't good enough for me. Crazy as I am, I want more. I want *you*."

Maxim disappeared down the hall, leaving her stunned.

Every time she thought she had him pegged, every time she thought she had handle on herself . . . *wham!* Maxim went and said or did something so out of the ballpark, she was left stumbling to catch up. Sputtering like a fool. Acting like a jerk.

One thing was for certain, as far as being dominant went, she unarguably sucked. Hard as she tried, she always ended up clay in his magical hands.

She'd just have to try harder.

Yeah right. She was crazy for even thinking she could use him and lose him. How she'd behaved and how she *wanted* to behave toward Maxim were polar opposites. Deep in her heart, she sensed there was something more to him and what he'd just told her had confirmed it. Maxim had a dark side.

The front door slammed, marking his exit. Now what? She couldn't just stand here, feeling like a jackass. She needed a distraction.

Lizzy.

Probably the last person on earth anyone should take advice from in the relationship area, yet, Lizzy had an odd way of putting things in perspective, of being real. Elisa needed that right now.

Still naked, she walked to the great room and retrieved the portable phone, then returned to her now-cold cocoa, banked fire, and the blanket she'd abandoned when Maxim had returned. Curling up, she dialed her sister's number. Lizzy answered on the third ring. "Hey, Elisa."

A chill ran down Elisa's spine at the ESP-like hello. "You know that gives me the creeps. Can't you just say hi? At least hear my voice first?"

"No." Lizzy gave a short laugh. "What's the fun in having caller ID if you aren't going to use it?"

Exactly why Elisa didn't have them: caller IDs, answering machines . . . she couldn't stand them. She didn't care for the idea of her actions or words being recorded—her mistakes could potentially be permanent.

But she hadn't called Lizzy to debate the necessity of modern conveniences. "Question." Other, larger matters on her mind, Elisa steered the conversation. "Do you think I'm too uptight? Maybe bitchy?"

"Yes." Lizzy chuckled. "Oh yes, but what a way to start a conversation."

"You didn't even hesitate."

"Well, why would I?" Lizzy laughed again. "Is everything okay, Elisa?"

Ouch.

Lizzy might be teasing, but Elisa couldn't help but take her words to heart.

"At least I've had a boyfriend in the past decade," Elisa snapped, then immediately felt guilty. What was wrong with her lately? You'd think her period was on the way, except it was at least three weeks off. "I'm sorry, Liz. My nerves are on edge, ever since . . ."

"Since?" When Elisa didn't respond, Lizzy made a tsk-tsk sound and laughed again. "See? Bitchy. But not that that's a bad thing, mind you. Being nice is being weak. Remember that. And, by the way, just because I choose not to tolerate men doesn't make me boring."

"So now I'm boring?" Elisa raised her brows. Boy, was Lizzy putting things in *perspective*.

"Well, the whole porn fiasco did sport a certain measure of excitement, but not the good kind." Lizzy's voice echoed slightly and made Elisa question if she was in the bathroom. "What's the matter, Elisa? Getting lonely? Tell you what . . . the club is the last place I feel like hanging out tonight. There's this guy who won't stop hitting on me. Yuck. Should I skip work and get some DVDs and chocolate and come over?"

"No!" Elisa practically shouted, catching her overreaction a moment too late. "I mean, that's all right. *Play* needs you more than me. Things never go smoothly when you're not there. Don't let that guy get to you. Besides, we'll see each other on Monday. But I wondered . . ." Her question trailed off. While she was hesitant to ask Lizzy anything that might spark her curiosity, she needed to talk with someone. Someone who would tell her how it was, not gussy up the conversation with a bunch of pomp and circumstance, or worse, romanticisms.

"Hurry up, Elisa. I have to pee," Lizzy announced.

Take that for example—Lizzy didn't hold back, not anything, not ever. In fact, sometimes she revealed far too much.

Elisa could just imagine Lizzy, with her pink hair and big black boots, doing the pee-pee dance around the bathroom. But she'd called her a bitch, so she could hold it.

"I just thought you might remember . . . you probably don't. It was such a huge campus and you and I didn't study for the same degree. Heck, our classes weren't in the same building, much less the same rooms, but—"

"Elisa—" Lizzy interrupted with an exaggerated sigh. "I'm going on the phone. Deal with it."

Used to Lizzy's blunt behavior, Elisa continued to ramble. "I don't know. You probably didn't know him. How could you have? I'm just being silly and—"

"*Who?*" Lizzy demanded. "Get to the point already!"

God. Why couldn't she just get it out? She was exhausting herself with this nonsensical beating around the bush.

Truth be told, as much as she craved Lizzy's blunt opinions right now, she was half-afraid to bring up Maxim's name, for fear Lizzy *did* remember him.

"Well?" Lizzy questioned again. "Who is this man I'm going to shoot for getting to you?"

"No one is getting to me. I was just thinking about him."

"Right."

Elisa sighed. Maybe if she said his name fast enough, Lizzy would mishear. "Maxim Cox," she blurted.

Silence.

Tap, tap, tap.

Silence.

"You stay away from him, Elisa," Lizzy suddenly snapped.

"You remember him?"

"Sweetie, Maxim wasn't studying anything but females in college. I didn't know him personally, but my friend, excuse me, *friends*—"

"No. Don't. Never mind. I don't want to know." Invaded by tortuous jealousy that squeezed her heart and prickled her nerves,

Elisa swallowed at the knot suddenly lodged in her throat. She was a fool for even dwelling on Maxim. She knew better, damn it.

"Why? What's going on?" Lizzy's voice lifted a notch, becoming high pitched with worry. "Elisa, you better spill whatever you're hiding, or I swear—"

"Nothing," Elisa quickly cut her off, feeling bad for fibbing, but knowing if she told Lizzy the truth, Maxim would be hoisted from her cabin by his ears and ass-kicked into the nearest trench. "I was just thinking about him, that's all. Out here, I have lots of time to think and not much else."

Besides have mind-blowing orgasms produced by a dildo-wielding hottie that she wanted more than she should.

"But why him?" Lizzy questioned.

"I don't know." Elisa sighed, trying desperately to remain nonchalant. "Did you ever get the notion there was something more to him than one-night stands?"

"Absolutely not." Lizzy's voice was firm. Undoubtedly, in Lizzy's opinion, Maxim Cox was nothing but a walking, talking dick.

"Really?" Somehow, she didn't *want* to believe it, true as it likely was. "Nothing at all?"

"Sweetie, are you being honest with me? Are you sure you're simply thinking about him?"

"I want a serious answer."

"Okay . . . serious." Lizzy sighed as she thought about it. "Call me crazy, but any guy who has as much of a commitment issue as Maxim has is either stupid, or has issues. Big ones," Lizzy answered, more truth, more *help*, in her scorning words than she could ever imagine. "And you're sure everything is all right?"

All right? Not really. Not even close. Her heart was pounding furiously.

Lizzy might be right. Maybe Maxim had issues. Maybe all along she'd judged him too harshly.

Maybe she was a bitch.

"Everything's fine," Elisa answered quickly. Knowing damn good and well she couldn't maintain lying to her sister, she rapidly fired, "Except he's here and I think I'm falling for him and um, don't you dare come here, love ya, bye!"

Elisa quickly hung up, feeling so confused . . . yet not. She had a new perspective, a new outlook on Maxim that she never imagined she would see.

Could there really be something more to Maxim? Considering what he'd said, the way he'd actually respected her, she could almost think . . . almost believe . . .

Maxim *was* more than just a man-slut.

seven

*B*y the time Maxim calmed down enough to come back inside, Elisa was snuggled in bed, fast asleep. Teeth chattering, he stood in the doorway to her room, soaking in her serene, sensuous appearance.

A heavy quilt covered her up to her chin, tucked snuggly at her sides. Her long, dark hair flowed around her body, stretching across the mattress like a thick, silky curtain. The slightest smile curved her lips. An angel sent straight from God couldn't have looked more peaceful . . . or beautiful.

On the floor, her box of dildos and vibrators sat open, disproving the presence of a heavenly creature in this room. Elisa was a vixen through and through . . . a fact that would be ever-clear when she roused.

Could he take any more of her game?

He shook his head as he thought of the torment his poor penis had endured at her insistence. And yet, crazy as it seemed, he couldn't wait for more.

Drawn to her, he took another step inside the room. His tongue darted out, wetting his lips as he fantasized about ditching her rules, hopping on her, and fucking her without mercy.

Maybe he couldn't do that, but he could lie next to her. Soak up her warmth. Touch her soft skin. He had to have lost his mind, but all he wanted was to snuggle next to her. He was so cold, so wet, and her bed looked so inviting.

Sure, there were other rooms he could sleep in, not to mention the couch, the bearskin rug, even the tub. He had his options. But none of them sported a very seductive angel that he wanted to get to.

Unable to stifle a long, stretching yawn, his cock twitching in protest at the thought of being close to her—physical torture he likely could not withstand in his condition—Maxim went to the side of the bed and sat down. Here went nothing.

He stripped off his boots, then his pants. The notion of sleep seemed impossible, the prospect of sexual relief too tempting, but his worn body begged to differ. He'd been up almost twenty-four hours, had barely eaten, and had exhausted his stamina pleasuring her. Not to mention that within the past week, he'd flown here from Egypt, completely switching times zones, then hunted her down, traveling in the thick snow.

Hard as it was, hard as *he* might become, he was sticking to his plan. He *would* prove himself. No matter how severe his lust became, or whatever dildo-induced, desire-fogged opening she gave him, he wouldn't fuck her. Not until she was truly ready, heart, body, and soul.

Elisa might find it easy to emotionally reject him, but he was no blind idiot. Every time he talked sweet to her, every time they kissed, he touched something in her, whether she wanted to admit it or not. She'd likely try to push him away again, but he wasn't budging. He intended to be everywhere she was: in her face, on her body, in her bed, driving her nuts until she couldn't pretend anymore.

With numb limbs, Maxim shrugged off his coat and shirt, then yanked off his boxers. Gently, so not to jolt her, he slipped under the covers. To his shock, she lay naked. He slid a finger along her length, searching. Nope, she didn't have as much as a stitch of underwear on.

A bolt of need shot through his loins. Where was her flannel nightgown? Why didn't she have it on?

Had she expected him?

Gulping, he commanded himself to adapt to the situation. Make the best of it. The change in temperature felt like he'd just lain down in paradise and he snuggled closer to her warmth, intending to enjoy the contact, even if she wasn't aware of it.

Sure, he'd expected her to be wearing something—panties at the least—but she wasn't and naked or not, he chose to sleep next to her. He chose torture over denial.

His cock pulsed in disagreement. Turning, he lay flat on his back, so that his growing erection would not touch her. Normally, he'd have pressed his hard dick right between the crevice of her ass cheeks, to make sure she was aware of him. But being that physically insistent wasn't part of his plan.

Keeping his hand on her upper thigh, he forced himself to lie there, *just* being close to her. While seducing her really wouldn't be all that difficult, not if he really pressed matters, he wanted her to want *him*, not just his body.

It was cheesy and ridiculous, but some deep, dark, hungry part of him required nothing less. With every hour that he remained at this cabin, his need for her grew. He'd come here with the simple intention to seduce the one woman who'd got away. Now . . .

His fingers flexed, pressing into the flesh of her thigh. Every instinct in him warned him to stay clear of the wave of feelings inundating his mind and body. His heart.

Until Elisa, he'd managed quite effortlessly to stick to his guns, to avoid relationships and the downfalls they undoubtedly would bring. After Keaton had died in the car accident as a direct result of discovering his wife cheating, Maxim had easily avoided closeness with one night stands and flings aplenty. Elisa had been a fluke . . . he hadn't meant to fall, yet suddenly . . .

His fingers dug even deeper into the soft skin of her upper leg as he realized what he'd almost just admitted. He wasn't falling in love with her. Jesus, no.

Why was he actually thinking the two of them could have some sort of future together? Ridiculous.

His grip on her caused Elisa to stir. She wriggled, tossed her head to the side, then sighed in a throaty, lust-invoking manner that left him in a panic. Thankfully, a moment later, she calmed and her gentle, even breathing returned.

Maxim stared down at the tent his cock made in the blankets.

Hungry. Sure, he was hungry, famished, needy for her. But love had never been, and would never be, a part of his life.

Oh God. *Ohgodohgodohgod.*

Awoken by his touch, Elisa fought to keep from gasping. Maxim's cold palm pressed into her thigh, burning her flesh, searing hot and fast need through her.

So much for catching a few winks.

She'd lain in bed for hours, unable to get any shut-eye as she'd pondered her new outlook on Maxim Cox and his wild ways. Wondered what to do about it. Sometime, somehow, she'd miraculously drifted off, only to be jolted back to consciousness by his very *naked* presence.

Had she expected company, she would have left her nightgown on. But it had smelled like him—it seemed everything in the house did now—and she hadn't expected him to climb in her bed uninvited. Certainly not naked.

Again, his nails lightly caressed her skin. A bead of sweat rolled down her forehead as she fought to remain composed. Silent. Pretending to be asleep.

If he knew she was awake . . .

Maxim wriggled and the coarse hair covering his legs rubbed her smooth skin, creating erotic friction. While his fingers were still cold enough to cause her skin to goose bump, his body was quickly heating against hers, killing Elisa's will with his presence. Her every nerve was aware of him and firing demands throughout her.

Why was she putting herself through this?

How easy it would be to roll over, climb aboard, and fuck him right now. To stop fighting and start enjoying.

But *easy* wasn't a good thing where Maxim was concerned; easy equaled trash. If she fucked him now, he'd toss her aside and never look back.

Then again, she had to give the dog a bone, or in this case, a boner, if she wanted him to stick around. If she kept giving Maxim hell, he'd give up. Leave.

The prospect should make her happy. After all, she wanted Maxim gone, didn't she?

Yes! Of course!

No. The truth resonated through her. The thought of being in this cabin, alone, without him, was suddenly unfathomable. She needed him to stay. She needed to be with him, if only once.

The reality of her situation closed in around her. It felt as if she had nothing left, but here Maxim was, wanting to be with her.

The thought of playing with Maxim was so much more welcoming than being alone, worrying about who might be watching her on porn.

Elisa shifted her lower body, driving his fingers dangerously close to her pussy. If he'd just cooperate a little . . . be a little more aggressive . . .

"Maxim, I—" She cleared her throat. "Okay. Fuck me. Please."

To her surprise, he responded with a snore. His fingers drifted downward, resting lower than before.

The asshole!

She'd bet he wasn't even sleeping. He was probably toying with her, giving Elisa her just rewards for stopping him from jacking off. She peeked over the blankets, noting the spike propping them up. Just like she thought. He was *very* awake.

Why wasn't he seducing her like a good man-slut? Shouldn't he be on top her by now?

Elisa lay there, fighting a forming clump in her throat. Damn Maxim! Had he gone crazy? He should be all over her like a kid on candy!

Seconds turned into minutes turned into an hour. A hundred times she almost reached for him, almost said screw her damn plan to become stronger; if sleeping with a man she desired was weak, she welcomed weakness.

But she just couldn't make herself go through with it.

Maxim's breathing became even and steady, telling her he'd really fallen asleep. Quietly, she slipped from the bed and threw on a robe. Tiptoeing from the room and down the hall, she made her way to the kitchen.

Their disastrous meal of burnt tofu still lay on the table, reminding her of the poor way she'd behaved the night before. She didn't want to fight with Maxim anymore, but neither did she want to relinquish what thin thread of control she did possess.

Her eyes drifted to the wasted, full glasses of milk also left untouched, reminding her of the age-old saying "why buy the cow when you can get the milk for free?"

Elisa picked up the glasses and carried them to the sink, dumping out the contents. Why indeed? Maxim was used to free milk, used to flashing a dimpled smile and having women spread their legs. Yet despite all the females at his disposal, here he was, persisting in his attentions. Why? She wasn't about to let the horny bastard guzzle her milk for free.

Her mouth stretched in a yawn. It was too early to think about this. She needed to wake up, clear her mind. Try to think rationally.

Leaving the dirty glasses in the sink, Elisa grabbed a pot and boiled some water for tea. Five minutes later, she was mindlessly flipping through the paper when the telephone rang.

Elisa glared at the noisy interruption, contemplated not answering, but knew no telemarketer would be calling at eight in the morning. She answered on the sixth ring. "Hello?"

"Elisa. I'm sorry to call so early, but I wanted to get right on top my day and I know you're an early bird. Well, how are you doing?" Her typically serious and stern boss, Nora Moning, asked sweetly—too sweetly. Something was up. "Enjoying your time off, I hope?"

"You could say that." Elisa lifted her chin, concern flaring in her gut. "I'm managing."

What was this all about? After the tabloids had hit the shelves, Nora had been politely sympathetic, telling her to take a few months off until it all blew over. Elisa had always anticipated that Nora would eventually tell her not to come back, while she questioned if she even wanted to.

So here it came. She was officially being fired.

She wasn't sure she cared.

"Good, good," Nora cooed. "Listen, I know I encouraged you to take a few months off. But Elisa, I need you to handle a case for me."

Return to work?

Now? The request hit her hard, almost knocking her from her chair. Her chest grew tight.

She'd expected to be let go, not to be invited back. Oddly, she'd have rather been axed. There had been too many comments. Too many looks. She could never face her peers again.

Could she? Did she even want to?

"What's the issue?" Elisa couldn't help but ask, the fighter in her instantly needing to know. "Who are we up against?"

"The state of Colorado," Nora declared, her tone switching from charming to no-nonsense. "They're trying to put a highway right through my parents' ranch. The amount they offered for the land is a pittance, especially when you consider the fact that my family has lived and worked there for generations. The house is practically a museum and it'll have to be torn down. It isn't right. My parents—my family—deserve better. That's why I thought of you."

"Me?"

"After the way you settled the Robert's suit, I'm certain you could be beneficial to their lawsuit, and how convenient, Aspen is only two hours from their farm. I'd consider it a personal favor."

Settled.

The words sunk like a rock in her stomach. Nora didn't want her to save her parents' land. She didn't want her to fight for what was right. She didn't even want her *back.*

She just wanted to get the most money for her parents, without having to bother to fly to Colorado herself.

That was what her job had become. Rarely was she working to save anything, or anyone. Her job had become about getting the largest payoff and she couldn't stomach that. Being a cash cow wasn't what she'd imagined herself doing with her life. She wanted to save forests, farms, *lives*.

Inside, she felt as if she was falling apart all over again, but difficult as it was, Elisa knew what she had to do. She had to quit.

"No," she answered, her voice firm. When she thought about who she'd become lately, she didn't like herself. It was time to get back to being Elisa. "And I'm sorry, Nora, but I'm afraid I won't be returning to Moning and Fielding. You'll be receiving my official resignation shortly."

She needed to start fresh. She could always put her degree to use some other way. Work for other causes that meant something. If only she could decide what those were or where she wanted to be.

And get up the nerve to show her face in public again.

"I'm very sorry to hear that, Elisa," Nora's reply was stiff and cold. "Is there anything I can do to change your mind?"

"No. But thank you." Elisa swallowed a final knot of uncertainty that was lodged in her throat, emotionally acknowledging that her career as an environmental lawyer was officially over, at least at Moning and Fielding. "No. Good-bye."

Elisa hung up. Maybe she'd eventually go back to practicing law, maybe not, but it was time to move on. Once upon a time, she'd loved her job. But not anymore. She wasn't satisfied with where her life had gone thus far. It was time to make a change. She certainly could do better than fighting for huge settlements in exchange for permitting the environment to be destroyed. Moreover, she had other dreams. Maybe it was time to fulfill some of them.

But what? Right now, deciding the direction of her future seemed impossible. Nora had been right about one thing. She needed some time off and away from it all.

Elisa took a sip of tea, glancing down the dark hallway that led to where Maxim was sleeping. She really was glad Maxim was here. Glad she wasn't alone. Glad she had him as a distraction. Even glad they could finish what they started back in college.

But how was she going to handle him? She didn't want them to get carried away. She also didn't want him running away, at least not too soon. If she couldn't be more to Maxim than a woman he'd conquered, she didn't want to go there.

Maxim wanted what he couldn't have. She wanted to give it to him.

But if she did, his thirst would be quenched.

That left one solution. She'd just have to make him work for her. And once he had her, she'd have to make him work even harder to have her again.

Ah yes, she was in the mood for a little sport. A game—one that would keep her mind off her woes and make staying in control not only possible, but fun; one that would keep him interested.

Walking to the fridge, Elisa took the pad of stationery magnetized to its side and a pen from the kitchen counter. *Dear Maxim*, she wrote, then blanked. Now what? She tapped the pen against her teeth as she debated. *The best things in life are worth working for. I know how very much you want me. I want you too, like I never dreamed possible. Let's forget our stupid agreement. Forget the rules. Make new ones. A game perhaps? One of hide and seek—so come find me. I've got something special for you. It won't be easy, as nothing with me will ever be, but it will be worth it. Remember that. Elisa*

Folding the letter, Elisa walked down the hall to the bathroom and took her perfume from the vanity. Spraying the paper, she smiled to herself, never feeling better about his presence or her own sexuality.

eight

Her earthy, exotic scent permeated the kitchen, but Elisa was nowhere to be found. Inhaling deeply, Maxim followed his nose and wondered through the room, curious where his reluctant lover might be, and what there was to eat in this cabin other than burnt tofu.

She sure hadn't changed since college. Never could be normal. But then, until right now, he'd always loved that about her.

His stomach growled a demand, one not even Elisa could fulfill. Apples sat in a bowl on the counter and he grabbed one, taking a huge bite. Disgustingly healthy, but better than the crap she'd fed him last night. What he needed was a nice, thick bowl of Egyptian meat soup. Maybe some beef kofta. His mouth watered at the thought of the fried minced meat and onion patties.

God, he missed home. Hearty meals. Warm weather. Willing women.

He'd settle for some milk. From the fridge, he claimed the almost empty jug and guzzled straight from the container. The rumbles in his abdomen quieted, but the dull ache of hunger persisted.

He rummaged the pathetically stocked icebox. More tofu, lettuce, carrots, tomatoes, leftover rice . . . cheese! He claimed the block and slammed the fridge door shut. It wasn't bacon and eggs, but it would suffice.

Where was Elisa anyway? Wherever she was, he sure could smell her. He just couldn't see her.

Had his presence in her bed driven her to flee? No matter. This was her cabin. She'd be back and he'd be here—waiting in her bed.

He turned around, surprised to see a box of Cocoa Crisps sitting on the table, along with a bowl and spoon. Forget cheese! A smile spread across his face, stretching from ear-to-ear as he tossed it back in the fridge and walked into the breakfast nook. So the rabbit-woman was half-human after all. And even better, she cared enough about him to leave him something tasty to eat.

In the dish lay a note, folded neatly. Lifting it, he brought it to his nose. Ah, the source of her scent. He drew in the spicy yet feminine fragrance, then opened the letter. Reading her words, his smile broadened. His heart lifted.

Elisa *did* want him . . .

The promise of *something special* permeated his mind, suffused his body, filling him with longing, lust, and need. Would she suck him off? Wrap that luscious mouth around his cock and drive him insane with her tongue? Spread her legs, let him fuck her? Even better, bend over and bare all to him?

Arousal blazed through his instantly hardening cock. His body heated with the furious need for that *something special* and desire like he'd never experienced practically knocked him off his feet.

Find her? Easy. Piece of cake. He just hoped she was ready for the fuck of a lifetime.

Three hours later, icicles hanging from his nose, Maxim officially dubbed *easy* a cuss word. He sniffled, his lower lips shaking in tune with his muttered foul language. He should've known . . . should've read her letter twice . . . should've taken the time to let her words completely sink in.

He really should've heeded Elisa's warnings.

Eaten a second bowl of cereal. Stolen an extra pair of her jogging pants.

"F-f-fucking cold." Maxim eyes scanned the tall, never-ending forest of pine trees for any sign of her, slipping as the trail scooped. Using the poles to stay upright, he struggled for balance. The last thing he needed was to fall. Again.

Standing up on the damned skis wasn't easy and he'd taken them off too many times to count, choosing to wade through the knee high snow instead. For him, traveling on the sloped

alyssa brooks

mountainous landscape was the equivalent of Elisa walking through the desert. But though clumsier, skiing was faster and he always ended up trying again, desperate to find her.

"Th-h-his is crazy."

He'd searched the inside of her house first, foolishly hoping she'd have been kind enough not to drive him outside again. Then he'd donned his skis and combed the area surrounding the cabin. She'd been nowhere in sight, forcing him to take the trail leading away from the cabin in hopes of finding her.

Now, he was pretty sure his lips were frostbitten, his balls were ice cubes, and he knew he was lost. His earlier hard-on had melted, his hopes of *something special* withered away.

He slipped again, grappling for the poles. Where did she get off teasing him like this? Getting his hopes up, only to smash them down?

A bear in him rose up and he growled, thinking if he found Elisa now, there'd be no stopping the animal in him. Fuck her rules, fuck proving himself, because he'd long since earned the right to fuck her.

As if in divine answer, her soft, melodic voice reached out and snagged his attention. "Hey, little guy," she cooed. "You like your nuts?"

Huh? Of course he liked his nuts, though currently they were swollen from days of built up need, inflicted by her. And what did she mean, "little?"

The cold must be making him delirious.

"Come here. Come on, come on . . . that's it . . ."

He followed her voice, not able to see her, though from the closeness of her voice, it sounded as if she were right there. His eyes searched the woods. To his surprise, while he didn't spot her, he saw the distant shape of her cabin in a clearing about two hundred yards ahead. Hallelujah! He was going to sit right in the fireplace . . . and the box of Cocoa Crisps was *his*!

"I think I'll call you Mr. Hungry." Her voice echoed with laughter. "You sure do like your nuts."

What? Of course he was hungry. Famished. *Starved.* He had her tofu-ass to thank for that. And he'd never met a man who didn't appreciate his nuts . . .

But what game was she playing now?

Another bout of laughter filled the air. He whirled around, trying to pinpoint where the sound came from. Nothing.

Damn it.

"Want more, Mr. Hungry?"

Despite how freaking cold he was, the sound of her sweet voice talking about nuts sent a streak of heat through his loins. His cock fought against the confines of his snow pants, insisting upon standing upright, at attention.

For a woman he could only hear, not see.

Where the heck was she? Was he imagining her?

He had to be. She'd driven him to insanity. He was imagining an oasis in the middle of the damned mountains.

"Hey, squirrelly squirrel. Come back here, Mr. Hungry!" she pleaded loudly. "Darn it! Don't leave me!" A frustrated sigh followed. "Alone again."

This time, he placed the sound of her very real voice. She was underneath him.

He should be committed.

"Elisa?" he called out.

"Maxim?"

No way. She really *was* below him.

Reaching down, Maxim unfastened his ski boots and stepped free. He strode to the edge of the trail, looking down the sloped mountain side. Sure enough, a deep, dark cave was tucked into the hill.

On a large rock, Elisa sat in the cave's mouth, staring up at him. A slight smile curved her lips, marking her humor at the situation. "You found me. About time."

About time? The woman had no idea what she did to him.

"Damn right, about time," he growled, all too ready to devour her. "You were hiding from me."

"Hence me calling the game hide and seek." She shrugged. "I said it wouldn't be easy. I think you looked too hard."

Maxim scoped the area for a way to reach her, and decided no path was better than straight down. He threw himself over the edge, landing on his hands and feet right in front of her.

"You made it impossible." Standing, he brushed snow from his gloved hands and stared at her hard, expecting some sort of explanation. An apology. "And what the hell do you mean by little nuts?"

"I was talking to the squirrels, silly." She raised a brow, looking guiltless. "And you found me, didn't you?"

Did Elisa have no clue what she'd put him through? What he was going to do to her now that he'd found her? Finally!

Whipping off his gloves, he walked toward her. "I want my something special. Now."

*M*axim——" Elisa barely eked out the futile protest. A determined man, he stalked toward her, his jaw clenched, a certain glint to his eyes, a rage—spurred by her sexual starvation— that could not be controlled.

Tiny icicles hung from his nose, snow clinging to his shaggy hair. He looked almost mad, like a rabid animal attacking prey.

Oh dear. She was in real trouble. She'd pushed him too far this time . . . there was no way she'd get away with giving him a simple hand job to fulfill her promise of *special*.

When she'd invented the game, she'd decided the best way to go about it would be to let him climb a ladder: a hand job, a blow job, actual sex, then more complicated positions. Such a lead-on would keep him around for weeks, but she was never going to get away with her plan.

Even if she could stop him, she couldn't stop herself.

"Maxim, you look like you're freezing. Let me . . ." *Warm you up.* Not exactly what she meant, though she wasn't positive he'd appreciate her pocket warmers. He had something else in mind for heat.

Elisa swallowed the offer, well aware of how sexy her innocent suggestion sounded. She took a step back.

"You'll be my heat," he ground out, taking her by the shoulders and lifting her to her feet. His fingers clenched her jacket, holding her dangerously close to his body, a kiss lingering in the air.

Too easy.

Wrenching away, she sidestepped him, though she knew he'd catch her. Knew he'd take her. Knew she wouldn't do a damn thing to stop it.

But at least she could enjoy the chase. Taking off running, she darted into the woods with him right on her tail.

"Hey! Don't think you're getting away from me this easily!" He lunged for her, but she quickly turned away. Tripping, he landed face-first in the snow.

"If you want me, you've got to catch me!" She kept right on running, not slowly for a second.

He growled in protest and she laughed, feeling as if someone was tickling her from the inside out. Having Maxim pursue her was more arousing than having her clit sucked.

Though, damn she couldn't wait for him to do that either.

Pure, unadulterated excitement fluttered in her stomach, arousal making her hot.

In no time, Maxim was on his feet again and coming after her at full speed. He closed the distance between them in half a heartbeat. Encircling his arms around her waist, he hulled her against him.

Her feet dangled in the air as she struggled, *caught*. His mouth went right for her neck, kissing and suckling. Driving her crazy.

"You forget the rules, Maxim," she told him, leaning forward in a feeble attempt to put some space between them. "You forget yourself."

Suddenly, every breath she took, every brush of the fabric covering her skin, even the slight movement of the thin strap of the silk thong nestled between her ass cheeks, seemed intensely erotic. Elisa sucked in a sharp breath, never more aware of a man's mouth on her.

"You threw them out, remember?" He caught her arm and whirled her around, yanking her against his chest. Driving her backward, he pinned her against a tree. His body smashed hers and he yanked off her knit hat. Her hair fell free and the wind blew the long locks between them. Winding the stray strands around his fingers, he brushed her cheeks with his knuckles. "And you promised something special when I found you. I want it. Now."

Tucking her hair away, he pinned her arms above her head, his erection pressed against her upper thigh, prominent despite the thick pants she wore. He ground his lower half against her.

"Feel that?" He pressed into her once again. "I *want* what I'm due."

Elisa shuddered. "But I didn't say what. Now did I?"

Innocently, she wrapped her arms around his neck. Oh, she was having fun. Damn, she was turned on.

He cupped her cheek in an almost endearing manner. "Well, I found you. So give."

Roughly pumping his cock against her cunt, he stroked his fingers across her jaw to her lips, toying with the plump flesh.

The combination of savage and sweet left her speechless. "I—"

"Tell me what the *something special* is, before I take it," he demanded.

Maxim afforded her all two of seconds before his mouth smashed down upon hers, knocking any sensible replies from her mind.

What she might have said didn't matter, nothing did, nothing except having him inside her, fulfilling her, erasing the ache.

Possessing her with his lips, his tongue swooped into her mouth, rubbing along her teeth. Their mouths tangled together in a fierce embrace, stealing her breath away. Elisa relaxed against the hard tree, welcoming his kisses, his touch.

Wrenching his mouth free, he rained kisses along her jaw, neck, and collarbone, slowly working his way down her torso as he ripped open her coat.

"Hurry," she told him, pushing his busy hands south. "Get to it."

Her demand made him pause. He looked at her with a dimpled, fresh smile, his deep eyes sparkling with pure joy. Filled with lightness she'd never seen before.

"Yeah, baby. That's what I want to hear." He kissed her fully on the lips, so fiercely, her lips swelled. "This is the best *something special* a man could hope for." His pressed his mouth to hers again, this time softer, quicker, then pulled away with a groan.

He jerked at the elastic waistband of her snow pants and tugged the bottoms down, which were quickly followed by the long johns she wore underneath, then her thong.

His stripping left her most intimate regions exposed to the frigid cold and her ass pressed against rough bark. She stepped from the garments, breathless as she watched him shove away the clothing confining his cock.

When he was completely bare from the waist down, he retrieved a condom from his coat pocket, tore the wrapper apart, and sheathed himself in rubber. He seized her thighs, reaching around them to toy with her pussy from behind. His erection nestled between the juncture of her thighs, a constant reminder of the ecstasy to come.

Holding tight to his shoulders, she leaned against his upper torso and enjoyed his delightful foreplay, the way his fingers whispered along her silky wet folds, the way he tapped ever so softly at her clit.

Tiny earthquakes shattered her body and she melted against him, mewing her delight. The pads of his thumbs caressed the tender skin on the underside of her ass. Fingers from both of his hands teased her entrance, plunging in, then withdrawing, plunging in, then withdrawing.

Her sheath constricted around vacant space and she moaned from pure frustration. His cock was the only thing that could provide her relief. Release.

"Maxim, please," she whimpered as his fingers again pierced her, then quickly withdrew. "I—"

"Say no more." Straightening, he cupped her bottom and lifted her. She leaned against the tree for support and he positioned his cock at her entry. "Your wish is my command, my queen."

With one full thrust he drove into her, his shaft stretching her sheath to accommodate his size. She cried out in glory, filled to the max, and dug her nails into his shoulders.

"Hold on, baby," he whispered against her ear, nuzzling her intimately before suddenly pumping into her, hard and fast, his strokes thumping her against the rough bark of the tree.

She bucked against him, driven wild as pleasure burst through her in a million tiny electric shocks.

They fucked in steady, quick rhythm, their lovemaking so intense she wasn't sure how much more she could take. Her body was on an all-time high as she rode a powerful wave of ecstasy.

Maxim slipped his hand along her bottom, sliding his finger in the deep crevice, and stroking the tender, buttery-soft skin. Without warning, his pinky pressed into her anus, driving her to the brink.

An orgasm vibrated through her, her pussy convulsing around his cock, the pleasure trapped in her nether muscles discharging in quick, furious spasms. She clenched her core and held tight to his shoulders, crying out.

Maxim slid his hand free, drawing her tight against his body as he plunged deep within her, then quickly yanked his cock free.

Her sheath continued to quiver in tiny aftershocks as he drew her into his embrace, hugging her. His hand stroked her long hair from scalp to end. "I . . ."

He better not say it. Better not cry wolf and claim love. Not now.

Her every muscle tightened in emotional protest. She didn't want a bunch of heartfelt bullshit from him. Just honesty. Affection. A good fuck. Sweet talking trash she couldn't take.

"Maxim, don't," she warned, but Maxim held her even tighter, unrelenting, his eyes studying her intensely.

"Thank you," he murmured, surprising her as he placed a gentle kiss to her head. "Thank you."

nine

Releasing his suddenly tense lover from his embrace, Maxim stepped back, giving Elisa room to dress.

Mind-blowing orgasm or not, he wasn't satisfied with his *something special* yet. Not even close. But he did want to get Elisa back to the cabin, where he could romance and pleasure her properly, in a bed, in the warmth, rather than up against a cold, hard tree.

"You good"? Maxim asked. After slipping off his condom, he reached for his pile of discarded clothing lying on the snowy ground and slipped his feet into the legs of his stolen jogging pants. He pulled the bottoms up, awaiting her answer.

Screwing her had moved him so much he'd just *thanked* her, yet Elisa had clammed up. Her lips were flat and pressed tight. Her eyes hooded by her thick, dark lashes. Even though he wasn't touching her, he could sense her anxiety. Her withdrawal.

Elisa drew up her pants with quick, jerky movements. "Well," she huffed. "I can see what all the fuss over you was about."

"*Was* . . . that's right, Elisa." Forgetting the coat he was about to zip up, he winked at her. "I guess you should have gone on that date with me, explosion or not."

"Yeah. Right." She rolled her eyes, trying to stifle a smile.

"I was a boy. No control." Stepping forward, he pressed his palms to her biceps and hauled her body against his. "I'm a man now. And think of all we've missed."

"If I'd have dated you, Professor Hobbs would have failed me."

"Hey, he didn't hate me that much. He let me stay lab partners with you."

"Let? He forced me to, because he was hoping I'd straighten you out. Much to my dismay."

"Much to your fun." He kissed her forehead. "You know I made you laugh."

She chuckled again, memories dancing in her eyes. "I know you ruined every experiment we did."

"Not true." He rotated his hips, rubbing his cock against her. "We just made chemistry, baby. And I'm not done *experimenting* with you, yet. Not even close."

"Pfff." She looked away, shaking her head, and trying to control the smile threatening her lips. "What a line."

He placed a hand to her shoulder. "Don't do it again. Please don't shut me out. A minute ago, you were getting all—"

"Bitchy?" She gave a quick, seemingly sincere laugh and shook her head. "I'm fine. And I'm sorry. You're right."

"I was going to say uptight." He stepped back, allowing her to finish dressing.

"Well, you do know how to talk to a woman." Her pants in place, she met his gaze. A grin widened as she gave the zipper of her coat a quick tug. "It was a natural reaction, I suppose. After an experience like that, it's hard to know how to act." When he just stared at her, she continued to ramble. Her words practically poured out all at once. "I mean, the sex was great . . . better than great . . . I guess I just didn't know what to say. And I thought for a minute that you were going to—well—" Her smile fell. "You're gawking at me like I'm weird."

"That's what I lo—like about you," he stammered, feeling like a fool for the slip he'd almost made. Had he completely lost his mind? No, just his dick; a part of him that was currently growing hard all over again from her little speech about awkwardness and great sex.

She gulped and glared at him like he was a lunatic. "What's that?"

With a growl, he seized her shoulders and hauled her against him. Her breasts smashed against his torso, barely perceptible through their thick coats. He pressed the growing lump in his pants against her pelvis, trying to redirect their conversation— into another fuck against the tree.

"You're so different. Unusual. Incredible," he told her, trying to cover his almost-slip with enough bullshit to distract her. "Damn, I want you."

Shaking her head, she pulled back. "I thought you were going to say something else . . . something stupid . . ."

Damn. She'd caught it. He'd better clean this up, before she got any ideas in her head. "Like I love you?"

"Yes."

"That's one line you'll never hear from me, Elisa."

Surprise flickered in her gaze, and she exhaled, widening her grin. "Good."

"I'm glad you feel that way." Releasing her, Maxim returned to dressing in an attempt to ignore the strange feeling in his gut. "Really glad."

"Not that I thought you would . . . fall for me . . . just that you'd use the line. You know, like your others." Elisa tossed her long, wavy hair over her shoulders and wiggled her knitted cap into place. Such a simple, innocent gesture, but combined with her lift in spirit, so damn adorably sexy.

"Nope. Not me. Not ever. That's not the kind of line that should be *used* by anyone. When said, it should be meant." Maxim studied the raised curve of her mouth, the dimples in her cheeks, the pink glow to her flushed skin, wanting her reaction at its fullest. "And I'll never mean it."

Their gazes met once again. With a blank look on her face, she nodded slowly. "Good."

"Good?" The question slipped from him before he could stop it. "Can I ask you why that is?"

"Are you kidding? You saw the tabloids."

Yeah. He saw them. He still wanted to strangle the guy who did that to her. Now, he wanted to even more. "So you loved him?"

"No, not truly. But I came close enough. What about you?"

"Me?"

"Why won't you ever mean it?"

"I'd rather not talk about it," he grunted. "I just can't."

He zipped his coat up. They'd done quite enough talking for now. It was high-time they got back to her cabin, to a warm bed and a hot fire. He wanted to take things slow, to handle her right. Physically. Forget all this emotional bullshit.

"So, you want to know how you should act, Elisa?" Stepping forward, he wrapped his arms around her, letting his hands rest on her ass.

"Ho—"

"Just like this." Quickly bending at the knees, he caught her by her upper legs and tossed her over his shoulder.

She squealed, kicking in protest. "Maxim!"

His hand swatted her bottom. "It took me three hours in the freezing weather to find you. I do believe that means I get at least three hours of hot, *something special* from you." He grabbed her ass cheek firmly, keeping a tight grip on the muscle as he walked, his thumb pressing into the crevice in sensual promise.

"But our skis!"

"Screw 'em. I can wade faster through this shit than I can ski. The cabin is close. I don't want to waste a moment of time, not until we get into your bedroom. Then, things are going to move at a much, *much* more leisurely pace."

Naked, Elisa stretched, lying on her back atop the bearskin rug. She watched Maxim stoke the fire, jabbing at the glowing coals with a poker, moving the burning wood so that flames burst forth.

She'd allowed herself to be taken against a tree, hauled inside, and stripped naked. She didn't regret a second of it . . . except when she'd expected a second go-around, he'd turned his attention to fire and food.

Since Maxim had already eaten more than his fair share of the apples, she might as well enjoy some sustenance herself—she couldn't make love without energy. Plucking a slice from the bowl beside her, she popped it in her mouth, chewing the juicy flesh.

Maxim lifted a log, bending to carefully place the wood on coals. His motions granted her an intriguing glimpse of his taut ball sacs. With a sigh, she brazenly studied the muscled definition of her former adversary's fine ass.

Wasn't life ironic?

"I can't believe I just screwed Maxim Cox," she murmured, more to herself than to him.

Once upon a time, she'd avoided him like he was the devil himself; a pure shame. He was quite the lay. Hell, he'd *thrust* her right out of her self-commitments and concerns. No wonder he was so popular with the ladies. No wonder so many females had been wounded by his abandonment. She'd be hurt too if she didn't get laid again real soon.

"Oh yeah?" Maxim turned his attention from the fire, a gleam in his intense gaze. "Correction, Elisa, screw*ing*. We aren't finished, no way. I still have at least a couple of hours left to my *something special* and by the time they're up, I'm positive I'll have persuaded you into needing more of this." Grabbing his dick, he winked at her.

Cocky as ever. But somehow, right now even that was sexy in an adorable sort of way.

She raised a brow. "So, I take it I'm your longest relationship ever?"

He'd already stuck around much longer than she'd ever expected. Unusual, given his bad boy history.

"Probably." He grinned wide enough to show his pearly white teeth. "Okay, definitely. But don't turn me away and I won't stop."

"Deal." Elisa smiled, rolling onto her side. At the moment, nonstop orgasms sounded damn good to her. Whether they knew it or not, his parents had named him appropriately. She just wished she'd discovered his talents sooner, like before meeting her asshole ex.

No matter what came next, she wouldn't regret having sex with Maxim. Back in college, there'd been no telling this side of him existed. Maybe she'd been too preoccupied with wanting to strangle him to notice—mainly because she was so damned attracted to him despite his behavior—but something haunted Maxim and she had to know what.

"Can I ask you a question?"

"Depends." He covered the few feet between them and lay next to her, flat on his back. "About what?"

Elisa fingered the fur directly above his shoulders. "When I told you that you couldn't masturbate, you hinted that maybe you'd been hurt."

"Yeah."

"You said I didn't understand you."

"Yeah."

Good grief. She felt like she was pulling teeth.

"So, I'd like to."

He cleared his throat. "I don't know." His voice dropped, thickened by the slight, exotic accent he often slipped into. "Have you ever wanted someone so badly, you hurt?"

"Yeah," she chuckled, thinking back to when he'd screwed her with the dildo. "Oh, yeah. But you never had to come here. Never needed to play this game. To hurt so much. So, *why* . . . really?"

"Because," he grunted, again dancing around the truth.

There was something more going on, something he refused to reveal. Something she needed to know.

Elisa abandoned the rug, instead wrapping his hair around her pinky. "That's not an answer."

"Have I told you how beautiful you are?" His Adam's apple bobbed up and down, revealing more than his slapdash words ever could.

"A hundred times, but that's still not an answer."

He rolled to his side, facing her, and glided his hand over her hip. "I think it is."

The touch set off mini fireworks as he trailed his fingers along her bare skin, gently caressing over her ass, her thighs.

With a shiver, she caught his hand, ceasing his seduction. "No, Maxim. I really want to know. I *have* to know. What's your deal? Why all this trouble for me?"

"I'd tell you, but the answer sounds silly. Like one of the lines you're always accusing me of."

She raised a brow. "Tell me anyway."

"Okay. First of all, you're right, you know. I understand how to talk to a woman . . . or at least the average one. Not you, though." His tongue darted out, running over his lower lip. "But I'm not toying with you, Elisa, I swear. When I saw that tabloid, I don't know what happened to me. I changed. Went crazy. I kept thinking of our college days. The way I drove you nuts. The way you drove me nuts. How much I wanted you. You're the only one to tell me no and mean it. I couldn't stand that . . . Suddenly I just had to come. To finish what we started."

"But there was never anything between us. I told you no, remember?"

"There should have been and you know it."

"I think we're past a date at this point."

"Yet, I still want it. I still want you. You make me feel . . . differently than most females. Like I shouldn't." Taking her hand, he pressed her palm to his chest, directly over where his heart beat. "You don't just interest my cock. You touch me here."

For a second, Elisa was speechless. She concentrated on the steady pulse thudding against her hand.

He was right. It did sound like a line. A big one.

Yet, this time, she almost bought it.

Her fingers curled in his chest hair as questions rose to the surface. "I affect you differently than other women? Hmmm. And it took you since college to realize that? We haven't seen each other in a long, long time, Maxim and we never really got along even back then. You're right, it doesn't sound . . . sane."

He scoffed with laughter. "Thanks."

"Are you sure you're not going through a midlife crisis?"

"Sure seems like you are," he chuckled. "I'm not the jobless one hiding in a cabin."

"Hey!" she protested, play hitting him. "You're the one who flew around the world to get laid."

"Not to get laid. To get you." He pulled her closer. "I guess we're both kinda losing it, huh?"

"Maybe just a little."

She snuggled against him and he wrapped an arm around her. "Elisa, I know I shouldn't want you like I do." He pushed her hand south, to his rigid cock. "I know it's dangerous. But I just can't stop how I feel. Not anymore."

Her fingers curled around his width as even more questions wrapped around her heart. "Why is it dangerous?" she whispered. "Why stop it?"

"Because like you, I know better than to get involved."

"But *you* weren't turned into a porn star against your will. So who hurt you?"

"No one, Elisa," he brushed her off, his tone completely changing as he caught her by her upper thighs, hefting her on top of him. The head of his erection pressed against the wiry hairs protecting her mons. "Are we talking? Or fucking?"

Shifting his lower half, he pressed his cock into her folds and wriggled, tickling her clit.

"Talking," she protested with a giggle. Despite her denial, sensation shot through her.

"I disagree. There was nothing about conversation in your letter. I want the rest of my *something special*." His cock slid downward, resting against her slit.

So *damn* close.

"Remember . . ." She spoke through clenched teeth, tightening every muscle in her body as she battled the urge not to plunge down upon him. "I think we still need new rules for our little game."

"Rules? No more, please." His cock pressed a fraction into her. "I won't let you."

"Oh?" She gulped, searching for inner strength when she had none. "What do you think you'll do about it?"

He brushed his nose along her cheek, sensually making his way to her ear. "I can be rather persuasive when the occasion calls," he murmured and nibbled at her lobe, then suckled the flesh, making her whimper.

"Tell me something I don't know," she asked.

Distract me.

The presence of his cock, threatening to spear her, to fulfill her, yet not, had her in sheer agony. Elisa bit her lower lip, practically drawing blood.

She was so ready. So ripe.

But as much as she wanted to fuck, she wanted to talk. To *know* him. She needed to.

He traced his tongue along the inner rim of her ear, his voice soft. "I love the way you never wear a bra. The way your nipples are dusky around the edges and pink in the center. I love the taste of your pussy."

Oh God. She was losing this battle of wills. Bad.

"But not my burnt tofu."

"No." His laugh was deep, sexy, his breath raising tingles over the already nerve-ignited area he kept licking. Passion blurred her mind.

Forget discovering his dark, well-kept secrets. Forget talking. There was always later.

Assuming he stuck around. "You earn me, you can have me," she told him. She turned to face him, her lips hovering over his. "The rest of the rules I'll make as we play. Now kiss me."

"Where?" he asked. His tongue darted out, licking around her mouth.

"Everywhere."

"Gladly, my queen." Winding her hair around his fingers, he rolled her onto the bear rug. He claimed her mouth in an open embrace and swooped his tongue along hers, gently coaxing her passion. She welcomed his soft, slow kiss, wanting more.

The ache between her legs increased, her need, exploding. She lifted her hips, pressing them against his pelvis, and tore her mouth free. Her hands grappled for his cock.

"Uh uh . . ." Maxim took her wrists and pinned her hands above her head. "You said to kiss you *everywhere* and that's what I intend to do."

ten

Kiss her *everywhere*, he would.

Holding her wrists firmly, so that her hands stretched above her head and rested on the bearskin rug beneath them, Maxim kissed her palms, then her wrists, working his way down one forearm to her elbow.

She whimpered in weak protest and he increased his tongue movements. "Don't think I'm going to quit," he murmured. "Tasting every inch of you sounds all too heavenly."

"You know, I always thought you were a 'wham, bam, thank you ma'am' type of fuck. You went through so many women." Her eyes fluttered shut and a sigh escaped her lips. "Oh God."

Releasing a short chuckle, Maxim continued devouring her. "Not a chance, baby, at least not when it comes to you."

Not even though his cock was threatening to blow. No matter how *hard* kissing every inch of her became.

"You have my full, undivided attention," he whispered. Suckling the rough skin of her elbow, he teased it with his teeth.

Behind them, the fire sputtered. Between the flame's heat and his combustible lust for Elisa, he was sweating, a welcome change from chilled skin and goose bumps—one he intended to relish until she was screaming his name.

Peck by peck, nibble by nibble, he continued his trek straight to her underarm. He nuzzled the sensitive area with his nose, blowing with his mouth, and Elisa squealed, jerking from ticklishness.

"Maxim!" Giggling, Elisa twisted in protest and attempted to roll away. "What are you doing?"

Maxim held her firm, arresting her struggles with more kisses. She was *his*, completely and thoroughly, until his mouth—hell, his cock—was satisfied.

"You said everywhere," he murmured. Lifting his head and sliding to the left, he applied the same treatment to her other arm. Their torsos brushed, his chest hairs creating friction against her smoothness. "And everywhere sounds damn good to me."

"I didn't mean literally." She wriggled against him and a streak of inferno need blazed along his dangerously swollen cock. "That's—"

"Glorious. Delicious." Maxim kissed her biceps, licking up and down the length of her arm. "I want my mouth to touch every single last inch of you. From your head"—he planted his lips to her forehead—"to your toes."

Elisa yelped at the suggestion. "My toes?"

"Which I shall suckle until you scream, my queen."

Praise God, he was enjoying this. Enjoying her. Two days ago, he wouldn't have imagined such playful passion between them. Wouldn't have dared to dream his *queen* would ever relinquish her reservations, much less allow herself to be pinned down and kissed all over.

Of course, he'd intended to seduce her and he'd succeeded— but the end result was much, much sweeter—no, *rewarding*—than he'd ever expected.

He *had* her. Finally.

How could simple kisses—even gross ones—be so insanely erotic? Tingles danced across her skin, shivered down her spine. Her body was burning, the ache in her loins so deep, her womb felt hollow.

Heaven help her, she wanted *more*. She wanted his mouth upon every last inch of her, just as promised.

At the same time, she wasn't sure she could take even one more kiss. Part of her wanted him to stop. To get on with larger— longer, *harder*—matters.

Maxim placed his lips to her nose and then planted tiny pecks over her cheeks, her jawbone, her chin. His mouth slid down her neck, stopping to suck at the indentation at the base of her throat.

"Maxim, you've made your point!" Elisa's nails dug into her palms. "Please!"

"Not hardly." He kissed along her collarbone, swiping his tongue across her shoulders. "Not even close."

He released his grip on her wrists, slowly gliding his fingertips along her arms until they reached her breasts. Cupping the mounds, he pushed them together and rained kisses down upon the flushed flesh, licking and nuzzling, his whiskery cheeks causing her to shiver.

Oh God. She was going to lose her mind.

Her clit pulsed, eager for the same attention that her breasts were receiving, and her pussy flooded with readiness. Spasming, her tunnel rebelled against its empty state.

Reaching to her left, she grabbed one of the condoms lying next to the bearskin rug and tore it open. Sliding her hand between their bodies, she slipped the protection on his cock and then tried to guide him inside her. He didn't budge. She fell back with a whimper. "Come on, already!"

"Damn, Elisa, you are sweet," he said softly, claiming her left nipple and drawing it between his teeth. He sucked hard, milking the bud like a babe nursing his mother's breast. His tongue darted out and caressed the dimpled rose-colored circle, creating electric shocks through her.

Easing his grip, he licked around the outer rim of her areola, and slowly worked his way back to the center. Sexual excitement burst through her, stronger than was tolerable, and she clutched his hair, holding on for strength.

She jerked his head back, demanding he listen to her. "Maxim, fuck me," she insisted, the arousal controlling her body and mind like storm waves crashing against a ship in a hurricane. "Now!"

She'd pull every inch of his hair out if she had to. She wanted this man in an impossible way and she'd had it with being denied.

Her nipple popped from his mouth and he rested his head against her breast, breathing heavily. "I can't believe I'm saying this, but no."

She gave his head a demanding tug. "No?"

If only he would kiss more *effective* parts of her, maybe she could stave off this rage, but damn it, she didn't need her nipples sucked at the moment. She needed an orgasm.

Reaching up, he peeled her fingers free of his hair. "Not until you're good and ready."

"But I am," she moaned.

What power did this man have over her? No matter how bossy, how *demanding* she became, once again she was at his mercy. Suffering from pure pleasure.

He pushed her hand south, between the heat of their bodies. "Well then, I'm not."

His cock met her hand and she gripped the head between her two fingers and squeezed gently. Maybe he needed a little coaxing. She'd like to see how much of her attention *he* could tolerate sanely.

Her thumb flicked across the tip of the wide mushroom top, then smoothed across the tender area underneath.

"I disagree. We're both ready. *Please*."

His jaw hardened and again he seized her hand. "Pleasure yourself, not me, because I'm not done kissing you yet." He nipped at the creamy skin of her breast. "As long as I've waited to have you, I intend to make a meal of you."

"But—"

He pushed her fingers into her mons. "Play with your pussy." He encouraged her with strokes of his own hand. "Don't be shy."

It certainly wasn't the time for that.

Too aroused to be embarrassed, Elisa followed his lead, pleasuring herself. She took her swollen clit between two digits, gently squeezing, then rubbing the bud in a circle. Biting her lower lip, she searched for the fulfillment she so needed, as Maxim returned to kissing her breasts ever so softly.

He moved to her waiting nipple, nursing it as he had the other. Sensation burst through the bud as she pressed two fingers into her tunnel.

They weren't enough. Nothing but his cock would be.

Why was he torturing her like this? Maxim should *want* to fuck!

She groaned and pressed deeper inside herself, desperate.

"Christ, you're incredible." Maxim released her breast and slid his mouth along her chest to the bone in the center. He sucked and licked his way to her belly, pausing to dip his tongue in the tiny indentation and swirl.

"Oh God." She bucked against him and drove her fingers deep inside her cunt. Her nails scraped her G-spot and her loins tensed with the promise of an orgasm.

Continuing to pleasure the sensitive spot, Elisa attuned herself to his physical appraisal. This was too good not to enjoy. She had to stop fighting. Relax. Take all he had to offer. She might never be loved like this again.

Maxim kissed her hips, his tongue brushing the dark hairs covering her mons, but disappointingly not coming into contact with her now soaked pussy. Not dipping into her folds.

When would he, already?! Did he have any idea what he was doing to her?

More than likely.

With his mouth, he trailed down her left thigh, over her knee and her calf, to her foot. Lifting it by the heel, he sucked on her pinky toe. She writhed from the acute pleasure blasting through her.

"Ma—" Elisa whimpered her delight. Sensation shot from her toes to her head, knocking her senseless. "Ma-Maxim!"

Her hand fell from her pussy, her grasp knotting in the bearskin rug underneath her.

"You like that, eh, baby?" He claimed a second toe, softly drawing on the digit. "You have beautiful toes. So tiny. So soft."

Ludicrous, but she couldn't find her voice to protest.

Toe by toe, he individually applied exquisite suction to each, then stroked the soft spot under her foot. By the time he moved to the opposite leg, she was near tears and fighting to hold in unreasonable emotion. She didn't feel like she was being screwed by the world's biggest slut, she felt like she was being loved, by a man who touched her very heart.

He teased her baby toe with his tongue. Elisa squirmed, howling in protest. Not that Maxim let that stop him. The bastard was enjoying his torture. More than he had a right to.

A man-slut wasn't supposed to be this good in bed. To be this irresistible. She'd expected him to fuck as quickly as his flings usually lasted. Not to be so slow . . . and so damn good.

How much more was she supposed to take?

She was falling and falling and . . .

"Delicious. I could eat you up." Maxim continued to execute the same torture to the rest of her toes, leaving Elisa sure she would come before his cock ever entered her.

"Maxim!" she cried. "Please!"

He cradled her foot, licking the thin bone along the top. "Do you have any idea how sexy your feet are? Not a single callus. So slim and smooth. Dainty. You have angel feet."

"Oh, please!" Her grip on the bearskin rug became dangerously fierce. She was close to ripping the fur right from the hide. *"Maxim!"*

The fire in the background was nothing compared to the heat generated by his touch. She was a ball of flaming lust, so close to detonation, he'd be smart to either plug her up or stand back, before her pussy exploded in his face.

He chuckled, low and deep. "You toes are more delicious than candy. I could just suck on them and suck on them . . ."

"Hurry up!" She pounded the floor with her fist.

What the hell was wrong with him? She wanted to fuck! Damn it!

"But I can think of another part of you that's even tastier." His tongue stroked upward, along her shin. "Mmmmmm ... mmmm ..."

"Yes!" she pleaded.

She was losing her mind, her body was going crazy, her heart ...

What was she saying? Her heart had nothing to do with matters!

She spread her legs wide as Maxim slowly delivered his mouth to her pussy. The trip up her leg, kissing and sucking, took a lifetime, but eventually, his lips landed gently on her mons.

Thank God.

Elisa wrapped her legs around his back as he rose to his knees and propped himself on his elbows, enjoying the up close and personal view of her pussy.

His cock was so hard that it practically touched the ground. Hell, it could act as a prop. A third leg. The damn thing was more erect than the taut skin could take and the head pulsed from agonizing engorgement—a swelling that could be easily relieved, just by simply sliding into her willing body. Taking what she begged him for.

His mind spun with the possibility, but his will rebelled. Not yet. Not for quite a while.

The self-inflicted torment was more than worth the pain if it meant keeping Elisa in the lust-controlled rage she currently battled.

He wanted Elisa to want—no—*need* him, like she'd never needed a man before. Like she never would. When she dreamt, he wanted it to be of him. When she fantasized, it would be of his touch. His cock. He wanted to brand her, to make her his. Forever. And most of all, he wanted to be certain she'd never be capable of turning him down again.

Spreading her folds, he opened her cunt wide, this time placing a kiss to her clit, then another on her slit.

"As expected, most delectable." He licked the salty desire that swamped her pussy. "Indeed, a gourmet meal."

"Probably the best one you'll get in this house." Her words were strained as she reached for his head and attempted to return his face to her intimate regions. Her legs tightened around him, preventing escape. "Better than the salad I'll feed you later."

"Indeed." He chuckled, again savoring a lick of the creamy, thick liquid. "I better enjoy."

She thrust against his mouth. "Eat your fill."

It would be his pleasure . . . but doubly hers.

His thumbs keeping her spread wide, Maxim slipped his tongue along her labia, slowly, thoroughly, stroking the length of her cunt.

He licked her from top to bottom, and back again, lapping at the sticky liquid flowing from her inner depths. Rotating his movements, from fast to slow, to nibbles and wide, hungry licks, he consumed her pussy.

Elisa moaned for more, her pleas desperate and weak with passion. What *more* he'd give her, she'd get slowly. So slowly, it hurt him, but that was the way of it.

Aiming to keep her teetering on the brink, he claimed her clit, drawing the tiny bud from its hood and flicking it with his tongue. Pulling on the bundle of nerves with his teeth, he drove her to scream out.

Elisa slammed her fist into the bearskin rug beneath her. "Oh God!"

Ah, satisfaction.

He sucked and teased harder. Only when she was panting and thrashing beneath him did he release her clit and move his attention to her entrance, spearing her with three fingers. He licked around them as he thrust in and out of her vigorously, purposefully driving her to a climax.

He couldn't believe she'd lasted this long, but he was going to force her over the edge. Make her orgasm.

And when she finished, he was going to push her to the brink all over again.

He pulled his hand free and rammed into her again, this time with four fingers. She cried out and her loins constricted around him, growing tight as he searched out her G-spot.

Reaching deep within her, Maxim curled his fingers and rubbed the sensitive spot in circles. Her whole body shook, her pussy convulsing as she screamed out, coming in a whole-body experience.

Oh yes, oh yes, oh yes, OH YES!

Maxim maintained steady hand movements as she exploded in a violent orgasm, her whole body lurching with the release. Her pussy shook, her cum spilling over his fingers as she gasped for air, her fingers holding the fur tight.

After several moments, the sheer, blinding, almost paralyzing ecstasy began to clear. Elisa collapsed, glorious vibrations humming through her body as her world whirled from the powerful climax.

So good . . .

Mind-blowing . . .

Incredible . . .

Sighing, still half-delirious, Elisa murmured something unintelligible. Even without his dick being involved, it had to have been the most intense sex she'd ever experienced. Maxim touched something in her no one else had, ever since the moment their professor had paired them together all those years ago. This . . . this was too good to be true . . .

Maxim slid his fingers free, slipping them under her ass and cupping her cheeks. He tilted her pelvis, jolting her to awareness as he plunged his cock inside her without warning.

His wide shaft demanded entry to her body, forcing her sheath to expand and accept him. Without preamble, he thrusted into her hard and fast. Her relaxed state was literally *thrust* back into a heady, need-charged whirlwind as she scrambled to meet his physical demands.

"Maxim! Oh yeah, I need this!" she cried. "I need you!" She matched his passionate fucking and wildly bucked her hips against his, taking every inch Maxim had to give. They mated violently, nothing soft or sweet about the experience.

Elisa quickly found herself on the verge of yet another orgasm, her mind unable to stifle her body's burning need to climax again.

She clutched his shoulders, hanging on for dear life as her pussy spasmed around his shaft, her body jerking from ecstasy. Her muscles contracted and released so many times, she battled to remain conscious.

Totally blown, she fell into a pile of useless mush as he continued to fuck her like a caveman. He drove into her even harder, abruptly jerking as he climaxed.

When he finished, he rested his hands on his knees, taking deep breaths. "Fuck."

"No kidding." With a groan, Elisa pulled free of him and curled in a ball.

"I wanted you to come again," he gasped, shaking his head. "But I couldn't hold out."

She chuckled, unable to hide her amusement, even as her world blurred around her. "A third orgasm? Maybe later." Her heavy eyelids curtained, sleep claiming her and erasing all possibility of any more physical activity.

eleven

Even after a full night of rest, Elisa could still feel the after-effects of the powerful orgasms Maxim had driven her to.

Damn, the man was good. Too good. So good, it was scary.

Cleaning the steam from the mirror, she stared at her reflection. How long had it been since she'd seen her eyes dance with such excitement? Since she hadn't been able to wipe the smile from her face with self-enforced negative thoughts?

Stick her in a loony bin and label her crazy, but she couldn't wait to make love to Maxim again.

Her pussy screamed in keen agreement.

So much for vowing off men. Even secluded in the middle of the woods, she'd fallen prey to the worst of the worst and was currently *smiling* about it.

Her hands shook as she attempted to comb her dripping wet hair, starting at the bottom of the knotty mess and working her way upward. Within seconds, she dropped the comb. Forget it. Her heart was fluttering like a hummingbird's. She couldn't function correctly to save her life.

She was lucky to even be clean. She'd barely soaped herself up and rinsed off before she'd hopped from the shower, eager to return to Maxim and their bearskin rug.

Seriously, she had to get a grip.

The chase was officially over. Chances were, Maxim would soon get bored. Leave.

No. He'd stuck around this long and there *was* a reason. Plus, she didn't want him to go, at least not yet.

She just couldn't allow that to happen.

If she played him correctly, surely she could manage to keep his attention, at least a while longer.

Elisa squared her shoulders. She had to get it together. Stop acting like some lust-struck teenager and start acting like a woman.

If there was any hope of him staying around, she needed to regain control. Be the queen he called her.

And she knew just how.

If Maxim wanted to fuck her again, he needed to earn it. Earn *her*.

Hair a mess, without a stitch of clothing to cover her body, Elisa marched from the bathroom, resolved to take control of the situation.

*D*id they deliver pizza on skis? Hell, Chinese would be better. He had a serious craving for anchovies.

Wholly disappointed at the empty space next to him, Maxim stretched his limbs, his mind on nothing but his empty belly and ready dick.

He'd woken with the worst morning erection ever, and Jesus, he was famished. This time, fruit wouldn't do. It was either more hot sex or fattening, unhealthy, oh-so-delicious take out.

Where was Elisa anyway?

He swore, she better not be toying with him again. He was getting *really* tired of waking with worries and a hollow stomach.

Leaping to his feet, Maxim stretched again, commanding his hard-on to chill out. As typical these days, his cock didn't listen.

On to the kitchen. Not bothering to dress and barely able to walk, Maxim headed toward food, surprised to find a naked Elisa silently stalking down the hall, her arms crossed, her hair soaked and in knots. She carried the air of a lunatic on a binge—he could only hope it was sex she was crazy for.

"Morning, baby." He walked toward her, meeting her mid-hallway. Taking her by the shoulders, he swung her around, pressing her against the rough-wood, oak-paneled wall.

"*Good* morning." She gazed up at him, a hint of amusement curling her lips, a twinkle in her eyes. The merry madwoman look punched him in the chest, knocking him breathless. How could she look so sexy and so dangerous at the same time?

He tangled his fingers in her wet knots, bringing the locks to his nose. "Mmmm . . . vanilla . . . cinnamon . . . so exotic . . . what is that scent? I could eat you up."

She retrieved her hair, patting the tangled strands neatly back to their mess. "It's my favorite shampoo. Cinnamon buns."

"Mmmmm . . ." He was practically drooling. Weak at the knees. "Breastfast . . ."

"Did you say *breast*fast?

He chuckled at his mistake, grabbing her by the bottom and hauling her closer, so that his erection pressed against her pussy. "My mind is being controlled by my smaller head."

"I see. Hard again?"

"I was dreaming of you," he murmured. "I have, every night since college, you know."

She rolled her eyes and gave him a hearty shove backward. "Oh, bullshit." Free of him, she walked gracefully down the hallway, her sweet ass swaying as she laughed under her breath.

"It's true. Most days, this goes away once I rouse. But with you around, I think my cock is sticking it out for the duration." He panted after her, moving as fast as he could with his still ragingly aroused cock.

Damn, she did it for him like no other woman could. Even tired and hungry, he couldn't stop.

Elisa flicked on the kitchen light. "Well, I hope you slept well. It's going to be a busy day."

"Sounds good, angel." After the vast amount of time he'd waited to have her, an all-day sex affair sounded damn good to him.

"I don't mean having sex." Going to the fridge, Elisa swung the door open, showing no sign of any desire to hop back into bed. "Let's get you something to eat."

Food. He could settle for that.

He stopped angling for more sex, allowing his fantasies to dissipate, along with his softening cock. Leaning against the breakfast bar, he tapped his fingers on the marble top. "Please say you have something real to eat."

"Hmmm . . . how about scrambled eggs and cheese? Sausage?"

"You have sausage?"

"It's soy, but yes." She took some items from the fridge, tossing them on the counter. Maxim eyed the products—they weren't anything close to what he longed for. Resting his head in his hands, he groaned with despair. "Soy sausage? And the eggs are in a milk carton? Have mercy."

"The eggs are still eggs. They're just yolk-free. And the sausage is good, trust me."

Damn it. She was really sexy—really, really sexy. And cute. And endearing. And smart.

But she was not a large supreme pizza complete with a beer.

Damn it, one couldn't live off lust alone. His stomach growled in protest, his mind roared. "I am a man, you know. If you don't start feeding me, I'm going to lose consciousness. Then the only sex we'll be having will be in my dreams."

She laughed at him as she poured the ingredients together and placed the pan over a flame, shaking it around. "Don't worry. I'm going into Aspen tonight to meet my sister and I'll pick up some groceries."

He breathed a sigh of relief. *Thank God.*

He grabbed a stool and sat at the breakfast bar, resolved to eat whatever she had to offer. *For now.* "Great. That sounds like fun. I'll get some of my clothes while we're there."

And meat. And wine. And a television.

Elisa was silent as she scraped the food onto their plates. After a moment, she said, "I didn't say *we*. I said I."

"But—"

"Trust me, you don't want to hang out with Lizzy. She doesn't like men." She handed him his plate and sat down. "Besides, you're going to be way too busy today to have the energy to ski tonight."

Busy? Well, hell, if sex was involved, then he'd forgo the protests. "Sounds like fun, my queen. Will you tie me up?" He winked at her, but she didn't even smile.

"And as for clothes . . ." She sighed, looking him dead in the eye . . . and all too serious for his taste. "I think it's high time you learned to live without frivolities."

"Clothes are frivolous? You're tough."

What was Elisa up to? To say the least, she was acting weird. Not angry and indifferent, like a couple of days ago, but changed. Combined with the fact that she wanted to do something *without* him . . . he didn't like it. After sex, women usually followed him around like puppy dogs.

Oh yeah, he was worried. And tonight, he was following her into town, whether she knew it or not.

"If you want to be with me, Maxim, you're going to have to work for it. Dance to my tune." She took a bite of the white eggs and pointed the fork at him. "You know what I think? Your outdoorsman skills are pathetic. I want a man who can take care of me."

Really weird.

He cleared his throat. "Hey, we aren't getting married."

She shrugged and continued to eat, like their conversation was normal. "Of course not. Why buy the cow?"

Maxim practically choked on the sausage—which really wasn't that bad—and stared at her. "What?"

Really, really, really weird.

Elisa pushed aside her plate and laid her hands flat on the breakfast bar. "I'm not angling for marriage. But if you want to stay here, you're going to earn your place . . . and me." Biting her lower lip, she contemplated a moment. She pointed to the left rear of the cabin. "In fact, there's a tree fallen out back. It isn't large. My father cut it up last time he was here, but he never got around to chopping it. You will, and stack it too."

What!?

Forget weird. That was mean.

He'd never chopped wood in all his life. He wasn't about to now. "And if I don't?"

"No nookie for you."

"Yeah. Right." Maxim chuckled. Elisa was bluffing. Even if she thought she could resist him, she couldn't. They'd already proven that.

Did she really think she'd get away with making him do manual labor for sex? It wasn't his style. With the money his family had, he'd never been forced to do menial chores and he wouldn't start now. If Elisa wanted wood, he'd buy her a truckload. But lift an axe? No way.

"Go ahead. Try." She slipped off the stool and opened her arms, the motion lifting her bare breasts as she welcomed a sexual attack. Damn, her naked body looked so much tastier than his breakfast.

He stared into her steely eyes. She glared back, unyielding. Maxim studied her—the set of her jaw, the way she didn't move, didn't shake—shocked to realize she *meant* it. She wasn't budging. He could sweet talk until his throat hurt and kiss her senseless— she wouldn't open her legs. Not this time.

She *really* wanted him to chop wood.

Why was she doing this? Was she was trying to piss him off? Push him away?

He wasn't ready to go.

Nor was he prepared to let Elisa Cross get to him. He shrugged, acting unimpressed. "I'll chop the damn wood. It's nothing."

"Oh yeah?"

"Piece of cake."

He'd never been a good liar, at least according to his mother, who ended more of his escapades than he could ever start. And based on the glimmer in Elisa's smile, he wasn't pulling off his nonchalance very well.

Damn it.

Funny, but it was said that a man falls for a woman just like his mother. As far as strength and resolve and seeing right through him went, she and Elisa could be twins.

Maxim pressed his lips shut, deciding to play it cool and calm, and not give Elisa any more fuel for her fire.

Her smile broadened as she dropped her arms. "I also feel like going for a ski. So after you finish your chore, you can come find me."

"What?"

"I'll be hiding, of course. That's part of the game, remember?"

"You've got to be kidding me!" A natural reflex, Maxim slammed his hand into the counter, knocking his stool off balance. Before he could steady himself, he tumbled backward, landing on the floor with a big bruising blow to his left side.

Freaking crazy crap!

Holding his shoulder, which screamed in pain, he moaned and rolled over, looking up at his drill sergeant. "Are you enjoying this? You really want me to do all that just for sex with you?"

"Yup." Bending, she planted a kiss on his shoulder. "But I'll tell you what. We'll up the reward with a new rule. Once you find me, you'll also get to use your choice from my toy box." With that, she stood and walked from the kitchen, leaving him lying there, injured and frustrated. "Provided you chop the wood."

"Infuriating woman," he muttered to himself, nonetheless resolved. As far as his dick was concerned, he wasn't about to allow some wood and snow to stand between him and scoring with Elisa Cross again and again and again—especially not when toys were involved.

"I heard that!" Elisa called from the next room. "You don't want to make me mad, now do you?"

She'd half expected him to leave, to at least put up some resistance; but to comply so easily?

He had to have better things in his life to do than struggle to please her. Forget *things*, he had better women—more willing women to be precise—at his disposal. Why her? And what about his job? How could anyone just leave his life behind as he had? Wasn't he worried? Concerned about his hotel?

That was the thing about Maxim. He didn't stress over anything. He did what he wanted . . . and apparently that was *her* at the moment.

From the window, Elisa watched Maxim haul a large piece of round oak to the chopping block, then raise the axe high. He swung hard, knocking the wood in two. Favoring his left shoulder, he picked the sections and threw them on the stack, then retrieved another log.

Despite the fact that he'd hurt himself falling from the stool, he was moving quickly. Too quickly.

He'd be through that pile in an hour. That didn't leave her much time to implement the next stage of her "prove how much you want me" plan.

And yet, she was enjoying the view far too much to budge. He looked so strong. Resilient. Tough. *Pure male.* Even injured, he was fighting, fast and furiously, to have her.

He was nothing like the man she'd believed him to be.

A little drop of drool threatened to slide from her smile and she swallowed, loving it as he swung the axe again. Too bad it wasn't summer and he wasn't shirtless, but even with his padded clothing, witnessing *him*—rich, spoiled, womanizing Maxim— chop wood was distractingly sexy.

Was he really so determined? She couldn't believe he was actually doing it. He wasn't just working—something she wondered if he were capable of—he was proving himself to her through and through. And earning her.

If she based the outcome on yesterday when he'd found her, there was no doubt left. After all she was putting him through, he'd want *full* payment.

twelve

"*Elisa!*" Maxim shouted from directly behind her. "*Elisa!*"

Maxim was right—skis were clumsy and slow. And since when was he such an expert on them?

She'd barely set off into the woods and already he was closing in on her fast. Worse, he'd spotted her. In all fairness, she should probably forfeit. After all, the game was for him to find her, not chase her down like a fox after a rabbit.

But where was the fun in being caught five minutes after leaving the cabin?

Damn it, she shouldn't have drooled over the sight of him chopping wood for so long.

No, she should have recorded it.

She topped another hill, flying through the air and landing safely, at least for about three seconds, before she caught sight of the sudden drop off looming in front of her. *Oh no!* Elisa twisted her skis to the left and dug her poles into the snow-covered ground, barely escaping a plunge over the edge.

Holy shit! Where had that come from?

She stared down, not knowing what to do. Her heart pounded in excitement and her breath came in heavy pants. Blood pumped through her veins so furiously, her skin heated.

In her excitement, she must have taken the wrong path. This certainly wasn't the awe-inspiring clearing with a guaranteed perfect view of the sunset she'd intended to lead Maxim to, hoping for a peaceful moment between the two of them.

This was a dead end. The jagged mountainside practically dropped away, creating a gorge with steep sides littered with half-grown, spindly pine trees and hints of dangerous rocks peeking from beneath the blanket of snow. Excellent skier that she was, she doubted her ability to successfully navigate the slope.

What's more, she knew damn good and well Maxim couldn't.

He might roll down the hazardous incline, but no way could he ski it. Likely he wouldn't even try. Not with his luck on skis.

His loud whoop broke the air. She jerked her head up, knowing she had to make some sort of decision. He was so close, she could hear the sliding of his skis in the snow.

"Elisa, baby, don't you dare move!" he called. "You're mine!"

This chase was far too thrilling to end now.

At least, that's what she told herself.

She felt cornered. Trapped. She wasn't just fleeing from Maxim, but reality. If he caught her, if he proved himself, how could she possibly continue to pretend? She couldn't.

Deep down, she knew all her promises to herself were fleeting. Maxim was forcing her to face things she'd already dealt with. Handled. She hadn't dreamt he'd go this far and now that he had, she was in serious trouble. She couldn't resist him . . . physically or emotionally.

She just didn't know what to do. How to face the truth settling in around her.

"Oh, what the heck!" With a shift of her poles, Elisa threw caution to the wind and leapt into the chasm.

A second later—the direct result of her ski catching on a hidden rock—*she* was rolling. Tumbling and catapulting downward, her feet locking together, her body ramming into the surprisingly hard ground despite the fluffy blanket that covered it.

Distantly, she heard Maxim follow her into the gorge, his curses echoing off the mountainside.

Oh God. What had they gotten themselves into?

Talk about a stupid decision. Dying wasn't worth a thrill . . . wasn't worth escaping him. Didn't she secretly want him to catch her anyway?

Dumb, dumb, dumb . . .

"Uff!" Butt-first, Elisa slammed into a small pine tree, her descent brought to an end. She barely caught her breath and lifted her head before she realized that Maxim was skiing *directly* toward her.

"Oh no!" she squealed. "Maxim!"

"Watch out!"

Where was she supposed to *go*? Down? No thank you . . . as a rule, she never made the same mistake twice.

Except when it came to men.

"Whoa!" Struggling to keep his balance, Maxim opened his legs, so not to hit her head on. He stretched his hands out and caught the top of the pine tree, halting his flight. The action thrust his hips into her face, his groin knocking her backward.

"Caught ya." He chuckled, rolling off her.

"That wasn't pretty." Riddled with so many aches and pains that she felt like she'd been hit by a bus, Elisa moaned.

The only thing keeping both of them from plummeting to the bottom of the gorge was a pathetic baby pine and with their combined weights, the tree's strength wouldn't hold out long. They needed to regain control of the situation and fast.

Elisa attempted to sit up, but her skis locked with his, preventing her from moving far. "Damn."

Maxim reached down, untangling the mess. "What were you thinking?"

"Thinking?" She followed his lead, freeing her feet, and scooting so her feet propped against the pine's base. "Was I?"

"Probably too much. Like always." He moved behind her and attempted to gain a footing on the hill, but he quickly slipped, landing on his knees."

"Hey," she protested. "Be nice!"

"Nice? Like you?" He tried to stand again and slipped. "Shit!" Giving up, he sat down in the snow and scooted behind her, claiming the tree she braced herself with. His arms enveloped her waist and drew her onto his lap, hugging her tight.

"I'm always nice," she protested.

"You made me chop wood!"

"You want to stay warm, don't you?"

"Oh, so that's the way of it?" He nuzzled her ear. "Far as I'm concerned, you're all the warmth I need."

Elisa battled shivers as he licked along her jaw line. His mouth pressed firmly to her cheek, wetting her cold skin, the kiss so simple, yet so sensual. "Your silly chores are worth it though, this ridiculous fall too, as long as I can carry you off to our rug and have my way for several hours."

"Provided we can get out of the gorge." Another shudder racked her body, her nerves crawling with excitement, the sensation whirling through her body like a storm, wetting her in an area that didn't need to be wet while they were in the woods, about to roll to their deaths on a very steep incline. Couldn't he give seducing her a break?

But despite herself, she leaned into his decadent mouth, welcoming more.

"You got us into it this mess, baby. Assuming you can get us out." His breath blew across her nerve-ignited cheek as he spoke. "You know, finding you was a piece of cake."

"Not fair. I never really got to hide." The weakened pine tree started to give way and she felt herself sliding. "Uh, Maxim? I think—"

"Shhh . . . you'll be fine. I got you. And forget hiding." He scooted her further on his lap, right atop his cock. "Far as I'm concerned, now that I've caught you, you're mine, to take *however* I please."

An anxious flutter tickled her stomach. "Oh, and how is that?"

"A little spanking may be in order after the way you've behaved." His left hand roamed along her thigh, stroking the side of her ass. "I definitely want to slide my cock into that tight bottom of yours."

The flutter burst into a full outbreak of nervous trembling. "B-but—" Her stuttered reaction dropped like pebbles rolling down a hill, disappearing into thin air. She was speechless.

Never had a man spoken of such things so bluntly to her. And while she'd experienced anal sex before, never had a man laid a hand to her bottom.

Her pussy swelled, welcoming the thought. *Eager.*

Just knowing he *might* do such things to her suddenly had her so physically excited, she couldn't think straight.

So much for her being the dominant partner.

His hand squeezed her bottom firmly through her thick clothing. "Don't worry, I'll make sure you enjoy both," he whispered in her ear.

"You will?" She gulped. She felt them slide a small fraction downward. Maxim dug in his heels, but that didn't make her feel better. They were so going to end up at the bottom of this hill. This slope was going to spank the both of them.

His arms tightened around her, practically squeezing her breathless. "Why the fear? Don't you trust me yet, Elisa?"

"Not particularly, no."

She wanted to. She even thought she might. But she knew better. Men like Maxim were not the type to put faith in, except maybe when it came to matters of the bedroom.

"Why?"

"Your history . . ." she began and then changed her mind. "You've never given me any reason to."

"Do you think I'll hurt you?" he asked in a gentle voice.

Yes. When you decide you're done with me. When you sleep with another woman. Or two. Or three. Or twenty.

But she couldn't admit that. Couldn't confess that the biggest reason his flings made her so angry was pure, unadulterated, unreasonable jealousy.

The insane desire to be the only female he'd *ever* wanted, from yesterday into eternity.

"Yes. No." She swallowed again. "Let's just say that you're slowly winning my confidence."

He chuckled lightly. "And you're slowly winning my h—"

His words fell away, once again, but her mind easily filled in the blanks. *Heart.* Is that what he almost said?

"What?" she questioned, oddly wishing he'd finish his sentence. Bombard her with sweet bullshit nothings. Lie if he must. She wanted him to say it. *Love.*

Even if he didn't mean it, part of her wanted to hear it. Oh God. She was lost.

"Nothing."

Awkward silence fell around them. For several moments they just sat there, his embrace around her midsection tight, though the connection between them suddenly felt as if it stretched between two planets.

They lived in different worlds. Their lives were dissimilar, their personalities, night and day.

So why did it keep feeling like they were meant to be one?

She coughed, clearing the air. "Well, how are we going to get back up?"

"I guess, Elisa, you're going to have to trust me."

Fifteen minutes later, still cradling her like a baby, he had her safely away from the canyon as promised and practically swooning with *trust*.

My shoulder is killing me. I don't know if I can even spank you. First my fall from the stool earlier, then chopping the wood and then our tumble . . ." Maxim moaned and groaned, feeling like he had been hit by a train. Belly down, he stretched on her plush, queen-sized bed, his toy of choice—a small but effective one—clutched in his hand and hidden from her eyes.

The delicious scent of hot cocoa filled the air as Elisa carried the tray to the nightstand and set it down. She sat next to him, her hand lying on his ass. She patted his bare butt affectionately.

"Oh, what a shame," she cooed. "No spanking. Whatever shall I do with myself this afternoon?"

"You know you want it."

"Oh?" She gave his ass a sudden, sharp smack. "Perhaps I shall spank you."

Maxim chuckled. He didn't think so. After carrying her out of that canyon and half the way home, he *deserved* to spank her sweet ass. He'd earned it—and he intended to cash out. Soon as he felt like moving.

He stretched again, wanting a sip of the cocoa, but feeling too lazy to even reach for it. "Massage me."

"With a dildo?" She chuckled, pressing her fingers into his crack and dangerously close to his rectum.

An awakening zap of arousal shot through his body and his cock jerked at the touch.

"No, smart-ass. With your hands." Uncomfortable, he quickly shifted away from her daring hand. "Does everything have to be about sex with you?"

"Me!"

Scooting down on the mattress, he forced her hand higher on his back. "Besides, I've already made my choice from the toy box while you were showering and making our drinks."

"Oh?" Elisa raised a brow, more curious at his reaction to her probing than what toy he may have picked. Again, she slid her hand south, over his firm, well-defined buttocks, and kneaded. "I think you liked that, didn't you?"

"I think *you'll* like these." Turning his hand over, he opened his palm, revealing a string of three vaginal beads, each plum-colored, egg-shaped, and about two inches in diameter, connected by a smooth cord.

They appeared, compared to the other, more complex dildos and vibrators in her collection, to be simple. Plain. Then again, she'd never tried them, simply because she didn't know what to do with them. Not to mention that before this week, she'd never been into toys. Oddly, it took being with a man to really enjoy them.

But Maxim had such a way with . . . everything. Women, toys, *her*.

"Mmm. I give. You've quite distracted me."

"Uh. I demand my massage first." His hand closed around the beads. "So get to it, woman."

She smiled, actually enjoying the prospect of some intimacy between them that wasn't sexual.

"I think I have some oil." Moving to the floor, she rummaged thru her exposed box of goodies, silently amazed by how very comfortable she felt with Maxim now, even with the presence of sex toys. A wall had fallen between them, one that allowed him to lie naked before her and for her not to think twice about it; one that had her bubbling with anticipation, rather than shaking with apprehension.

If Lizzy knew what she was doing with her gifts, she'd shoot her.

Elisa found the bottle of oil and some protection and climbed on the bed, tossing the condom on the pillow. Straddling Maxim's back, she unscrewed the cap and poured some of the perfumed liquid onto his shoulders. Her fingers met with rock hard resistance.

"You are tense." She kneaded his muscles slowly, working the knots in his shoulders gently. "I think you did too much."

"Yeah. Because you worked me like a dog today." He moaned, practically falling to pieces beneath her touch. "Mmmm . . . God, that's good. I'm turning into mush."

"If I didn't know better, Maxim, I'd think you'd enjoyed your day."

"Hard work?" he mumbled. "Never."

"Then why haven't you left?" she chuckled, drumming her fingers over his shoulder blades.

He sighed at the touch. "I'll grant you this—you're interesting."

Interesting? Well, at least he didn't say bitchy . . . or pathetic.

"I'll take that as a compliment." She pressed her fingers a little deeper.

He groaned. "You're pretty too."

"Pretty and interesting . . . hmmm . . ."

"And smart."

"I'm beginning to like this."

"Sexy."

"Sexy," she repeated in a whisper. Something in her welled up and she smiled to herself. Somehow, Maxim calling her sexy was much more moving than his other compliments. It made her feel good. It made her feel . . . *sexy*.

Before he'd come here, she'd felt used and sorry for herself. Bitter. But, oddly enough, his presence was giving her a strength she might not have found on her own, secluded in the middle of nowhere with nothing but bad memories and hopeless feelings.

As surprised as she'd been when he'd shown up, she was glad he'd come. Maybe it had just been *time*.

"So I take it I've convinced you?" he asked. "Are you finished with your silly vow to be done with men?"

Was she? The sting of the porno fiasco was certainly fading. What's more—she was beginning to trust him.

"I don't know," she answered honestly. "I don't know how I feel about anything right now. Men. My future."

"Me?"

"Yes, you." Unconsciously, her grip on his muscles tightened, squeezing hard as she rolled the flesh in her hands.

"Too much," he protested, pulling away. "Elisa. Does that mean you think I'll be a part of your future?"

"I don't know. What makes you ask that?"

"I could offer you a job at my parents' hotel."

Her heart skipped a beat and her massaging came to a complete halt. A job? What did that mean?

Did he actually want to keep her around? Or just help her out?

"I can't believe I just asked you that." He cleared his throat. "But, um, what do you think?"

She swallowed, commanding herself not to read too much into his suggestion. He wasn't presenting her with forever—not even a commitment—just a job. One she could never take.

"You know that's not the type of work I want to do, Maxim."

Forget the fact that she wanted to do positive things with her life—what if Maxim wasn't truly changed? What if they broke up? How could she possibly consider resigning herself to watching him fling through women like trash after the time they'd shared together at this cabin?

Ultimately, even if she could tolerate such heartache, it wasn't part of her plan for life. She'd been thrown a curve ball with her porn star status, but she couldn't let it stop her from doing some good in the world.

Ever since she was a kid, Elisa had promised herself she'd serve a purpose in this world. *Hands on.* Before she died, her mother had made a career of funding organizations to help save rainforests and the indigenous people in them . . . but she talked about doing more. Touching the world . . . the *real* one. Unfortunately, those dreams were never realized, her mother's existence cut short by a car accident.

Elisa wasn't going to end like that. She wanted to live . . . to make a difference. Save those rainforests and so much more for her mother.

Maybe she didn't know exactly what she would do with herself now, but her future *couldn't* involve running away to Egypt with Maxim. She couldn't center her life around any man.

She'd trusted once before . . . and been hurt terribly. She couldn't, wouldn't, go through that again. And somehow, she knew with Maxim it would be so much more painful.

Derrick hadn't mattered. Maxim did.

No, the last thing she needed was to imagine them with any kind of future. Lately, she'd lost sight of her goals. But confused as she still was about Maxim, she saw matters clearly now. She could enjoy him for a while, but then she had to move on. Get her life back.

"Elisa? Did you hear me?" Maxim asked, jolting her from her deep thoughts. "What kind of work are you looking for? I know some people. Actually, a lot of people."

"No, thanks, Maxim. I'll find something when I'm ready."

"Just think about it, okay?" he insisted. "I mean, maybe a move would do you good and I have a lot of contacts in Cairo."

"No."

"Why?"

Elisa shook her head. It was time to curtail this conversation. Maxim's first priority was himself. He only wanted her in Egypt for *his* pleasure. Someone like him could never understand her and her reasons. She couldn't expect him to. They were just different . . . they had different expectations in life. That was that.

"Come on, tell me," he insisted. "What kind of work are you looking for?"

She ignored him.

She returned to kneading his shoulders, lowering herself to plant kisses along the sore area. "Feel better?"

"Tons. But—"

"Good. I like this position I have you in." Elisa willed herself strength. Hard as it was, she was shutting him out of her life. She had to remember that the only thing between them was sex, nothing more, nothing less.

Reaching down, she swatted his bum twice in quick succession. "It just might be me giving the spanking."

"I don't think so." He reared against her and then flipped over, knocking her off balance. The beads he held dropped to the floor as he reached for her and caught her arms, dragging her onto his lap.

Sitting, his hard cock dancing between her legs, he grasped her hair tightly and pulled her head back. His hold was rough and tough. Unrelenting. He stared into her gaze, not allowing her to look away. "I'm onto you, Elisa Cross. I know—"

Her poor heart . . . it was under such stress. Unable to beat properly.

"Oh?" She swallowed, feeling caught, trapped, though she didn't even know why. "What's that?"

Thankfully, before he could answer, the telephone rang.

thirteen

*L*et it ring!" Maxim stared in shock as Elisa clambered from his lap, running naked from the bedroom. "Oh, come on!"

She had to be kidding him.

"Elisa!"

"It might be important!"

It might be ninety degrees in Aspen tomorrow too.

Jesus. Any other woman would have taken the phone off the hook or let it ring . . . at least shown annoyance at the untimely interruption. But apparently, not even the presence of his hard cock between her legs could prevent his "lover" from fleeing when the opportunity presented itself.

Of course not. Not Elisa. *Never Elisa.*

"Oh, come on!" he groaned. He'd been so close to busting down a wall between them. So close . . .

But getting through her barricades was like trying to take down the Great Wall of China. Once up, always up.

Man. Did she seriously care who was on the line?

Yeah right.

Sure, they'd had sex multiple times in multiple ways, but when it came to real, intense conversation or sincere moments between them, she always shut down. As far as relationships went, she was worse than him.

And what was going on in his mind? It seemed he was becoming a man obsessed. He couldn't believe he'd asked her about their future. Asked her to work for him. Suggested she move to Egypt. He'd been talking without thinking.

Did they have a future?

Did he, the man who would never settle down, actually want one?

Perhaps he'd hit his head in the fall.

With a pathetic whimper, he let himself sink into the mattress. Of course she was answering the phone. She'd found a temporary escape from the intimacy blooming between them and she was taking it.

But temporary it would be.

He didn't intend to let her off so easily. He intended to make her face her feelings. Her desires.

Elisa was no dominatrix, no queen, but a sweet woman who was ultimately turned on by a powerful man.

Maxim listened to the pitter patter of her footsteps as she fled down the hall, tempted to follow her. *Too* tempted.

Who was she speaking to? Was it important? Why?

Guilt rose up in him, followed by quick shock. Damn it, he was actually thinking about spying. What was wrong with him? How could he even consider it?

He was this far gone . . . over a woman?

He shouldn't eavesdrop. He shouldn't even care what the phone call might be about. He knew that.

Nonetheless, the urge wouldn't be tamped down. By God, he was too intrigued not to follow. Elisa refused to share her life with him—hell, her affairs weren't any of his business—but oddly enough, he wanted to know her. Very much. Too much.

"This is stupid," he swore to himself. "Stay in bed."

But he never was very good at taking advice. Not even from himself.

Before he could stop himself, his bare feet hit the wood floor. Quietly, he wrapped a blanket around himself and crept from the room to the end of hall. Leaning against the wall, he listened.

Are you going to make it tonight or what?"

Elisa cringed at what her sister's annoyed tone and direct question insinuated. Did Lizzy truly believe just because she was involved with a guy that she'd lost all sense of self?

She'd done that once and it wouldn't happen again. Ever.

Lizzy should know that.

But as typical, when it came to men and relationships, Lizzy was quick to be cynical.

Squeezing her thighs together in an attempt to block the desire flooding her pussy, Elisa twirled the kitchen phone cord around her thumb and breathed in relief at the thought of having some free time away from Maxim this evening. While she enjoyed being with him, things were getting so intense. His insistent behavior, as well as her desire and even worse—*her growing feelings*—were increasing . . . to the point of danger.

"Of course I'll be there." Shaking away the troublesome thoughts, Elisa burst out the answer, finally replying to Lizzy's question about tonight. No wonder her sister doubted her. She was acting like an idiot. "Since I've been in Aspen, we've met every Monday night for wine and poker. Now why would I miss it?"

"That was an awful long pause." Lizzy voice dripped with sarcasm. "Need I remind you that you have company? Company you're *falling* for?"

Company she needed space from so she could breathe. Think. Make sense of the situation before it exploded in her face.

Besides, even if she did feel the urge to cling to Maxim, she'd never ditch her own sister.

Elisa squared her shoulders and firmed her voice. "Lizzy, I promise you, just because I'm foolishly falling for some guy doesn't mean I'm going to—"

Thump!

What was that? Elisa whirled around, her eyes seeking out the cause of the sudden noise in the hall. Her gaze found nothing, which only caused more concern.

Was Maxim spying on her? Worse, had he heard her say that she was *falling* for him?

Crap.

In a bucket. Dumped over his head.

A smack of bubble gum cracked over the line, regaining her attention. "No kidding, Elisa. I'd shoot him before I let him steal you from me."

A bark of laughter escaped Elisa. "God help anyone who gave you a gun. Though, if he gets to be a problem, you know, gets too *nosy* . . . well, fire away, by all means."

"I have an idea. Instead of cards, why don't we meet at your cabin tonight? I know someone willing to supply me with anything I want. I can bring two guns. We'll blast him to bits."

"You better not shoot him, you brat, at least not until I'm done with him." Elisa raised her voice, determined that Maxim hear everything she said, especially the part regarding his well-deserved death. "I promise you, I'm having some sex. Off camera. But that's it. I know better than to get involved. And if I do, blow him away with a machine gun."

"Good thing. I wasn't going to tolerate another episode like the last." Lizzy popped another bubble and chewed loudly. "Speaking of which, have you given any thought to what you'll do with your life now? And please don't say it might include him."

"It won't, that I can swear to you." Elisa held off saying anything more, because it was none of Maxim's concern. "We'll talk about it later tonight, at your club—after hours, same time, same table."

"Right. And, Elisa?"

"Yeah?"

"Leave him behind. Please."

"Don't worry. He's not coming."

Like hell he wasn't.

Sure, there'd been references to shooting him—but he didn't care. Fill him with holes. If the conversation tonight was anywhere near as good the one he'd just listened to, he wanted to hear more.

He was going into Aspen with Elisa and she couldn't stop him.

Maxim ran a hand through his hair, aware of the way his very being was glowing with delight. If his smile grew any wider his freaking face would crack.

He just couldn't believe it. Elisa Cross was *falling* for him.

Hallelujah, his whole world had just shifted.

But if he didn't start running right now, his ass might just be blasted into small bits. He better escape back to the bedroom before he was officially caught. After hearing her confession, he'd lost his balance and fallen into the wall like an idiot. No doubt Elisa already suspected him of listening.

Maxim tiptoed down the hall, positive he could fool her. Or at least distract her.

With any luck, she'd simply believe she'd just been hearing things.

Liar.

Maxim shook his head, surprised at the unfamiliar voice in his head. It was as if the little devil had disappeared, replaced by an angel—no, worse, a cupid, complete with bow and arrow. And his little cherubic brat was steadily firing in the direction of his heart.

Damn, he needed to get a grip.

Her footsteps fell into place behind him. "I never pegged you as the intrusive, eavesdropping type, Maxim," she called.

Damn it. So much for sliding under her radar.

"Hey, baby." Caught, he turned around with a wry smile. "I was just using the bathroom. Can't make love with a full bladder." He held out his arms. "Come here, sweet thing."

"And now you're bullshitting me." She lifted a brow, continuing to stalk toward him. And she looked *pissed*.

He forced a smile. "Can't fool you, huh?"

"You asked me earlier today to trust you, Maxim. Do you not trust me?"

Her eyes were steely with anger, her jaw set. She snorted with distaste and shook her head, trying to brush past him. He caught her, drawing her stiff body into his embrace.

"Of course I do." Swiping her bangs from her face, he kissed the top of her head gently. Despite her anger, he just wanted to smother her with kisses. To rejoice. To sing and dance.

She was falling for him!

His insides swarmed with a feeling he'd never experienced before. Anxious to move past the ugly and into the bedroom, Maxim searched for the right words. "It's just . . . well . . . there was a lot of talk of shooting me."

"Which would be well deserved." Her voice was cold as ice.

"Hey!" he protested. "That's not nice!" He quickly scooped her up and cradled her in his arms. Her muscles were so tight it was like carrying a board. He kissed her again, this time fully on the lips, and she struggled.

He held her tight as he walked to the bedroom. "I just wish that you would talk to me more. You're so aloof, so—"

She rolled her eyes. "Just shut up, Maxim. Right now, I really don't want to hear it. I can't believe you. In fact, put me down."

"No."

"No?"

He nuzzled her cheek with his nose. "I do believe I'm still owed a spanking, not to mention some anal sex."

"Just what you deserve."

His posture straightened, the lighthearted tone to his voice vanished at the threat. "Funny."

"Well, you won't be spanking this behind. You're owed sex and that's what you'll get. My way." She looked away, clearly in "queen" mode. "So get on the bed."

"I don't think so." Not this time. This time, he wasn't allowing her to put up walls. To keep her distance. To pretend she was something she wasn't.

He firmed his hold on her. He was taking her, the way they both wanted. "By the time I'm through with you, I'll have you begging for my hands on your bottom and my cock up your ass, baby. That's a promise."

"What?" she screeched.

Not loosening his grip, he sat on the edge of the bed, locking her in his embrace and forcing her to remain on his lap. He wrenched her legs apart, demanding she straddle him.

If she was truly falling for him, then there was only one thing to do. Drive her over the edge of reason and straight into his arms.

"I want to continue our conversation from earlier," he whispered in her ear and then seized her chin, forcing her to look at him. His eyes met her defiant glare. "And don't think for one moment I'm forgetting your spanking."

"*You're* the one who should be spanked." A flutter of anticipation danced in her belly, heat filling her loins. Elisa shifted, wishing she could look away from his sharp, all-knowing gaze. But he held her true, forcing her to face not only him, but herself.

"And maybe that would turn you on." His free hand smoothed over her hips and to her shock, he gave her bare bottom a smart slap. "But not near as much as being spanked yourself."

She sucked in a breath, hissing through her clenched teeth as she fought against the explosion of desire that followed his unexpected assault. "You're wrong."

"Please, angel, I can sense your yearning. I breathe your need. Even if you deny it, I know." The intensity in his eyes was too much. She jerked her head uselessly. How she wanted to look away, but he refused to release her. "The whole dom, in charge, Queen Elisa act . . . it's bullshit."

She swallowed back tears. "Correction. It's an attempt."

"So you really like to be bossy in the bedroom? You really enjoy commanding me . . . and having me obey?"

"It's satisfying." Her jaw ticked as it always did when she lied. Damn it.

Why did he have to be so right?

Why did she have to be so wet?

"But not mind-blowing." He released her face, sliding his fingers along her cheekbone. "I know a true dom. She can get off just from giving orders. You can't."

Sudden insecurity swamped her. She looked away, thanking the high heavens she no longer had to look into his eyes.

He knew a dom? What did he do with her?

"Of course not," she snapped. "That's perverted and I'm not perverted."

"Not you, little Miss Innocent with your box full of dildos," he laughed. "And not to mention, the dom I know, she never sways. Never falls to pieces at a man's touch. She has control."

"The world is full of different people. Each to his own. If I'm not good enough for you, you can always return to your dom."

"Not a chance, angel. I want you, not some hard dom." His words were like little hammers, driving nails of truth into her heart. "I think you're trying to guard your heart, acting all tough, but what truly turns you on is—"

"Maxim, please . . ." she begged, no longer averse to childish pleading if it would turn off the faucet between her legs. The beating in her chest.

"Nope, not this time Elisa." He scooted back on the bed, stabilizing his legs, and encircled her waist with his hands. "This time, I'm completely in charge." *Umpphh!* He forced her over his knees. "But good boyfriend that I am"—his hand gripped her ass firmly—"I'm going to give you an out."

"You're not my boyfriend," she ground out through clenched teeth.

She sucked in several deep breaths, blank as far as a plan went. All she could think was that he'd called himself her boyfriend—so not true! A boyfriend cared. Was part of a woman's life. Took her on dates.

Maxim was sex. Nothing more.

He patted her exposed ass. "I disagree."

"I don't."

For hell's sake. A man had her over his knees. Was she really debating?

She wriggled, her resistance futile against his strong grasp. Not that she was trying all that hard, mind you, but she was trying. A little bit. As much as her hungry cunt allowed.

Her breasts rubbed his steel cock, jolting awareness through her pebbled nipples to her very being. "Let me go!"

"I disagree." Maxim delivered a sharp, swift smack to her left cheek. "If I'm not your boyfriend, then what am I?"

"A gigolo! A man whore! You're just sex to me and nothing more!" she insisted.

He swatted her bottom again and she reared against him, all too aware of the way that the pleasure/pain flooded her with the need for more.

"Maxim!" she cried, though she wasn't sure what for at this point.

Relief.

He forced her down, pinning her firmly.

This time he sent a stinging slap to her opposite cheek. His thumb stroked along the crack of her ass in decadent threat. "If you *really* don't like being spanked and you *really* want me to stop, I will, Elisa. Just say the word."

"I—"

"But know this, stop me today and I'll stop forever." His tone was gruff. Solid. *True.* Maxim wasn't making threats. He really would stop if she wanted him to.

Damn it.

Fuckfuckfuckfuck!

She was lying there with her ass exposed to him and she couldn't bring herself to move? To say no? *Ughhh!*

Talk about inner struggles. Her cunt—her inner, naughty self—craved his hand upon her bottom, no matter how much her mind begged to differ. The two warred, her body and brain in an all out tug-of-war.

Forget that she was an advocate of woman's rights eager for a man to spank her. Maxim should not have her over his knee five minutes after eavesdropping on her. It wasn't right!

But damn, did it feel good.

"Tell me I'm your boyfriend," he demanded, his hand rising in threat. "Tell me you're falling for me."

God, she couldn't do it. She couldn't ask him to stop.

Elisa whimpered, knowing she was trapped. She wanted him to spank her so much, she was forced to oblige.

"Say it!"

He slapped her ass again and she cried out. "I'm yours!"

"And what do you want?"

"You!"

"To do what?"

"Spank me!"

He delivered a softer, almost loving blow to her already tender skin. "That's my girl," he said softly. His hand ran softly over the smarting area, caressing her. "You've been naughty, but I'm going to teach you to be good."

With that, his sensual punishment continued, leaving her ass stinging, her every nerve standing on end, ignited, flared, ready to combust.

Her pussy was dripping wet, suffused with sexual need. Her clit pulsed rapidly. Her slit yawned, open to take him. Even her anus puckered in awareness, also wanting in on some of the pleasure.

"Keep saying it," he commanded. "Who do you belong to?"

"You . . . I'm yours," she cried, knowing she was betraying herself, but not giving a damn at the moment. "All yours, Maxim! Take me!"

He groaned from deep within, sounding like a hungry animal. His spanking came to a sudden halt. "Get on the bed. On your knees."

He lifted her off of him and she crawled into position, thrusting her ass in the air. She didn't know how much more she could bear, but she was at his mercy.

f o u r t e e n

To Elisa's surprise, it was not his hand that delivered the next blow, but his mouth. Maxim kissed her flaming bottom and then licked every inch of the tender area.

When he finished with her left cheek, he moved to the right, his mouth melting her very core as he loved all over her ass. Slowly, attentively, he made sure his tongue and lips came in contact with every inch of skin that his hand had punished.

Meanwhile, his thumbs caressed the undersides of her knees, creating little electric shocks that bolted through her, making her want to wriggle away.

"Maxim." She whimpered under her breath, trying desperately to stay still so he wouldn't stop. "Oh God."

She'd never had a man kiss her ass before . . . and she liked it. A lot.

With a moan, she shifted her weight, propping on her elbows to better support her upper body and keep her ass high in the air.

"That's it." He kneaded her bottom, continuing to lave her rounded cheeks with his tongue. "So sweet."

His tongue stroked along the deep crevice between her butt cheeks, sending shooting sparks through her. Alarm flared in her. What was he going to do? Dare she hope that he'd place his mouth to the sensitive skin surrounding her rear entrance?

A knot formed in her throat. She wanted to scream, to plead for more, to protest his every touch, but silence owned her. She was barely hanging on. His attentions were too much. Too glorious. She was primed to detonate.

"Hang on angel. I'm going to give you exactly what you need." Maxim took the condom from the pillow and opened the foil package, rolling the rubber on. Spreading her legs, Maxim opened her from behind and pulled her cheeks wide apart. Air hit her asshole and cunt, making her gush with need.

Gently, he planted his lips to her center. "You're all mine, right?"

"Yes," she hissed, despite all logic. "All yours."

"Then I'm going to take all of you." His breath blew across her pussy. He dipped into her folds with his tongue, then withdrew. "*All*, angel. Are you ready?"

Ready?

How could one ever be *ready* to give themselves up to passion . . . to ecstasy . . . to love? It wasn't something you could prepare for. When it hit you, it came fast and hard and explosive.

She moaned her permission and thrust her rear against him.

His hands palmed her ass, halting her action. "No. I want you to say it. No hiding, Elisa."

"Yes," she whispered, her words barely audible. "I want you."

"Louder," he insisted. "Say it!"

"I want you!"

"*Louder!*" Roughly jerking her toward him, he spanked her pussy, slapping her bared mons just enough to slightly sting. "Now."

"I'm ready. I want you. Fuck me!" she cried, her fingers knotting the comforter beneath her for strength. "Please!"

"How do you want it?" he demanded.

"Take all of me."

"That's what I want to hear." Grasping her bottom tightly, he bent and slid his tongue along her pussy, slowly tasting every inch of her before pressing the oral muscle into her slit. He probed her depths, drinking her dripping juices. Driving her to the brink of insanity, he abruptly pulled free.

Maxim gently nibbled her clit, milking waves of need through her. Just when she could bear no more, he slid his tongue along her cunt, over her perineum, to her anus. He flicked the tip of his tongue over the puckering bud and then kissed her fully, pushing her over the edge.

"Maxim!" She screamed as a totally unexpected, uncontrollable orgasm bolted through her lower regions, sending her body into spiraling convulsions. "Oh . . . oh . . . oh God!"

"That's it, angel, come good for me." Several of his fingers pressed into her shaking pussy, fucking her without preamble, driving in and out of her, hard and fast.

The pads of his fingertips reached her G-spot, caressing the sensitive area each time they plunged into her. He explored her most intimate area with broaching strokes, as if searching for ways to drive her crazy. And boy did he find them, over and over and over.

Her whole world turned upside down and inside out as she climaxed repeatedly around his hand, feeling lost in the powerful waves.

Without slowing his hard thrusting, Maxim moved onto his knees, angling his cock so that the tip touched her rear entrance.

"You sure about this, Elisa?" His erection pressed ever so slightly into her anus, applying pressure.

"Yes," she whimpered.

"Beg me."

Heady anticipation twisted in her gut. Her bottom twittered in longing.

God, she wanted his cock up her ass . . . badly . . .

Elisa opened her mouth, wanting to scream, "Please, fuck me in the ass!" But her throat tightened. Nothing came out.

Did he really expect her to *beg* him?

Heat rose to her face and spread through her every limb. Damn the bastard, always being so talkative. Astute.

She turned her head to the side so that she could see him, groaning as he withdrew his fingers. Drawing some of her liquid lust with him, he spread it along his shaft. "Well, Elisa?"

"Maxim . . ."

His wet thumb flicked over the puckering bud, torturing her. "Yes, angel, what would you like?"

"You know," she practically pleaded.

Damn, she was really going to do it. She was so close to begging him, she could taste the words in her mouth.

"I don't." With his other hand, he reached down, and found her clit, rubbing the bundle of nerves in tiny circles. "You have to tell me."

"I can't."

"Then you don't want it." Hands on her bottom, he started to withdraw. "I guess we're done here."

The walls of her anus spasmed, protesting. Without thinking, she thrust her bottom in the air. "Wait!" Forced to the pinnacle of intimacy with him, whether she wanted to be or not, she swallowed, searching for the right words. "Take me . . . that way. Please."

"What way? Where do you want my cock?"

"In my ass. *Please*, Maxim."

"How?" His thumb pressed into the tight circle, gently opening her up. "Is there a certain way you like it?"

"Very slowly."

"Lie down," he directed, sliding a pillow under her hips. He planted a gentle kiss to her shoulder, then nestled his cock between her cheeks, probing her back door.

"Don't tighten up. Stay relaxed." His hands gripped her wrists and pulled her arms above her head. "And if it's too much, just say so, and I'll stop. I promise."

His body melted against hers as he slid slowly into her bottom, opening the tight hole inch by inch with his thick member.

She whimpered, knotting her fingers in the bedding as her body accommodated him. Tiny pricks of pleasure/pain shot through her, but nothing severe. Nothing that didn't turn her on. Big time.

After a moment, his cock was fully inside of her. He propped up his body with his left hand and slid his other arm beneath her, cupping her mons.

He dove into her folds, finding her clit. Pressing the bud, he played with her pussy and gently rocked inside her. The measured, slight strokes into her bottom, in addition to the exploration of her pussy, were so damned erotic, actually beautiful, she could cry.

She'd been taken this way before but it had been hard. Fast. *Dirty.* She'd been embarrassed.

It was nothing like this.

Nothing so pleasurable. Intimate.

She relaxed, accepting all of him. He nuzzled his face in her hair and massaged her cunt in wide circles. "Are you all right?"

She inhaled, drawing in his masculine scent, his tenderness making her feel like pure woman. "Yes."

The head of his cock circled against a tight gathering of nerves hidden within her that she hadn't known existed. New sensation rippled through her. She'd never known anal sex could feel so good . . .

He stilled, rotating his hips gently. "Am I going to make you come?"

"I want to . . ." A moan escaped her. "But I need . . ."

"I know, baby." He pressed two digits into her slit, searching deep and finding exactly what she needed.

He teased the orgasm blooming at her core, drawing it forth.

"Damn, I'm so close," he told her through gritted teeth. "You're so tight."

Heat washed over her, ecstasy igniting her every last nerve from her fingers to her toes. She tingled, clenching her loins and ass muscles as she climaxed.

Maxim pressed his fingers into her hips, holding tight as he grunted and drove into her with sudden force. His cock jerked and he filled her with his cum. "Elisa, you're heaven-sent. Say it one more time."

"I'm yours," she murmured, reading his mind. Elisa melted into the mattress, sexually spent. "I'm yours . . ."

There was such a thing as too tired to move. And for the first time in his life, he was experiencing it.

Maxim commanded his limbs to function. Just like all his other previous attempts, they didn't obey. Instead, he lay there in a pile of mush, his mind protesting.

Damn it!

How could one little lady have completely worn him out?

Well, it wouldn't work. So he couldn't walk . . . he'd roll after her. She'd see. He was freaking going to Aspen.

He tried to throw himself from the bed, but he couldn't even do that.

Damn it. Elisa was leaving. He had to . . .

Ufff!

Suddenly his body gave way and he flopped from the thick mattress to the hardwood floor with a nasty blow to his shoulder.

"Ohhhhh . . ." He rolled to his side, moaning as deep pain radiated through his upper body. "Elisa . . ."

He never should have tried to move. It was impossible.

"Oh, come on, why me?" He curled his knees, groaning. The sound of the door shutting slammed through him. "Damn it! Elisa . . ."

He didn't want to miss going into town. He wanted steak and fresh men's clothing and wine and more than anything, to know what she was up to with Lizzy.

It wasn't fair.

He commanded the pain to stop and his body to stand. He needed to stop being so wimpy and whiny. But nothing. Nada. Only the dull, consistent ache in his shoulder.

He was stuck. Tired. Helpless.

Despite his battle for consciousness, he was rapidly descending back into sleep, right there on the floor. Fighting only made his fall faster. He gave in. If he couldn't have the real thing, then hell, he was ready for heavenly dreams of good food and spirits, and as always, Elisa.

Within moments, his snores filled the air.

fifteen

Brilliant moonlight created a subtle glow in the otherwise black, cold night. Since it was Monday, Play was closed and the street was eerily quiet. Oddly peaceful.

With a sigh of physical exhaustion, Elisa set down her over-loaded pack in the snow and unbuckled her boots. Stepping from her skis, she propped them against the back wall of Lizzy's club.

Shopping had taken longer than it should have and she was late. Not good, considering she'd have to leave early. A crisp, unadulterated scent lingered in the air, supporting the weatherman's forecast. Another storm would hit soon.

Lizzy was going to be pissed.

Lizzy was going to blame Maxim.

She couldn't even imagine how Lizzy might attempt to sway her from her latest sampling of the male gender, but it wouldn't be pretty. Elisa wouldn't doubt her sister had a whole truckload of dildos to give to her.

She could definitely use a strong drink. Or two. Or ten.

Leaving her pack in the snow so her groceries would stay cold, she kicked the snow off her boots and let herself in through the unlocked rear entrance.

"Hello, hello!" she called, surprised to find the kitchen dark. Silence loomed in the air. She whirled around, attempting to catch the door, but it slammed shut, leaving her in total darkness.

Well, this was weird. Where was Lizzy?

Damn it, she better not have gotten impatient and left. Just because Elisa had admitted she was falling for some guy—

Not just any guy, her mind corrected, *Maxim*.

Yeah. Right.

Elisa explored the walls until she found the switch then flicked it on. The overhead lights to the kitchen fluttered then smoothed out, creating a neon glow.

The contrast of cold and warm caused Elisa to shudder as she unzipped her coat. On the counter sat a dusty bottle of expensive wine straight from the cellar. A good sign. At least Lizzy was prepared for her, even if she was missing.

"Yoohoo!" Elisa called again. "Elizabeth Cross, where are you?"

Stripping off her gloves and coat, she hung them on a rack near the door, then bent, unlaced her boots, and pulled them free.

Opening the massive pantry, she reached under the shelving and found the box where Lizzy kept a spare pair of slippers for her. It was incredible fun having the club to their selves for a night—often times they turned on the music and danced like nuts just because—but Play wasn't always the coziest place to unwind, so they'd learned to bring some creature comforts.

Elisa wandered from the kitchen into the dimly lit club and scanned the room's wide expanse. Empty.

A brilliant yellow light streamed down on their table in the far corner near the bar, a stack of playing cards and pen and paper sitting atop its surface. But Lizzy was nowhere to be seen.

Where could she be?

Heck, if she had to kill time, she was helping herself to a glass of that wine. She—

"*Boo!*"

Elisa practically leapt from her skin at the sound of Lizzy's surprising shout. A mini heart attack clutched her chest. Spinning around, she found Lizzy standing directly behind her, grinning like a fool.

"What's your problem?" Elisa gave her a little shove. "Where were you?"

Lizzy chuckled, shoving her back. "I was lurking in the shadows." She waved her hands around, foolishly acting like a ghost. "Ohhhhhhh . . ."

"Funny." Elisa rolled her eyes and shook her head, her pulse beating too fast to appreciate the childlike behavior. "You scared the hell out of me. I swear, sometimes you're so immature—" Elisa's eyes flew open as she took note of Lizzy's new hair. "Good God!"

It just kept getting worse.

"Like it?" Lizzy fluffed her mass of frizzy hair, now not only a new, brighter shade of hot pink, but permed. Tight, crimped curls clung around her over-made-up but otherwise angel-like face.

Elisa's jaw dropped. "What did you do to your hair? And *why?*"

"My regular shade of pink was getting boring. I needed a change." Lizzy shrugged. "Don't you like it?"

Elisa raised a brow, still in shock. "A change? How about looking normal for once? What's wrong with you?"

When Lizzy had dyed her hair light pink a couple of years ago for Halloween, it had been quirky and fun. But then her wardrobe had changed, quickly followed by her nail colors, her makeup, even her shoe style.

The older Lizzy got, the crazier she became. One wouldn't even recognize her from the emotionally disturbed waif she'd been years ago. Though, even with the ongoing, increasing strangeness of her appearance, being different from *that* girl was probably a good thing.

Lizzy smacked her cherry-colored lips and chomped on gum. "Nah, sis. If you ask me, you could use a definite makeover. You've looked that way too long."

"No. Way." Elisa shook her head.

"Well, I have to keep scaring the men away, you know. This idiot who's a regular at the club keeps asking me out. Yuck." When Elisa just gawked at her, Lizzy waved her hands like she was talking to a fool. "Go shuffle the cards and I'll get the wine. I made mozzarella sticks too."

Ick. They were nothing but breaded, fried fat.

One thing was for certain, she hadn't managed to rub her health habits or fashion style off on Lizzy. But Lizzy did have her determination.

"Always trying to junk up my body and my sex life," Elisa muttered under her breath, shaking her head.

"I heard that!" In a flurry of movement, Lizzy disappeared through the swinging kitchen door.

With a half smile, half sigh, Elisa crossed the dance floor to the bar area and sat down at their table. Picking up the cards, she shuffled them slowly, thinking of her and Lizzy's history.

Though Elisa thought of Lizzy as her sister, she really wasn't, at least not in the biological sense. Lizzy's story was a true rags-to-riches tale. After spotting her on Hollywood Boulevard, a mere child trying to prostitute herself, her mother's heart went out to Lizzy and she took her in.

As Lizzy had no parents, the state granted Elisa's parents temporary guardianship. Almost immediately, Elisa and Lizzy became close friends.

Then her mother died. During the devastating time, Lizzy was a true angel to both Elisa and her father, helping them anyway she could, and the family bond had been sealed. Eventually, her father adopted Lizzy. Maybe they didn't share the same DNA, but Lizzy was a sister to her through and through.

How many times had Lizzy been there for her? Pulled her up when she was down? Elisa wished Lizzy would let her return the favor; but it seemed no one and nothing could tempt Lizzy into revealing the dark, hidden part of her that kept her dislike of the opposite sex at an all-time high.

Lizzy was successful; without any financial help from their father she'd made Play flourish all on her own. She was educated, beautiful, *strong*. But sometimes Elisa could see straight through her quirky dildo-loving, men-hating façade to the scared girl Lizzy still was. Lizzy didn't date for a reason, but Elisa still couldn't figure why.

"Are you staying the night?" Lizzy called. Cradling the wine by the neck and balancing a plate of food in her other hand, she skipped across the club. "Or returning home to lover boy?"

Elisa could just smell a fall coming. Lizzy moved faster than a five-year-old with ADHD and she wasn't the most graceful of women.

Tapping the cards on the table, Elisa evened out their edges. "Depends on how much it snows and how much of that wine I have to drink."

"And all that depends on how much cash I take from you tonight."

"Oh, are you planning to win for once?"

To her surprise, Lizzy made it to the table safe and sound. She emptied her load, placing her hands to her hips and smacking her gum in the most annoying way. "It's possible. You can't always win, you know. Tell you what . . . let's bet on it."

"You want to *bet* that I won't take all your money in a card game? Aren't you chancing enough just playing?"

"Fifty bucks." Lizzy walked behind the bar, retrieving two

glasses and a corkscrew. "No, let's make it a hundred." An ear-to-ear smile on her face, she glided to their table. "What do you say?" With a chuckle, Elisa took the bottle opener from her, twisting and pulling until the seal popped. "Lizzy, my dear, poker is my game. I've beaten you every night that we've played since I arrived in town."

She filled the glasses to the brim as Lizzy slid into the chair opposite of her and lifted a silver charm from around her neck. She swung it in the air, pretending to be a hypnotist. "But tonight, Elisa, ohhhhh . . . ohhhhh . . . Elisa! Elisa?" When she paid her no attention, Lizzy leaned across the table and placed the necklace directly in front of her face. "Elisa Cross, you will lose the card game. You will give all your money to Lizzy. And most importantly, you will dump the loser Maxim." The necklace fell away. "When I snap my fingers, awake!"

After three pathetic tries, Lizzy snapped her fingers.

Elisa glared at Lizzy, surprised to realize she felt a little defensive. "Maxim isn't a loser. And if you're going to try to be a hypnotist, learn how to snap your fingers first."

"Okay." Lizzy shrugged, leaning back in her chair and taking her wine with her. She guzzled her drink, her eyes keen. "Slut. Whore. Waste of time. Whatever you want to call him. You shouldn't be with him."

Here we go . . .

"Do you think any man is good?" Elisa followed her lead, drinking like a fish. The wine poured through her, infusing her blood and instantly flushing her with warmth.

"Of course not." Lizzy picked up a mozzarella stick and popped it in her mouth, chewing like a cow. "The male species should be wiped clean from the earth."

"Deal the cards." Elisa pushed the deck across the table and continued to sip the bittersweet liquid. "Don't worry, Lizzy. I'm not planning to lose myself this time. I'll admit, Maxim is touching me—literally—in ways I never imagined existed, and certainly not from him. But he's not the relationship type and now, I'm not either. Honestly, Lizzy, cocks are much better when they aren't fake. I'm having some sex, that's all."

"Twos and tens are wild." Lizzy dealt them each seven cards, then set the stack in the middle of the table. "You sure about that?"

Lifting her cards, Elisa was happy to see she had two aces and a wild card. Oh yeah, Lizzy was going down big time tonight.

She rearranged her cards to the order she preferred—high to low—and nodded. "I have my career . . . or lack thereof to think of. I can't stay at that cabin forever and we both know it."

"But I like you being here in Aspen!" Lizzy protested, nibbling on her lower lip. Suddenly her blue eyes sparked brighter than the glittery shadow covering them. "I know! You could help me run the club. I'll make you a partner."

"Me?"

"Or you could start a ranch. Open a ski shop. Marry Maxim and have lots of babies and raise them, right here in town."

No, no, and double no.

"Anything to keep me, huh?" Elisa shook her head, taking her turn. "We both know those things wouldn't make me happy."

"Yeah," Lizzy groaned in agreement. "You're always out to save the world."

"I'd settle for a few rainforests for mom. I just wish I knew what to do." With a wry grin, Elisa laid down three aces. "Beat that."

Lizzy eyed her cards, but her face showed no disappointment. "I hate to even mention this, but what about the Peace Corps? That would certainly whisk you away from the rumors and you've always talked about joining."

Join the Peace Corps? Shit. *Now?* At this stage in life? She was nearing thirty . . .

"Why not?" a little voice in her whispered. It wasn't as if she had anything better to do with her life.

Providing aid in third world countries was one of her biggest dreams . . . second to being an environmental lawyer and right now, her career felt like it was forever scratched from her future.

Surely the Peace Corps could put her degree to good use. She could teach environmental awareness . . . work hands on in the effort to promote forest conservation . . . the list went on. By joining the Peace Corps, she could still save forests.

But did she really *want* to? Elisa grappled with the idea. She had really wanted to once upon a time—she'd even thought about taking a year off in between college and law school—but she'd been afraid of missing out, of losing her momentum, so she'd skipped it.

The desire had never completely faded from her mind. Now though, it seemed almost overwhelming. Fantasizing about it was one thing, doing it another. She wished she could just go back to being a lawyer.

But she couldn't.

Lizzy was right. Now was the time. She had nothing better to do and nothing holding her back. Maybe she wasn't as into the idea as she'd once been, but she was certain the Peace Corps could really use her. Not to mention that it would take her away from all her problems.

But also Lizzy.

And Maxim.

The thought made her heart stop beating. She sucked in a sharp breath. Jesus. What was wrong with her, thinking like that? She was nowhere near prepared to give up her dreams for a man-slut.

Forcing herself not to even consider such a thing, she took another turn. "Let's just play and drink and laugh. I can figure out the next decade of my life later." She laid down a set of threes and smiled at Lizzy. "But thank you, dear, for the reminder about the Peace Corps. It means a lot to me."

"I know it does. Not that I want to see you go. Hey, if Maxim can keep you around, I may just grow to think he's good for you."

"Don't say that. I think you must've drunk too much already." Elisa took a big gulp herself. "But I'm just getting started."

And she meant it. Screw going home tonight. Right now, the last thing she wanted to do was think sensibly. Her mind was a wreck and the quickest escape she could think of was getting wrecked.

Life was too complicated. She liked living near Lizzy and the idea of traveling the world no longer appealed. She *should* want to join up, but deep down, she didn't.

God help her, but this past week, she wanted . . . everything she shouldn't.

To her shock, Lizzy suddenly laid down her whole hand, including a royal flush and set of aces. A brilliant smile dazzled her face. "I'm out. What luck I have. I win!"

Elisa eyed her cards. Several of them had bent corners. The cheat! "Hey, they're marked!"

"How else would I win?" Lizzy laughed. "Now pay up!"

sixteen

The delicious scent of eggs, bacon, and coffee roused Maxim
from his deep sleep. Tossing over on the hard floor, he sniffed
once, twice . . . Nope, it wasn't a fantasy. He smelled *real*
breakfast.

Stiff and sore, he pulled himself up and wrapped his arms
around himself. A shudder wracked his body. But damn, it was
cold. He'd fallen asleep with the light on, but outside, it was still
black as night. And snowing. Again.

"H-have m-m-mercy," he chattered under his breath. The sun
hadn't even risen and already she was driving him from
bed . . . er—the floor. That woman. "C-can't she ever be normal?
L-lazy?"

He shook off the urge to dive into the bed under the warm
covers, curl into a ball, and dream about food instead of actually

eating it. But his stomach growled its demand, leaving him no choice. He tugged a blanket free and wrapped it around his shoulders, sluggishly dragging his feet from the room.

For Elisa's sake, it better still be night, because if it were morning, he was pissed. Going to bed before dawn was a feat for him, but he *never* started his day before the sun rose. Not even for her.

Yeah right, the devilish little cupid that had taken up residence in his mind nagged him, *you'd chop wood and work like a slave at daybreak, starving and cold, just to please her.*

And that was what he wanted more than anything. To please her.

He groaned, every limb of his body aching with the desire to fall to the bed. But he wouldn't.

The ugly truth was, cupid was right. Elisa had him by the balls. He'd do anything to prove himself to her. That didn't mean he was in love though. Of course not.

Right.

The fulfilling aroma wafting through the cabin drew him to the kitchen like a magnet to steel. The smell could only mean only one thing: Elisa was home, ergo, he'd completely missed the trip to Aspen. Not to mention clothes. Steak. Beer. Television.

Why him?

Half-asleep, he stumbled down the hall and into the kitchen. Elisa sat in the breakfast nook, sipping from a steaming mug and reading the paper.

Her hair was pulled back in a ponytail, her skin was still fresh and dewy from a recent shower, and she wore a snuggly blue robe that reminded him of her beautiful eyes. What's more, she had food. Real, honest food.

She looked so cozy. Cuddly. Lovable.

"Good morning." She looked up at him with a dubious smile. "Would you like breakfast?"

Jesus! Her eyes were bloodshot, her face, pale as a ghost's.

Had she gotten drunk? Slept at all?

A knot tightened in his abdomen. What had she been doing all night . . . without him?

It wasn't fair! It wasn't right!

"You have to ask? You know I'm starving to death." He glared at her, wanting to gauge her reaction. "I'm surprised you can hold anything down."

An irritated sigh escaped her. "Yes, Maxim. I got drunk. I was up all night long, got two hours of sleep, then skied home like a nut in the snow when I should have stayed in bed until noon, so you didn't have to worry and could have breakfast. You're welcome." She returned her attention to the paper. "The food is on the stove. Help yourself."

"Great," he replied blandly. "Just great."

Got drunk with who? he wanted to ask.

He wasn't a jealous man. And hell, he despised a jealous woman—possessiveness sure didn't go over well when he had a female on each arm.

But seeing her eyes red from a night of fun without him had him ready to stomp his feet and throw a temper tantrum.

It *really* wasn't fair!

Why was this happening to him?

He clomped over to the stove. That he hadn't got to go to Aspen, nor the ugly fact that she'd had fun without him, wasn't what bothered him the most. Elisa had left here last night without a care. She didn't miss him. She hadn't even considered bringing him along. She'd enjoyed being away from him last night, while she'd danced through his every dream, plagued his every thought. And that stung.

He wouldn't have left her.

He pulled out a plate from the cabinet. Plopping the eggs onto his plate—all of them—he muttered under his breath.

"Are you actually pouting?" Elisa turned in her chair to stare at him, one brow raised.

"No." He took six slices of bacon, dropped his plate on the counter, and began shoving food in with his hands. The sooner he ate, the sooner he could go back to bed.

With a chuckle, Elisa abandoned her chair and came up behind him, molding her body against his. She rested her chin on his shoulder. "What's the matter?"

Instant sparks shot through him. What was this insane power she had over him?

"Nothing," he grunted, shoving more food in his mouth.

He shouldn't feel the way he felt and he didn't want to . . .

All along he'd known Elisa was more than a fuck. But that didn't mean he wanted to turn into some love-struck fool that lost all sense.

When he'd come to the States in search of her, he hadn't known why, he'd simply needed to be with her, if for only a moment in time.

More than a moment had passed.

He'd already overstayed his welcome and he should go home. Elisa would probably jump for joy at the prospect. She obviously didn't feel the way he felt about her. They had no future together. The longer he stuck around, the more he set himself up for a hard fall. He couldn't play her game anymore. He didn't want to.

Besides, he did have a life of his own and it was time he took charge of it. Being around Elisa made him realize one thing: he was wasting his life. He wanted—no needed—to change that.

"I'm leaving today." He told her between bites, his words muffled from his chewing. "I'm sure my mother is having a fit. She's been left to manage my work all this time. I need to get back."

"What?" Her voice was cold. Angry. "You're leaving?"

"Well, why not? You don't care."

Chomp, chomp, chomp.

"Oh." Her hands fell away from him. She stepped back and was quiet for a moment. When she spoke again, her words were soft. "We haven't finished playing our game, that's why."

Her reply gave him pause and he dropped his bacon. He'd expected rejoicing from her . . . not disappointment.

"I didn't think you cared."

"I do."

Her voice was firm. Almost desperate.

"Okay." He rested his hands on the counter's edge, cupid screaming *stay, stay, stay* at him, while reason begged to differ. Swallowing the apprehension lodged in his throat, he nodded. "If that's what you want."

What was he doing? Two words from her and his whole mind-set changed? *Way to be strong, Maxim.*

He really should go. Today. Now. If he didn't . . . he was in trouble.

Correction, he already was.

She closed the distance between them, pressing her body to his. Her face lay between his shoulder blades and her hands encircled his hips, the embrace so tender, so sweet.

She trailed her fingers along his biceps.

"I want you to eat your fill, my strong man. You're going to have a busy day," she murmured, as if her words were innocent, and not the threat they truly were; a whole different ball game from her actions.

This time, he knew she wasn't referring to sex.

Damn it.

"Oh yeah?" he asked stiffly. "What do you have in store for me?"

"I think we'll have fish for dinner. And you'll catch it."

Double damn it.

"That a fact?" Dropping the blanket around his shoulders, he turned, circled his arms around her, and grabbed her by the rear end. Drawing her to him, his fingers gripping her bottom through her thick robe, he backed her up to the counter opposite of them. His hips ground into hers. "And then we'll have sex?"

His cock turned to instant steel and he pressed it between her legs. She placed two hands to his chest, pushing him back in an attempt to keep some distance between them. Distance he wouldn't accept. He pumped his hips.

She gave up fighting him and relaxed, rolling her hips against his. The clever gleam in her eyes shouted "you're in trouble!"

"Right after you find me. That's how the game works." Her nails played over his bare chest, twisting in the tiny hairs and driving him crazy. "And of course, when you do, you can use me—however you'd like."

"I never did use my toy of choice from yesterday. Aren't I still owed that?"

"Who needs toys? We have our bodies." Her fingers traveled south, cupping his balls. She pressed her thumb to the tender area at the back of his erection. "This is all I need. But if you want a toy, go for it."

Maxim groaned with need. Fishing?

What choice did he have? Yesterday's tasks hadn't been fun, grant you, but not all that difficult either. The sex, however . . .

Praise the heavens, the sex had been mind-blowing. Unbelievable. Exhausting. So totally worth it.

What was catching a fish or two? Simple really.

But if he was going to stay, to continue to play her game, he wouldn't be shut out anymore. Elisa had been aloof long enough. He wanted something from her he'd yet to receive and it didn't involve toys. His request was . . . simple really.

He cupped her chin and lifted her face, bringing her lips a hairsbreadth from his. "I don't want a toy. I want a blow job, a good one. I want you to swallow my whole cock, all the way to my balls, until I come. I want you to kiss me. To make love to me with your mouth," he told her, his voice unyielding. "But that's not all. I want you to talk to me. To give me some answers."

She shrugged. "I can talk."

"I want to know what you plan to do once you leave this cabin. What you want to do with your life." His thumb stroked her cheek. "What it'll take to get you to come to Egypt."

She gave a little jerk, freeing herself from him. She focused on the floor. "We're playing for sex, not a future."

What? Why did she refuse to tell him?

"It's an uncomplicated question—don't complicate it. You refuse to open up to me at all. I'd at least like a reason. For hell's sake, Elisa, is everything between us *nothing* to you?"

She brushed past him. "Forget it. Let's not get all emotionally involved, okay, Maxim?"

"No. Caring about you isn't getting 'emotionally involved.'" Maxim caught her by the arm, whirling her around and yanking her against him. "So agree to my terms or forget your fish."

Caring about her wasn't getting emotionally involved? Then what did he call it?

"No fish, no sex." She shrugged. "Your loss."

"You forget, Elisa. I'm the one who came all the way from *Egypt* for you. I'm the one who pleasured you for days without taking for myself. I can wait. You however, are very eager." He hauled her closer, his erection nudging her pussy through her robe. "You won't just be denying me, but yourself."

Sensation shot through her, blurring her mind. Her cunt was already wet as could be, yet she felt her need gush from her at his rough touch.

"Oh really?" she ground out.

Fuck. She hated to be wrong . . . and that she'd become so very weak-willed.

Her head pounded from a hangover and too much to deal with. Worse, at such an inopportune time, her libido was raging like she was in heat. Even now, she wanted him so much she was sweating.

If she didn't play his game, she'd give in. He'd win. She'd lose.

And more than just a blow job.

The ground she held with him, her very heart, was at stake. Sure, obliging him was taking a chance, but denying him was an even greater one.

Besides, there *were* things about him she was curious to discover and in the interest of playing fair . . .

"Fish for sex," she reiterated, her voice firm. "Answers for answers."

He immediately looked nervous. "What is that supposed to mean?"

She looked him dead in the eye. "I'll answer your question, but I want to know what your deal is. Why you've avoided a relationship for so long. Maxim, I want to know the truth. The real you."

By no means was the trade fair. She was sharing her job interests, but asking him to divulge his deepest secrets. But that was the way of it.

He blinked slowly. A little muscle in his cheek spasmed. "I don't—"

"I won't budge. Take it or leave it."

He was silent a moment, and for effect, she reached down and cupped his cock. She squeezed gently. "An awful lot to swallow, but I'm sure I can handle all of you."

A sharp breath escaped him. "You are one tough negotiator."

"Damn right."

He released her and stepped back, a lopsided smile on his whiskered face. "Remind me to have you haggle for my next car. I could probably trade a Chevy for a Lamborghini with the way you bargain."

Elisa's heart kicked in her chest. The way he said that—like she'd be around for car purchases. Like they had a future.

They didn't, damn it.

Did they?

She dropped his prick like it was poison and turned away. "Is the game on or not?"

"You're on, angel, but you better be careful. You've no idea who you're toying with." He wiggled his brows at her. "Now, where's the fishing pole?"

seventeen

*C*ould fish smell? Maybe he stunk. Maybe something was wrong with his hook.

Maybe she'd deliberately set him up to fail.

One thing was for certain; catching fish wasn't as easy as it sounded. Not when the creek was frozen and his only bait was some sort of neon purple jelly-like plastic that wouldn't sink in the water. Who would want to bite that? Not him. And apparently not the fish in this creek.

Relentless snow once again dumped down on the earth like Mother Nature was trying to bury him alive in her bad dandruff, combined with a bone-chilling breeze that made his insides shiver. He knew Aspen was regaled for its winter weather and sports, but come on already. This was ridiculous. Who actually wanted to live like this?

"Elisa," he muttered to himself. "On-only Elisa."

Because naturally, she wanted everything out of life that he didn't.

He just couldn't imagine how there could ever be a "them" . . . how their worlds could ever connect.

Maxim wriggled his cold nose and sniffled, turning so the wind-whipped snow hit his back, rather than the delicate, chapped skin of his face. According to his watch, he'd been fishing for *two hours. Two miserable, shivering hours* in which he'd had too much time to think. To ponder on how he would reveal his deepest, darkest secrets to Elisa. If he wanted to. If he even *could*.

He never talked about his brother, not with anyone, not even his parents. Years had passed, but he still avoided the topic as if speaking about it would cause his tongue to swell in pain, because the memories plain hurt too much.

What's more, he was terrified once he got started, he'd pour his heart out. Make a fool of himself . . . start sniveling and all that bullshit.

Did he really want to let a female—even Elisa—have access to that part of him? He'd kept it hidden for a reason and maybe he should leave it that way.

Why did he need to know what she wanted to do with her life anyway? Her plans hardly affected him. For Pete's sake, he wasn't marrying her.

But . . .

Shut up, stupid cupid!

Maxim reeled in his line. The water at this spot was too shallow and his patience was wearing thin. He walked west, searching along the slippery bank for a deeper spot and a deeper meaning to life.

Bottom line, he had no desire to settle down, but the thought of going home to an endless string of one-night stands and partying didn't appeal either. Though he longed to return to Cairo, he also wanted to be with Elisa.

Somewhere along the line, he'd convinced himself that if he could find employment for her in Egypt, then he could keep her close to him. Perhaps forever wasn't in the cards, but he couldn't bear the thought of them living on opposite sides of the world. Of never seeing her again.

The creek widened and he set his gear on the pebbled bank. *Huh.* Maybe a stone would help get his bait below the surface. Selecting a small one, he weighed it in his palm. Couldn't hurt to try.

Close to the hook, he wrapped the fishing line around the rock in several directions and then tied it in a knot. He weighed it again. Perfect. He hoped. Hesitant but desperate, he stepped onto the ice.

"C-come on, b-b-baby, come on," he pleaded with the fishing god as he kicked at the frozen layer blocking the rushing water, throwing all his power into breaking the ice. Though the first several spots hadn't even yielded a minnow, this one had to contain some sort of life, and he was determined to get to it.

Suddenly, the barrier cracked and gave way, along with the ice under his feet. *Oh shit!* He leapt to the snow-covered bank, half sliding back into the creek before he regained his footing.

Elisa was going to get him killed.

But not before he got his blow job. The busted ice floated downstream and he stared at his new fishing hole, rather pleased with himself.

"Oh y-yeah, angel." He rubbed his hands together and grabbed his pole. "R-r-ready or not, h-here I come."

With that, he crossed his toes and dunked his fishing line in the opening.

"C-come on f-fishy, fishies, Maxim needs to get l-laid," he chattered. No bites came, even after several minutes of pleading, and his mind wandered to the hotel and his mother.

He couldn't stay in the States forever. In fact, he was being incredibly careless, and for once, he didn't want to be.

Elisa was an incredible, strong woman and being with her was changing him. Making him desire more out of life.

Sure, his mother was managing the hotel, but she had other businesses to attend to. She couldn't cover him forever and he didn't want to imagine the way his father was cussing him right now.

His dad was all business, no play, not ever . . . not even when Keaton had died. Maxim had always despised him for that, but for once, he was a little angry at himself for the way he constantly disappointed his parents. This time he'd gone too far for too long.

He needed, hell, for once *wanted*, to get back to his responsibilities.

As if someone upstairs agreed, the line jerked then bowed. "Whoa!"

A bite, finally! Maxim vigorously reeled his fish in, unable to contain the little dance his feet did. *Oh yeah! Oh baby! I'm gonna get some body heat! A blow job! Oh yeah! Oh baby!*

He caught the slimy wet fish by the tail. It immediately slipped from his fingers and nearly flopped away from him. He quickly seized it in a firmer grip, got out the wire cutters and pulled out the hook. Elisa better be ready to pay up and big time.

Pay up. Shoot. The other half of the deal . . .

Their talk he could happily forgo. Maybe instead of worrying about what she wanted to do, he'd offer Elisa a million bucks to come live in Egypt. What woman wouldn't take a million bucks?

Elisa.

Well, maybe if it were for some charity. But not him.

Wait! Hold the fish! A charity! That was it!

Grinning ear to ear, he held his catch in the air, whooping at the top of his lungs, for the world to hear.

Fuck yeah! He had a plan, and for once, a good one. Forget all this sharing and talking crap. He was taking Elisa home with him to Cairo. With what he had to offer, he knew she couldn't say no.

*S*o her hiding place sucked. Maybe it wasn't exactly original.

Okay. It was the same exact cave where she'd hidden the last time.

Elisa sneezed, sniffling uncomfortably. "God!"

She hadn't thought to bring any Kleenex and Maxim was taking forever to find her. She'd figured her plan could go either way: either he'd never consider looking in the same spot twice or it would be the first place he came.

She'd misjudged him, because it appeared to be the former. She'd sat here for hours feeding the squirrels and was darn close to wiping her nose on her sleeve, something she hadn't done since she was five. Last night, she hadn't had much sleep—barely two hours worth—and her head was still pounding from the hangover. Her throat was starting to hurt. Her nose was stuffy. It was all she could do not to curl up in a ball and go to sleep in the snow. She never should have skied home in the snow. She never should have started this stupid game again. Now she might freeze to death before he found her.

"Where are you already?" she whined, wishing he could hear her.

Sniffling again, she commanded herself to hang on. He'd get here soon and she was primed and ready for the truth about Maxim Cox. The reason behind his female escapades. And he wasn't getting his blow job or his answers until she received it.

Elisa stood up and walked from the cave, scanning the woods. Nothing. Not even a bird in sight. Everyone but her was warmly tucked away.

Wind blew snow in her face and she shuddered. The storm was really wailing and she was feeling sicker by the second. Worse, the silence surrounding her gave her too much time to think and ponder things she'd rather avoid, like her porn star status and worried sister. Maxim and the love she did *not* feel for him. Joining the Peace Corps.

Oddly, she didn't want to sign up. She *should*, but deep in her heart, it didn't feel right.

But neither did working at a hotel with a man she . . . did *not* . . . love.

Without warning, several violent sneezes escaped her, making her head jerk with their rhythm. Suddenly, her world felt blurry and strange. She stood and stumbled, instantly knowing she needed to get back to the cabin, that she didn't just fell unwell . . . she felt wrong.

She took a step and everything began to whirl. Losing her balance, she fell to her knees, and a curtain fell over her consciousness, black claiming her.

The music carried through the woods, prickling his every last nerve. She was home? Inside? Warm? Listening to an old eighties Madonna song? While he was out here struggling to find her?

Someone needed another spanking.

As he skied closer, the harsh wails of her terrible singing stung his ears. Horrific as her voice was, he couldn't help but smile, intrigued.

Elisa might rev his anger and push him to the limit, but never could he say she bored him. She was too fresh and honest and fun to ever lose his interest. Crazy as it seemed, he could spend the rest of his life listening to her shrieking attempt at "Causing a Commotion."

Maxim skied up to the cabin and took off his skis. Propping them at the back door, he picked up his pack, which contained the Igloo lunchbox holding his catch of the day and let himself inside.

Yanking off his hat and gloves, he set everything in the kitchen and took out his fish, holding it by the mouth directly in front of him. Quietly, he walked into the living room.

Only to find a petite, pink-haired lunatic flinging her body around like it was rubber.

Who the hell? What the hell?

He stared in shock. "Uh, can I help you?"

The clown woman dressed in polka-dotted clothes twice her size stumbled to a halt, spinning to face him. "Oh my God!" she squealed, clutching her chest and gawking at him like he were the intruder. "Oh my God! Max Cox? Oh my God! A fish! Ew!" Sucking in a sharp breath, she leapt onto the couch, as if would protect her from tonight's dinner. "You scared me to death! Get rid of that thing!"

Talk about weird. Dropping his catch to his side, he prowled into the room, looking around. The music boomed through the room and she remained perched on the furniture, gawking.

"Yeah, Max Cox. The one and only . . ." She remembered him, but he was clueless. He swept his gaze over her once again, trying to place her. "And you are?"

He glanced around the room again. No sign of Elisa in sight. What this some sort of prank?

"Lizzy," she answered in a cold tone.

Obviously, she was as wary of him as he was she.

He froze. Wait a sec. Lizzy? Only the woman who wanted to shoot him. He should be the one on the couch, half-terrified, not vice versus. Turning, he faced her again . . . after all, he probably shouldn't have his back turned to her.

"Lizzy, Elisa's sister. That's right. I hope you left your rifle at home."

"I wish now that I would have brought it."

"I really wish all these references to killing me would end. What did I ever do to you?" He blew out a frustrated breath. He didn't have time to worry about this right now. He wanted his blow job. Speaking of which . . . where was Elisa?

Finally, she plopped down on the couch, still staring at him and his fish like they were the enemy. "Where's Elisa?"

"That's what I was just wondering." He shook his head, flustered. "If she's not here, then she's still out there. Somewhere."

She *was* still hiding. That wasn't good . . .

His stomach knotted in fear. This didn't feel right. She'd been out there too long. The woods had been too quiet.

Was she tricking him . . . or was it something worse?

He ran his free hand through his hair. "I need to find her."

And he knew just where to look first. Fool him once, shame on her. Fool him twice, shame on him.

Maxim strapped on his boots and half waded, half ran toward the spot not far from the cabin where she'd hidden the last time. He'd already searched the rest of the woods before returning to the cabin—everywhere but this area because he'd never figured she'd use the same place twice. Now, he just prayed she was there. And all right.

If she wasn't . . .

He didn't want to consider the possibilities.

Fifteen minutes later, he navigated the trail through the trees, searching for a sign of the cave. The silence of the woods echoed around him. It was so quiet he could hear his own breathing, his pulse.

He spotted indentations in the snow. Footprints filled in by today's storm. Yes! This was it. He peered over the edge.

And his world stopped spinning.

Elisa lay face down, her body covered with at least an inch of snow. "Elisa? Elisa!"

No response.

His heart kicked in his chest, pumping a tidal wave of adrenaline through him as he jumped over the cave's edge and scurried to her side.

What was wrong with her? Had the little idiot passed out after being up too late last night? Why wasn't she moving?

He dropped to her knees. "Elisa? Elisa, wake up!"

She didn't budge.

eighteen

A wave of nausea threatened Maxim as he knelt beside her. She looked so lifeless. Almost . . .

Dead.

It couldn't be. Not Elisa.

"Elisa!"

Nothing. No response. No acknowledgement.

His heart pounded in his ears, his hands shaking as he moved to brush the hair from her face and press his palm to her cheek. Lukewarm. Not good. With the amount of snow covering her, she had to have been lying there at least an hour.

He turned her over and pulled her into his arms. Redness discolored the left half of her face where it had been pressed to the icy ground; a good sign her blood was still flowing, though her lips were deathly pale.

His fingers went to her neck and found a pulse. Relief poured through Maxim as he leaned in and placed his cheek to her mouth. Her breathing was even. Steady.

Thank God. She was alive.

If only she would wake up. Tell him what's wrong.

"Elisa!" he shouted, his voice weakening into a plea as he cradled her. "Damn it, come on, baby, wake up. What's wrong?"

He ran his hand over her bloodshot skin, then slapped her cheek. Her head lolled to the side. "Elisa!"

She'd be lucky if her face wasn't frostbitten, but that wasn't what had knocked her unconscious. Jerking off her hat, he searched her head for bumps. Nothing.

"Come on, angel!" He gave her a little shake. "Elisa, wake up!"

Suddenly she sneezed and her eyelids fluttered. Under her breath, she murmured something unintelligible.

"What, angel? What is it?"

She coughed and tossed her head to the side. "It's hot."

Hot? That didn't make sense. Unless . . .

Tugging down her zipper, he slipped his hand under her long john shirt and gauged her body temperature. Jesus, she was burning up. Sick. "You little fool! You're lucky you're not dead!"

Why hadn't she gone back to the cabin? If she hadn't been feeling well, she never should've instigated this stupid game.

And *she* was teaching *him* to survive in the wilderness?

"Sorry . . ." Her voice was weak, blurred. Her eyes opened then fell shut again.

"Sorry?" he ground out through clenched teeth. "What if I hadn't found you?"

He waited for a response that didn't come.

Anger and concern overwhelmed him and his throat threatened to close.

Maxim sucked in a deep breath, willing the emotions away. Now wasn't the time for a breakdown. Elisa needed to get warmed up. She needed a doctor.

Holding her tight, he stood. "Let's get you home."

"Mmmm . . . Maxim?" she whimpered. She buried her face in his chest. "Am . . . am I a-all r-r-right?"

"I sure hope so," he muttered, wading up the steep, slippery incline toward the trail. "But boy am I going to beat your butt when you get better."

Madonna music still blared through the cabin as he barged through the door. "Lizzy!" he shouted. "Elisa needs help!"

In a split second, Lizzy was standing before him, inspecting Elisa. Panic contorted her face. "What happened? What did you do to her?"

"I'll be okay," Elisa moved slightly in his arms, barely conscious. "Where am I?"

Okay? She was delirious!

He tightened his grasp on her limp body, drawing her snug against his chest. "She's not all right. I found her passed out in the snow," he answered. "She's sick. Under these clothes, she's burning up."

Lizzy shook her head. "Her fever is probably what saved her." Laying a hand to Elisa's forehead, she bit her lower lip. "I know she always carries pocket warmers and her body is likely warm from running a temperature, but her head is too cool." She ran her hands along Elisa's body. "Her extremities too." She gulped and stepped back. "Thank God you found her."

Their eyes met for a brief moment, then Lizzy jerked her gaze away. Anger radiated from her. If looks could kill, he'd be six feet under.

Let her hate him. He only cared about Elisa and making certain she was okay. "She needs a doctor. We need to get her to a hospital."

Disgust twisted Lizzy's lips. "And chance losing her to the cold? No. We have to warm her up slowly." Whirling on her heels, Lizzy waved for him to follow. "Bring her into to the bathroom. Strip, both yourself as well as her, and hug her tight. I'll run a bath."

"Strip?" Maxim raised a brow, following after her. He'd do anything to help Elisa, but Lizzy's request seemed a little odd.

Then again, she was odd.

Lizzy shoved open the bathroom door and stormed into the room, throwing back the shower curtain.

"Shy, Maxim? Plenty of women have seen what you have to offer. Keep your underwear on, but do as I say." She cranked on the cold water, then adjusted the hot. When he didn't instantly move, she threw her hands up. "She needs your warmth, Maxim, so get moving! It's your damn fault she was out there, so be a man for once! Oh, I wish I had that gun!"

His fault?

Shocked, Maxim laid Elisa on the floor and removed his clothes. He'd long since caught on to the fact that Lizzy didn't like him—a person only had to threaten to shoot him once for their dislike to sink in—but her blame . . .

It ate at him.

Was it his fault?

"Maxim . . ." Elisa sighed, sounding pathetic; something he'd never imagined her being. She was the strongest woman he knew, brought to her knees by *his* presence in her life.

Sure, Elisa had instigated the whole affair, but he'd pushed her to it. He'd come to her cabin, begged and insisted until she'd had to give in.

What's more, he'd been too slow. Had he caught that fish sooner, skied better, walked faster . . .

Been more of a man . . .

Maybe it was a sign. A sign he could never be enough for Elisa.

Maxim's stomach revolted at the thought and he looked to Lizzy, feeling desperate. Panicked. The evil gaze she rewarded him with did nothing to help.

She shook her head at him and knelt beside Elisa, untying her boots.

Swallowing back bile, he jerked his socks off. He couldn't think about this. Right now, he had to help Elisa. Nothing mattered more than getting her warm.

"Nice, Maxim," Lizzy snapped, rolling her eyes at the sight of his naked butt.

He ignored her. He hadn't had underwear on—one pair only lasted so long and Elisa's didn't fit—so bare-assed naked, with Madonna still booming in the background, he bent and began to undress Elisa, trying not to let his lack of clothes bother him.

"You're being too slow." Lizzy pulled over Elisa's socks. "I should know better. Never trust a man to handle anything. Not efficiently."

Maxim bit back an ugly retort. He was standing here naked for hell's sake!

But now was not the time. Besides, he wasn't properly dressed for his funeral.

Hugging Elisa's bare torso against his chest, her pulled her onto his lap and let his body heat warm her as Lizzy pulled down her pants.

"Not now, Maxim," Elisa muttered under her breath. "I have a headache."

He couldn't help his smile. Sounded like something a wife would say to her husband . . . every night. He cupped her head in the scoop of his arm, pressing it tight to his chest.

Following Lizzy's lead, he rubbed Elisa's hands as Lizzy massaged her feet. Welcome silence fell between them, the only noise in the room the sound of running water.

The iciness to Elisa's fingers was finally starting to thaw and he moved his way up her arm, the heat of her fever becoming more prominent, and the guilt plaguing him, burning hot.

He didn't want Elisa to be sick. He didn't want Lizzy to despise him. If only he could take it all back . . . start a relationship with Elisa the right way. Make it real, not a game.

He swallowed, needing to say something, anything, to ease the tension. "She is conscious and talking. That's a good sign."

Lizzy grunted.

Christ, the nutty woman had a mean streak—but why was it directed straight at him? He understood her blame, but it wasn't like he'd intentionally hurt Elisa. "Lizzy, I swear to you, I didn't mean for something like this to happen. I—"

"Men never mean it," Lizzy snapped, cutting him off. She scowled, her lips curled in a snarl. "Yeah. Jerk faces like you never *mean* to hurt women, now do you? It's always unintended, but it happens just the same." She shook her head in disgust. "Just shut up and let's get her in the tub."

Stunned speechless, Maxim followed Lizzy's directions, more worried over Elisa than anything, but Lizzy's harsh attack had him feeling like the world's biggest, most useless jerk. For the first time in his life, he wished he could be someone different.

An hour later, Elisa's temperature was normal and she was tucked in bed, napping. Maxim wanted to sit next to her, to hold her hand, but Lizzy had assumed that position and banned him from the room.

Enough was enough. Lizzy might be her sister, but he was Elisa's lover. He had every right to be in there!

Maxim paced the hall. To date, he'd never let anyone push him around—not anyone but Elisa—and he didn't intend to allow some pink-haired nut job to.

He should be with Elisa. Making up for letting her be out there so long.

That was it. He was going in. Facing the dragon.

Knocking sharply on the bedroom door, he promptly barged in. "I'm not staying out here any longer, Lizzy. She's my girl-friend, damn it, and I—"

"Please." Lizzy rolled her eyes. "Your girlfriend? Guys like you don't have 'girlfriends,' they have fast fucks."

Ouch.

"You don't even know me, Lizzy. That's a harsh judgment to make."

"Please, Maxim, I remember you from college. You dated—and abandoned—several of my friends," she snapped.

"Oh." Maxim looked at her. Funny, he didn't remember her.

"You don't have a clue who I am, do you?"

"Sorry." Maxim took a seat on the opposite side of the bed, trailing his fingers over Elisa's torso. She was fast asleep. His eyes met Lizzy's hard glare and he refused to back down. "Lizzy, Elisa is different."

"Until you grow tired of her."

"She's different. She makes me feel different. I won't grow tired of her." He cleared his throat. "I know you blame me for her being sick. I blame me. But I can't just turn my back on her."

"Please." An angry breath of air escaped Lizzy. "What do you really want with her?"

"I don't know," he answered honestly. "More than I should."

"Maxim, you are anything but a sensitive man. You're not in love, you're in lust. Don't play her."

"I'm not."

For a moment, something in her gaze wavered. Looking away, she chomped her gum, sarcasm warping her features. "Whatever."

She blew a bubble until it popped, then blew another. "Fortunately, I think she's going to be all right. Unfortunately, my club opens in an hour and I have to be there."

Thank God.

"She'll be fine," he assured her. "I'll take care of her, so don't worry."

She nodded and leaned down, placing a kiss to Elisa's cheek. Standing, she crossed her arms and headed toward the door. "I'm going to ask my doctor to make a special trip out. There's no way Elisa can ski into town and she should see someone."

"Great."

"Yeah. Great." Lizzy paused at the door, studying him hard. "You know, you're a jerk and all, but thanks Maxim."

"For what?"

"For being here for her." A devilish smile formed on Lizzy's lips. "For not being such an ass for once in your life, for giving her some no-strings attached orgasms, and for leaving, as soon as she's better."

With that, Lizzy walked out.

nineteen

She's different. *She makes me feel different. I want more than I should.* The conversation replayed through Elisa's mind over and over and over. Though she'd allowed Lizzy and Maxim to believe she'd been asleep, their harsh words had roused her, enough for his confession to have stuck like glue in her mind.

"I want more," she whispered to herself. What did that mean?

A tickle in her throat erupted into a cough and she covered her mouth, hacking. After a moment, the fit passed and she cleared her throat.

She felt awful and her mind was in utter turmoil. Could he have been for real?

This illness was getting to her brain.

With a sniffle, she rolled to her side and snuggled in bed. But she couldn't stop thinking about him.

Maxim was a sweet talker. He bullshitted women, always with one sole purpose: to get into their pants. But he already had plenty of access to her, and besides, he had no motivation to tell *Lizzy* such things. No motivation, that was, unless they were true.

Could it be? Was Maxim falling in love with her?

Her heart skipped with joy at the thought.

Elisa swallowed down the happy feeling. Good Lord. Was *she* falling in love with *him*?

Nah. Couldn't be. Shouldn't be. She knew better.

And when it came to matters of the heart, surely reason prevailed.

Hah.

Suddenly too warm, Elisa kicked the blankets down and flipped onto her back. Three days she'd spent in this bed and she was losing her mind. Though Lizzy's gracious doctor had paid her a visit and supplied her with antibiotics, not to mention Maxim smothering her with care and soup, she still felt somewhat feverish and headachy. But she'd had it with lying around.

She needed to get up.

Elisa threw her feet over the side of the mattress and sat up. Gingerly, she stood on shaky legs. It seemed forever since she'd stood on her own and gaining her balance took a moment.

Stretching, she walked to the window, not surprised to see that it was snowing hard. Again. This had to be the worst winter ever, but Elisa was thankful for it. She'd miss the cold weather when she joined the Peace Corps and was shipped off somewhere hot and buggy.

She'd miss Maxim.

But her mind was made up. It might not be what she *wanted* to do, but it was the right thing to do. For herself, and the world.

Footsteps sounded in the hall, and a moment later, Maxim walked into the room, carrying a tray with yet another bowl of steaming soup and mug of hot cocoa.

"What are you doing out of bed?" His stern voice was full of worry. "You're going to make yourself dizzy and fall."

Since when had he turned into Mr. Serious?

She shrugged her shoulders and returned her gaze to the window so he couldn't see her smile. "I needed to move around."

How was this the same boy she'd attended college with? He was being so sweet, so loving. Taking care of her like she was a precious commodity. Any woman would be lucky to have him.

She was lucky to have him.

If only it could stay this way.

Suffice to say, he'd proven himself. He was a far cry from Max Cox, the reckless, thoughtless jerk she remembered. She was beginning to think he was her dream guy.

Which was exactly why she would enroll in the Corps the moment she was feeling better; it was past time to end this crazy fling.

She glanced at him again, the thought of being separated from Maxim making her instantly sad. "I feel like I've been in bed a year."

"Well, you've gotten your exercise. Now back into bed. I want you better." He set the tray on the nightstand and closed the distance between them, taking her in his arms. "No protests."

Just the mere contact of his fingers on her upper arms, even through the thick fabric of her flannel nightgown, caused tingles to dance over her skin. It had been days—days and days and days—since they'd had sex. Probably why her thinking was so loopy.

Elisa lay against him and let him guide her to the bed, wishing they could make good use of it. "So you can get the blow job you're owed?"

She knew her insinuation wasn't accurate, at least not entirely, but she wanted to push him. To see how he'd react. There was definitely more to Maxim than sex. She enjoyed seeing that side of him exposed.

"No, Elisa." His voice was weary, confirming she was dead wrong to even imply such a thing. He guided her to the mattress and she lay back as he tucked her in. "In fact, I'll let you off the hook for that one. Honestly, I just want to see you get better."

Interesting . . .

Because she didn't want off the hook.

She cleared her throat. "You know, we may not be able to make love, but there was the second part of our deal."

Silently, he propped some pillows behind her back then set the tray on her lap. Steam from the soup rolled in her face, a welcoming comfort.

Turning away, he grunted. "Eat your soup."

He prowled to the window, his hands shoved in the pockets of his blue jeans. Completely clammed up. Again.

She had to know why. Never had she wanted to unearth the mystery behind the man more than she did right now. And this time, she wouldn't let the conversation end prematurely.

"Come sit next to me," she encouraged, patting the spot next to her. "Answers for answers, remember?"

"Right." His response was stiff and he didn't move toward her. Time to pull out the big guns.

"Well, here's your answer. I plan to join the Peace Corps."

That gained his attention. He turned to her, his eyebrows furrowed, his lips drawn tight. "You're kidding, right?"

"No."

Walking to the bed, he sat on the edge. "When?"

"As soon as I'm better." She stirred her soup in circles. "I'll probably leave the cabin in a week or so, get on with my life."

"No."

She raised her brows. "No?"

If only she could simply obey him . . . wouldn't that make the decision so much easier? But she couldn't. She had to do what she had to do. And number one on that list was getting away from him.

"I won't have it," he barked, not looking at her. Maybe he thought he could hide his anger, but his clenched hands were a red flag. "No."

Comments like that sure made moving to South America seem easier.

"Well, you can't help it. It's my life, Maxim."

Removing the tray of uneaten soap, he set it on the end table and leaned over her. Looking dead serious, he stared into her eyes. "What if I told you I could offer you something better?"

Not this again. "I told you, Maxim, working at the hotel isn't for me."

"No, doing good, just like you want to do, but in Egypt, for your own organization."

Yeah. Right. Like that could happen. He was grasping at straws.

She shook her head. "Maxim—"

"Listen to me." He took her hands, imploring her to listen. "There's a lot of poverty in Cairo and a lot of little kids running and playing in the streets. It's always driven me nuts. Forget the fact that it's annoying, it's dangerous. Unhealthy. But their parents are too poor to afford things like sports and after-school activities and babysitters. Sometimes they can't even afford school. What if we gave them a place, a place something like the YMCA, where they could come? Or maybe some sort of pre-school or sports activities? You could run it, I could finance it. Eventually, I could get corporate sponsors and—"

"Whoa!" She jerked her hand free of his, held it up to hush him. Her mind was whirling. This idea was coming from Maxim? *Maxim?* Why?

"I don't know Maxim. It's a good idea . . ." Elisa chewed her lower lip. "But not a good idea." As much as she'd love to be near him, as much as she'd love to participate in a charity like that, it would never work. Nothing good could come of it.

She shook her head. "You and I, we're temporary. We both know that. I can't base a future on temporary."

Moreover, she wanted to save the rainforests. To help protect the environment. Working with children was great, but it wasn't part of her dreams.

Was it?

He retrieved her hand, his thumb caressing the center of her palm. "Even if . . . this ends . . . we'll still be friends, Elisa. We'll always be friends, right? So what does it matter?"

"Maxim—"

"Hey, just think about it, okay?" He stared into her eyes, his gaze filled with need. "I'm not just asking you because I want you to come to Egypt. I really want to do this, so consider it. Please?"

She should stick with no. Leave it alone.

But damn him, he looked like a lost puppy dog. No matter how hard she tried, the word "no" wouldn't form on her tongue. What was it about Maxim she could never deny?

"I'll think about it."

"Good." With a nervous smile, Maxim stood and stepped backed. "Eat your soup. I'm going to go clean up the kitchen."

What? She didn't think so! Elisa grabbed his arm, almost throwing herself from the bed in an attempt to jerk his unwilling body back to the bed. "Oh no, you don't. You aren't getting away so easily. I want my answer." She pulled him down.

"Damn it," he grunted, falling over her.

"That's right buster. Fess up." She tugged his shirt, urging him to lie next to her. "Come on. Out with it."

After a moment, he released a heavy sigh and wrapped his arm around her. Unbuttoning his shirt, Elisa rubbed her fingers back and forth on his bare chest, feeling the coarse tiny hairs. "You really don't want to talk about it?"

"No. I do . . . but I don't. It's hard."

She'd never heard him sound so very grave. Reluctant. Hard. "Why?"

"Talking about death is never easy."

Death? Wow. This was big. A lot deeper and darker than one would expect hidden in a guy like him. Guilt seeped into her heart, reminding her of all the times she'd called him a man-slut.

"No. It's not," she told him softly. "What happened?"

"My brother was murdered, by his wife, if you ask me."

Wham! His admission delivered the final blow to her old opinion of him, knocking it out. And she'd thought she had a good reason not to want to fall in love?

She gulped, feeling awful. She'd judged him so harshly, for so many years. "That's terrible. I didn't even know you had a brother."

"It happened right before college," he continued, his voice hollow with pain. "Back then, Keaton was managing the hotel for my parents, working late nights. One day, he went home early and found his wife in bed with another man." His lips curled in disgust. "Keaton loved her, more than she deserved. In that moment, I think he must have lost his mind. He ran out of the house, hopped in his car, and went racing off. Witnesses say he must have been driving at least a hundred and twenty m-miles—" Maxim choked up, tears brimming in his eyes. He swallowed and sucked in a deep breath. "He was decapitated."

"Oh, Maxim—" Elisa rolled over and wrapped her arms around his torso, hugging him. "I wish I would have known."

"Yeah, well, I took Keaton's place at the hotel, but I vowed never to be like him. Never to fall in love." He sighed. "So, now you know."

She squeezed him tight. "I'm so sorry."

"Don't be. You didn't know." He kissed her head gently. "But I am sorry you're sick. I take the blame . . . and the responsibility of making sure you get better." He sat up and laid his hand on her forearm. "So you should get some rest."

He thought it was *his* fault she'd gotten drunk, not slept, and then become sick because *she'd* pushed him to play their game again? Why?

"Maxim, that's silly—"

He stared at the window a moment, then looked to her. "No, it's true. But it's okay, at least I think it is. Your being sick made me realize many things." He cleared his throat. "I think . . . I think by keeping my promise to myself, I was failing myself. Failing you. Failing lots of people. So you can consider me a changed man, Elisa."

"Changed?"

He smiled slightly. "You heard it here, first." Standing, he bent and planted a quick kiss to her cheek. "The milk is sitting out and you should get some sleep."

With that, he disappeared from the room.

Having gotten the truth off his chest, Maxim really did feel like a changed man. He felt real.

Talking about his brother's death hadn't been as difficult as he'd thought it would be. Maybe he even could've explored the subject more. Maybe he would open up to her again.

But right now he didn't want to be too much stress on Elisa. She needed to sleep and heal. Besides, after such a revelation, he needed to breathe a little.

Maxim strode down the hall to the kitchen, his mind spinning with the differences he felt in himself. He could never go back to the way he'd been. The parties and flings no longer appealed. He couldn't think about another female in a sexual way. Elisa was all he wanted.

Hell, the woman even had him cooking. For the first time in his life, he'd opened a cookbook and turned on a stove. And he didn't mind.

Grabbing the milk, he shoved it in the fridge and then looked at the huge mound of dishes he had to clean up. Afterward, he should probably bring in some firewood.

He smiled to himself. Funny, but he couldn't wait for tomorrow. No doubt it would bring hard work of some form, but it would also involve Elisa, and her presence in his life made everything blue turn rose-colored. If she didn't take him up on his offer to come to Egypt, he didn't know what he'd do. But he wasn't going back without her.

twenty

The game just kept getting better.

A thrill shot through Elisa as she ducked into the kitchen pantry and pulled the door shut behind her. Shaking with excitement, her body hot with arousal, she listened to the sound of Maxim's footsteps on the back porch, stomping off snow.

Now recovered enough to want sex, but still not about to step foot outside, she was hiding in the house and happily getting in a few more intimate, playful days with Maxim before she had to leave.

Leave.

An uneasy feeling crawled through her at the thought. Damn it. She should want to go! But each time she considered it, she liked the idea less. She actually found herself loathing the prospect of joining the Peace Corps.

Despite herself, she was leaning more toward taking Maxim up on his offer. At least, her heart was. Her mind knew better, but was losing control rapidly. Besides, he *did* have a good idea.

Elisa pressed her eyes shut. Right now, she had better things to think of. Like orgasms and plenty of them. Trying out the rest of her toys. After all, he never did use those beads.

Maxim's footsteps pounded across the kitchen floor. He was coming directly at her! How did he know where to find her so quickly?

Denying the urge to sniffle, she slowed her breathing, forcing herself to stand still in the small, crammed cubbyhole. Through the slats of the door, she saw his shadow. He prowled about, making her heart pound. Blood pumped through her, filling her with sheer adrenaline. Lust.

Damn, she couldn't wait to spread her damp thighs and take him.

"Oh, Elisa?" he called. "I can smell you, angel. Loud and clear."

Eek!

She smelled? He better mean good!

"Now where are you hiding?" He gave a turn, scanning the kitchen. "Huh. Guess there's only one place to look."

He spun on his heels and yanked the pantry door open, exposing her. With a gleeful cry, Elisa let him toss her over his shoulder. Finally, some dick!

She laughed out loud, thoroughly loving the moment. Loving the woman she'd become. Maxim had turned her into a wanton—she might even be worse than him now—but it felt good to be comfortable in her skin sexually.

He carried her across the kitchen and placed her on her feet in front of the breakfast bar. What was he doing? She wanted to go to the bedroom, darn it . . . to her box of dildos.

"Maxim—"

"Shhh—" He cut her off, catching her by her shoulders and spinning her around. Pressing down on her upper back, he forced her to lean over the counter, so that her feet lifted from the ground and her bottom was high in the air.

The counter's edge cut into her lower abdomen, but she didn't care. Having her bottom so exposed to him felt glorious.

"Ready?" he asked, wrenching her legs apart. His hands molded her ass, pulling her cheeks wide open. "Or not?"

"I'm ready." When he didn't immediately move, she whimpered. She was in no position for waiting. "Please, Maxim!"

"Good girl." He planted a gentle kiss to her bottom. "I think I want to eat you first. You're such a delicious woman. *My* woman."

The possessive insinuation sent a bolt straight to her heart.

Smoothing his tongue over her ass, he dipped between the crevice of her cheeks and found her pussy. His mouth suctioned her clit, nursing it powerfully, milking her desire for him.

Moaning, she clutched the counter. "My clit. Please, Maxim. My clit."

Pulling back, he chuckled lightly. "I see I've taught you to beg sufficiently. Good girl." His tongue flicked the nub, then swirled around it, torturing her. Finally, he gently claimed the sensitive bud between his teeth, gave it a little tug, then enveloped it. He sucked hard, so hard, the attention was almost too intense. She couldn't take it. "Maxim, please . . ."

Was that really her, sounding so desperate? Crying his name? Saying please?

Eagerly.

She wriggled against his expert lips. "Please, fuck me. Hurry."

"Mmmm." He released the bud and kissed his way up her buttocks. "Your wish, my queen, is my pleasure to fulfill." Reaching her lower back, he grasped her rear end in powerful hands. "You want fucked. Is that all?"

"No," she answered firmly. She wanted more. She wanted everything. She deserved it.

"No what?"

"I want you to touch my ass." Confident, she thrust her rear in the air. "Please."

Standing upright, he positioned himself between her legs. "That I can do."

His cock danced against her pussy as he pressed his thumb to her anus. Not entering her, he rotated his hips, rubbing his head against her dripping wet, ready slit.

Damn . . .

Her clit pulsed in awareness, heat flooding her loins.

"And play with my pussy." She ground out through her teeth. "Please."

"I may have to spank you. You're getting a little pushy, aren't you?" He chuckled again, sounding all too happy.

"And you love me for it," she blurted, realizing what she'd said too late.

Oh shit. Why would she make a comment like that? She knew how Maxim felt about love . . . not to mention how *she* felt about the dangerous emotion.

Love had no part of what they were doing.

Maxim stilled, not responding. Not saying anything.

Every one of Elisa's muscles tensed. What now? *Shit, shit, shit* . . . She hadn't meant what she'd said seriously, she'd just thrown the words out . . . but did they really affect him so powerfully?

She didn't have time to think on it further. All at once, he drove into her, thrusting his cock and thumb to the hilt. Crying out, she braced herself against his invasion. He took her in abrupt, demanding plunges, rocking her body to the steady beat of his fucking.

There was nothing sweet, nothing *loving*, about the way he drove into her. He was reminding her. They were about sex. Orgasms. Nothing more. Nothing less.

Her fingers clenched the counter's edge as she met his demands, pushed to the brink of ecstasy by his rapid, forceful thrusts into her body. This wasn't about anything endearing. But she needed him like this, she wanted him . . .

Too much.

Screaming, she welcomed the orgasm that vibrated through her, not slowing her thrusts even as her climax peaked. She sucked up every tingle of pleasure she could, because deep in her mind, she knew this had to be the last time.

She was losing herself to Maxim and that she couldn't allow to happen. Tomorrow, she left.

Maxim rammed into her, possessed by passion, possessed by her. *Love.* He was overcome by the word. Overcome by the feeling. All he wanted was to erase the way she'd hesitated after using the word.

To make Elisa his.

He took her as hard as he could, angry that she didn't love him, angry that he was afraid to love her, angry that she still wanted to join the Peace Corps.

He needed her. And no amount of fucking could fulfill him.

All at once, his cock jerked, spewing his seed into her, and he melted. His anger, his drive disappeared. He yanked free of her, bracing his hands on the counter. After several deep breaths, he stepped back.

What had just happened to him? He hadn't even remembered to use a condom.

Drawing a deep breath, he looked at her bared, beautiful ass, tempted to kiss her, to *make love* to her, but unable to move in her direction. He couldn't bring himself to touch her again right now. He'd lose his mind. His heart was already hers.

Emotion lodged in his throat, choking him. He needed to clear his head. Jerking upright, he fastened his pants and stormed from the cabin.

With all his might, Maxim swung the axe through the air, slamming it into the log that sat on the block in front of him. The wood shattered into two pieces, falling to the ground. Split.

Just like him.

Logic told him he was crazy. He could never be with Elisa. There were his old ways, his habits, his self-promises to consider. How could either of them ever get past such hindrances?

But then, they were *old* issues.

The way he felt, what he wanted; it wouldn't be tamped down. The stupid cupid that had taken up residence in his head was screaming like a raging madman bent on love.

He was divided. His feelings and thoughts clashed like ice in hot water, melting together to form one confused man.

What was this power Elisa had over him? If anything, her demands should make him want to flee. Over the past week or two, he'd chopped wood for her, fished, cleared brush, shoveled snow, cooked, hell, he'd even cleaned. The list went on. Never had he *worked* to be with a woman. Before, he wouldn't have considered it, but with Elisa . . .

Being with Elisa changed everything. His life felt fuller, meaningful; the sex, more poignant.

He couldn't lose her. He had to convince her to come to Cairo. *Had* to.

Maxim set up more wood and swung the axe. *Wham!*

He was no idiot. Her resistance had nothing to do with her career. It was him. She was afraid he'd go back to his old ways. That they'd never last and she'd be stuck in a sticky situation.

If he wanted her to come to Cairo, he had to commit to her.

Wham!

And he would. Tonight. This evening, he'd tell Elisa he was serious about her. That he wanted a relationship with her. That he loved her.

Love? *Love?*

Wham! Wham! Wham!

Admitting the deep feeling even to himself sent a charge of emotion straight to his chest, his ribs suddenly tight around his racing heart. Excitement infused his blood, heat rising to his face.

This was it. It was real. He loved her. Cared about her. More than just physically or in a way to get his cock off. He cared about what happened to her. If she was happy, satisfied in her life. He wanted—no needed—for her to care about him in the same way. Did she? Did it even matter?

He *loved* her.

He needed flowers and wine and a gourmet dinner. Jewelry. Chocolate. Music. Everything and anything romantic.

Tossing down the axe, he looked at the sky. Yeah, it was time; high time he fell in love, high time he lived his life. Quietly, he walked inside, straight to the bedroom. Standing in the doorway, Maxim peered in. Elisa was fast asleep, her hair billowing around her naked body like a silken blanket.

Damn, she was incredible. She looked like an angel . . . his angel.

Walking to her, Maxim covered her with a blanket so she wouldn't get a chill. There was no sense in waking her. He was getting pretty damn good on skis. Surely he could make it to Aspen and back in a couple of hours. With any luck, she'd never know the difference. That was, until he poured his heart out.

Footsteps in the kitchen jolted her awake. With a moan, Elisa rolled over, forcing her eyes open. She couldn't believe she'd fallen asleep so easily in the middle of the afternoon, but their intense lovema—*sex*—had knocked her out.

She really had to stop that shit.

Sitting up, she swung her feet over the side of the bed. "Maxim?"

The back door clicked shut.

Standing on wobbly legs, she walked to the window, expecting to find him chopping wood like he said he'd be. Instead, Maxim was on skis, headed toward the trail that led to Aspen.

"Where are you going?" Elisa wondered under her breath. Wiping the sleep from her eyes, she watched him disappear into the woods.

Her heart ceased to beat. What could he be doing?

Leaving her?

No. That couldn't be.

Could it?

He *had* brought up the need to return to Egypt several times. Not to mention she'd all but terrified him with her use of the word "love."

But surely Maxim wouldn't just leave. He'd tell her. Kiss her good-bye. Fuck her senseless one last time.

Oh, wait. He'd just done that!

But he wouldn't leave without telling her. After the way he'd proven himself, she needed to trust him. She *would* trust him.

Stifling the urge to run bare-assed into the snow and chase him down, she squared her shoulders and threw on a robe. Why, she bet there was a note explaining everything in the kitchen right now. She'd just go check.

twenty-one

*M*r. Cox, you have a message," the desk clerk called the very moment he walked through the glass doors of his hotel. Maxim didn't miss the wrinkled man's haughty tone, despite the crackling of age that distorted his speech. "Twenty actually, all from your mother, except for one from a Mr. Harold Cox."

Great. His father had called? Boy, he was going to get it. Maxim released a long sigh and marched to the counter like a good soldier.

"I had an unexpected engagement."

"I see." Gingerly, the man scooted around and retrieved a wad of papers from the shelf behind him, then handed them to Maxim. Clearing his throat, he leaned forward, resting upon the highly polished oak desk. "You're reservations, sir, I'm afraid they expired a week ago."

"I apologize." Maxim took the messages and flipped through them. *Mother, mother, mother* . . . Ah. Here was the one from his father. *Call. Now.* That was all it said. Not good.

Straightening, Maxim looked at the clerk. "I'll be checking out this afternoon. You have my credit card info, so please charge the incurred expenses."

"Very good, sir." The man cleared his throat, his eyes roaming over Maxim's two-week-old appearance and ill-fitting woman's coat. "Will there be anything else, sir? Shall I ring the laundry service?"

Translation: what the hell happened to you?

"No thanks. I won't be here that long."

But God, he missed laundry service. And cable. And good food.

With a grin, Maxim walked to the elevator and punched his floor number, then eagerly tapped the button that closed the doors. Maybe he'd gotten better at skiing, but the trip into Aspen had been no picnic. It had taken longer than expected by over an hour and now he had his parents to deal with.

He might as well telephone his mother first and then he could do his shopping for tonight. Had he been using his brain, he'd have left Elisa a note, but he hadn't, and he didn't want to give her too much time to worry. He should probably call, but he didn't want her to question his motives.

A few seconds later, he stepped off the elevator, walked to his room, and unlocked the door. He went straight to the phone. Picking it up, he dialed the access code, then the country code for Egypt, then his mother's personal number. After few rings, a curt message informed him he was being forwarded to her cell phone.

Great. She never answered the damn thing. He didn't even know why she had one.

Nonetheless, he didn't hang up. At least he could leave a message.

The phone rang three times and to his surprise, his mother picked up. *"Sa'ida!"*

Shit. He'd had a sweet but short message prepared, not a conversation. Caught off guard, Maxim tried to think of something—anything—intelligent to say. "Mother. How's the weather?"

Tense silence was followed by the click of her tongue. "How's the *weather?* Do you have any idea how long you have been gone this time?"

Too long. But not long enough.

Nervousness unfurled in him. From her tone, she was pissed. He couldn't blame her either, but at least she'd calm down when he told her about Elisa. She was dying for him to get serious about a woman.

"Yes, and I'm sorry—"

"No Maxim, sorry doesn't cut it," she bit his words off, chewed them up, and spit them out. Her voice rose. "I've been waiting for you to call me back for weeks! Have you any notion of the inconvenience your little disappearance has caused? I had a grand opening in Germany this week. Your father had to fly in to cover me. Do you think my time is worth nothing? That I'm at your disposal? When will you ever be responsible? And this hotel, Maxim—you must pay more attention to detail! This cannot continue. Your brother—"

Ouch.

Whatever she had to say, he didn't want to hear it. Not this time. "Mother, I—"

"Keaton would not be so careless."

Double ouch.

"Except when he was driving," he muttered in anger. "And in love."

"Maxim! Do not talk of him like that!"

It wasn't often that his mother threw such hurtful insinuations around, but when she did, he never argued with her. Keaton, until this week, had been a god in his eyes. Someone he could never compare to.

Someone he wasn't.

"How should I talk of him, mother? It's the truth."

And maybe it was time he faced it.

His brother had married foolishly. From the time the two had dated, Lila had a way of flirting with other men and making Keaton jealous. A history of sleeping around. Their relationship had been doomed from the get-go and Keaton had been too blind to see it.

It was time Maxim stopped comparing himself to him.

"You know, actually, Mother, you bring up a good point. One I never considered before."

Elisa was nothing like Lila. *They* weren't doomed. What's more, for once, he wasn't acting irrationally, a trait that appeared to run in the family. He hated to think badly of the dead, especially not one so loved as his brother, but Keaton had screwed up, and it was past time he stopped letting Keaton's mistakes screw *him* up.

A weight lifted from Maxim. "All this time, I've been comparing my life to his, but I'm not Keaton."

"Believe me, I know that." His mother clicked her tongue again. "Maxim, really. When will you ever grow up? And need I remind you—I secured you a date with the daughter of a very prominent man. You stood her up. I made excuses for you, rescheduled—"

"Who told you to do that?"

"Someone has to see you married. You've insulted their family."

Great. Another angry father. And when would his mother stop trying to arrange his love life?

Hopefully, after this phone call.

"I'm sure I can smooth the situation over with an invitation to dinner," Maxim suggested.

"Not this time, Maxim," she snapped, followed by a heavy, drawn-out sigh of defeat. "This time you've gone too far, for too long. You leave me no choice. I don't care where you are or what you're doing. You are to come home. Head to the airport right this minute."

"Not a chance in the world." He smiled, knowing she'd relish what he had to tell her next. "I'm in love, mother."

"I believe that," she said, her voice bland with sarcasm.

"Seriously."

There was a moment of silence, followed by a haughty harrumph of disbelief. "Then you are getting married."

Married? Whoa, doggie . . .

He cleared his throat. "I didn't say—"

"You see. You are lying to me, Maxim. If you are in love, then I expect you to bring home a wife. Within one week." Her voice was stone and she paused, allowing time for her demand to sink in. "Or you are disinherited. And fired."

"*What!?*"

Screw his inheritance. His job. Marry Elisa? *Marry Elisa?*

Marry Elisa.

Maxim forgot to breathe. The notion wrapped around him, hugging him tight and filling him with warmth.

Marry Elisa.

He would.

Not for his mother. Not for his inheritance. For love.

He'd never considered marrying her until right now, but he wanted to. With all his heart.

Why hadn't he considered it before? Because he was too busy running from himself. Hiding from love. Now that he'd found it, he wasn't letting go.

His mother cleared her throat. "Young man, did you hear me? I said I will disinherit you. You will be done with this family and the hotel. Penniless. Forced to make it on your own, Maxim. Unless you get married."

"I don't care about the money, Mother. I don't care about anything but Elisa," he declared. "But I am getting married. At least, if she'll have me."

His mother snorted, clearly doubting him. "We'll see. A week, Maxim. For once, I suggest you prove yourself trustworthy."

With that, she hung up on him.

Maxim sat on the edge of the bed, stunned. What was it with women and making him prove himself?

It didn't matter. He wasn't marrying Elisa for his mother. He was doing it for himself.

He ran his hand through his hair, feeling like his world was spinning out of control. This was huge. Huger than huge. Incredible.

But would Elisa say yes?

She had to. He had to ensure that she would . . . wooing her into a yes was going to take a lot of chocolate, wine, and hot sex, not to mention an expensive diamond ring. But above all else, he was going to need a good line.

He just prayed he could come up with one she'd buy.

*N*o note.

No note. No note. No note.

Why wouldn't Maxim have left a note? Why was she letting herself get so worked up?

Elisa drummed her fingers on the kitchen counter so hard it hurt. This was silly. She shouldn't be worried. Really. Truly.

But she was.

What if he'd left her? Good-byes are never easy and they'd made no commitments. What if he'd just decided to go?

Worse, what if he'd gotten hungry . . . for more than she could offer?

He'd come so far, *they'd* come so far. Future or not, she couldn't let him just disappear from her life . . . could she?

Hell no.

Leaping to her feet, Elisa rushed to the back door. She had to catch him, just in case.

Maybe bigger wasn't always better, at least not when it came to women like Elisa. Maxim wasn't sure whether to go with a huge, expensive rock or something simpler and more suiting a natural woman like her—but also cheaper.

Elisa deserved the best . . . but what was that?

Shifting his feet, he glanced at the ticking clock. He'd been at this an hour. It was taking him far longer than he'd expected and surely by now, Elisa was awake and pacing the floors. After this, he needed to look up Elisa's number and call her. Hopefully, she was listed.

He held up a four carat pink diamond to the light and reconsidered. Somehow, it just didn't seem right.

"You should get the very best you can afford," the persistent saleslady suggested, tossing her glossy blond hair over her shoulders. She drew another velvet-lined tray from the cabinet. "What about something framed with your birthstone?"

A neat idea. Maybe . . .

But a nagging little voice in his head—the stupid cupid maybe—insisted Elisa would feel such money was better spent. Like for some charity or . . .

That was it!

The idea hit him like a baseball bat to the head. Why hadn't he thought of it before? Forget this literal rock on a ring. He *would* buy something smaller, then he'd take the remainder of the money that he would've spent and donate it to the Peace Corps. Elisa could consider her intended service with them "paid" for and move with him to Egypt. And marry him.

Perfect. He had his line. Now he just needed to settle on the right ring.

A flash of hot pink caught his attention from the corner of his eye and he glanced up at the store's front window. Oh crap. Lizzy.

Talking animatedly Elisa's sister strolled down the street with a group of women, none of whom looked as nutty as her.

Maxim swallowed and debated letting her pass. Ignoring her would be easiest, but if he intended to marry Elisa, her sister would always be a part of their life. He might as well make friends. If that were possible. What's more, she could give him Elisa's phone number.

Setting the ring on the counter, he dashed to the door and opened it. "Lizzy!"

Her gaze narrowed. She glared at him a moment, then excused herself from her friends and barged into the jewelry store.

"Max Cox. Finished with Elisa?" she spat, following him inside. "Planning to buy some rich bimbo for a one night stand with some sparklies?"

"No." He planted on his best smile. "Actually, I—"

"Two rich bimbos?"

Where did she get off? She didn't even know him!

"No," he answered with strained patience. "I'm asking Elisa to marry me."

Silence.

Dead silence.

"What about this?" the saleslady interrupted. "The cut is exquisite." She showed him another excessively large ring, this one heart shaped. Tacky.

"That's just not Elisa." He shook his head and held up his hand. "Give me a moment, please."

An almost inhuman noise escaped Lizzy. "It won't work, you know."

"What won't work?" he scanned the case, looking for something smaller and more heartfelt. He did like the idea of his birthstone framing the diamond, just not so gaudy.

"Elisa can't be bought with a big diamond," Lizzy barked. "And you . . . you . . . what do you think you're doing?" She stomped her foot. "You should leave town! Now!"

He ignored Lizzy's pouting. Now that he had her attention, he intended to be treated with some respect.

His eyes settled on a marquis cut, half carat that was framed with rubies, his birthstone. Perfect. "I'd like to see that one," he requested. Looking put-out by his less costly choice, the saleslady handed him the ring and he took it between his fingers, turning it. He showed it to Lizzy, who eyed the jewelry like it was poison. "What about a hundred thousand dollars to the Peace Corps and a simpler ring? Would that make a more . . . appropriate proposal for someone like Elisa?"

Lizzy eyed the ring hesitantly, speaking through her teeth. "Elisa can't be bought. Not even with charity."

Maxim rotated the ring in his fingers, watching it twinkle from the overhead light. "I don't want to buy her. I want to love her for who she is, for the rest of my life."

"Oh, come on."

"I'm serious." He looked directly into Lizzy's eyes. "I respect Elisa, I respect her morals. I want to be more like her. I want her to know that when I propose."

"But—" Shaking her head, Lizzy looked flustered. "You . . . you can't. Elisa's right. You're full of good lines."

"It's not a line, Lizzy," he told her firmly. "It's the way I feel. I've changed."

"That's not possible."

"Come on, Lizzy. Give me a chance. I *love* her. Haven't I shown that? Doesn't this prove it?"

She swallowed deeply. A tear formed in the corner of her eye. Lizzy stared at the ring he still held between his fingers. "It's perfect," she whispered as if she were admitting the world was about to explode.

A smile spread on his face and he gave the ring one more turn. Damn, everything was falling into place. Turning to the saleslady, he nodded. "I'll take it."

"We have an insurance policy available and—"

"No, no, just check me out." He handed her the ring and reached in his pocket, pulling a credit card from his wallet. He gave it to her, then turned to Lizzy. "How about dinner?"

He was short on time, but he didn't want to let this situation between them go unchecked. He'd just call Elisa. Make something up.

"Dinner?" Lizzy squeaked. "I don't know. This is getting a little too weird, Maxim . . ."

"You and I, we may be family soon. We should get to know
each other."

She wrinkled her nose like he smelled. "Know each other?"

He shook his head. Getting through to her was like putting a
nail through a brick. "You see evil in everything I say, don't you?"

"Yes."

The saleslady handed him a slip to sign, which he did, then he
retrieved the jewelry box, tucking it snugly in his inner coat
pocket. He placed his hand on Lizzy's upper arm and guided her
toward the door. "I want your esteem, Lizzy, nothing more,
nothing less. I want us to be friends."

"Friends? I don't know . . . I have to admit, I'm not crazy over
Elisa being with you. I'm not sure I can support this 'thing'
between the two of you."

"Well, just give me a chance. What can it hurt?"

She sighed. "Okay. We'll see. But I'm headed to dinner with
some friends, so maybe another—"

"Great." Maxim clutched her bicep firmly enough that she
couldn't escape. He'd be damned if he gave her a chance to stall or
avoid him, not now, when he finally had her talking to him with
some measure of civility. "I'll trail along. I'm starved."

twenty-two

By the time she reached the edge of town, Elisa felt like a fool—a genuine, full-fledged idiot was on skis. It was snowing its ass off again, and she was still sick. She shouldn't be outside at all.

What would Maxim think of her desperately chasing after him? Good grief, he could *not* find out about this. At least when she'd come into Aspen he'd had the balls to wait at the cabin patiently. But then, she'd told him she was going.

Damn it, she really ought to turn back. It was the logical, sane thing to do.

But to hell with reason! She couldn't resist the temptation to spy on Maxim, not even to save her life.

Biting her lower lip, she tried to reassure herself that what she was doing was no big deal. She was here, so she might as well check Maxim out . . . assuming she could find him. Not that she was going on a big scavenger hunt. She would simply glance around. It wasn't a crime.

But then she was heading back to the cabin, no bones about it.

Elisa took the trail she always did, skiing up to the rear of Play. Taking off her skis, she left them propped behind the club and walked around the building to the sidewalk.

Elisa glanced at her watch. She couldn't believe how long he'd been gone. It would be dark soon. Dinner hour. Well, if she got caught, she'd simply claim she was meeting Lizzy for a meal.

Strolling down the street past small shops, cafes, and restaurants, Elisa walked blindly. Now that she was here, it occurred to her that she didn't have a clue where to look. He'd never told her the name of his hotel . . . so what was she going to do? Comb all of Aspen?

Not likely.

This was ridiculous. With a sigh, she relinquished her crazy quest. She'd just get a bite to eat and go home. If Maxim didn't come back to the cabin, then so be it.

The thought made her heart thud, but she forced herself to ignore the reaction. She was behaving like a fool . . . exactly the kind of woman she'd sworn not to become.

Joe's, her and Lizzy's favorite pub and grill, was tucked into a cul-de-sac right around the corner, so she walked toward the bar, her mind reeling with regret and confusion. No matter how she felt, the Peace Corps was looking more and more sensible—something she needed to be right now. Maxim—

Maxim.

Shocked, Elisa stared in the huge, front window of Joe's, stunned to see him there.

With four women.

Laughing. Talking. Drinking.

With four women.

No, no, no! The bastard! How could he?

Tears welled in her eyes and her vision blurred. She stumbled backward.

If her mind had been spinning before, a tornado was tearing it apart now. God! She'd been right from the start. She wasn't enough for Maxim. No woman was. No woman ever would be.

She walked blindly until she bumped into a wall. Clenching her fists, she just stood there, feeling like an idiot. Max Cox was a man-slut and nothing would change that. Not even her and her silly little game.

Not even her love.

Oh God. What had she been thinking? She'd slept with him, given him her heart . . .

Why? Would she never learn?

Sick to her stomach, Elisa turned and ran as fast as she could, needing to escape. She and Maxim weren't just over. They'd never existed in the first place.

Maxim eyeballed the pay phone in the corner. He'd called three times, but maybe he should call again.

Why wasn't Elisa answering? He needed to get home, and as soon as Lizzy returned from her excessively long trip to the bathroom, he would.

"Maxim? Do you agree?"

"Huh?" Lost in thought, Maxim commanded himself to snap out of it and smiled graciously at the group of giggling women surrounding him. Damn, he'd never missed Elisa more.

"We were talking about Jenny getting a perm. What do you think? Wouldn't she look sexy with curls?" Terri inquired, a twinkle in her eyes.

"Sure," he agreed. "I like curls."

This conversation, the female company, was putting him to sleep. These women had talked about their hair for twenty minutes.

"Don't you think I look sexy now?" Jenny pouted.

Jesus. What was wrong with these women? They were fine through dinner, but ever since Lizzy had gone to the restroom, they were hitting on him like he was the last man on earth. Perhaps they'd had too much to drink.

Jenny moaned. "No answer?"

"Of course you look nice," he answered stiffly.

All he wanted to do was return to Elisa. To make love to her all night long. To think, there'd been a time when he would've been in heaven being surrounded by four very friendly, very sexy women.

Not now. No one could hold a candle to Elisa. No female was as beautiful or intelligent as his lover. All he wanted, all he needed, was Elisa.

As soon as Lizzy returned, he was out of there. While she hadn't exactly pledged her faith in him, they'd managed to have an almost friendly discussion about Elisa. He got the idea that Lizzy was tolerating him, but coming from her that might be the best he could ever hope for.

"Hey! I've got an idea!" Jenny cried. "Let's play truth or dare."

"Fun!" Terri clapped her hands. "Maxim goes first!"

Maxim restrained a groan. Suddenly, a foot brushed his. "Truth or dare, Maxim." Cindy, the blonde across from him cooed.

He sure wasn't taking a dare from one of them. He'd end up naked.

Maxim tucked his foot under his chair and forced himself to continue smiling. "Truth," he grunted.

She grinned, ear to ear. "Which one of us is the sexiest?"

Maxim just stared at her. Did she have any idea she had lipstick on her teeth? That she sounded loose?

Clearly these women had had one too many margaritas and the last thing he wanted was Lizzy's friends to tell her he'd been rude. "All of you are appealing in your own way. I try not to pick favorites."

Carly, the redhead next to him, took that as an invitation to lean closer to him. "So you want to sleep with all of us?"

Whoa! Talk about aggressive.

"Uh, no." Flustered, Maxim leaned to the left. Carly's damn chair kept scooting closer and closer. Soon he'd fall off his seat from trying to avoid her busy hands. "No thank you. I'm seeing someone."

"Ohhhh . . ." Cindy caught her foot around his ankle and rubbed her toes along his calf. "Are you sure?"

Geesh! What was with these women?

"Positive," he grunted.

Was he giving off a scent or something?

He needed to leave. Now. Before he was raped.

"What about my hair, Maxim?" Carly questioned, practically flinging the brilliant locks in his face. "Do you like it? Do you want to touch it? Go ahead."

It's not as silky or as long as Elisa's . . .

"Uh . . ."

She turned to face him, her lips coming dangerously close to his. "My other hair . . . it's not red. It's black," she whispered. "Do you want to see?"

Awkward . . .

A bead of sweat rolled down his forehead. He cleared his throat and pulled back. Forget Lizzy. He'd had enough already. Placing his hands on the table, Maxim stood. "Ladies, I—"

"Leaving so soon?" Lizzy asked from behind him.

Thank God. He turned to her. "The steak was great, but I need to get going. Elisa isn't answering the phone and I'm certain she's worried."

"Really?" Lizzy's brow rose. "No bites, girls?"

Huh? He looked at the other ladies, surprised by the ornery smiles replacing their seductive ones. "Bites? I'm afraid I don't follow."

"No." Carly leaned back in her chair and sighed. "Unfortunately, he was an angel."

"Bites?" he asked again, looking to Lizzy.

"I told them to flirt with you. To act easy." She shrugged her shoulders. "I figured you'd jump into another woman's bed the first chance you got. But it appears I was wrong. You really do love Elisa and you really have changed."

"Yes." He nodded, annoyed by her test, but even happier that she was accepting him.

Lizzy gave him a wink and a rare, genuine smile. "Then welcome to the family."

Hot damn! Finally!

If he could get this harebrain to like him, surely he could get Elisa to accept his proposal. Suddenly, Maxim was on cloud nine. He felt like dancing. Singing. Making love all night long.

"Let's make that official." Giddy, he opened his arms for a hug.

The blank stare returned. Lizzy looked at him like he was a maniac. *Him.*

Shaking his head, he grinned. "Okay, no hug. Guess I was expecting too much at once. Listen, I better get going. It's late and I know Elisa is worried to death. I never even told her I was leaving."

Incredibly, her brows rose higher. "You think you're going home, *tonight?*"

"Yeah, why?"

"Look outside, sugar," Carly answered for Lizzy. "It's pitch black and snowing like God plans to bury this mountain. You try to go home and you'll kill yourself. Sure you don't want to rethink my invite?"

Maxim turned and stared out the window into the snowy night, filled with despair. *Damn it.*

twenty-three

Oh no, he didn't!

The bastard! The absolute nerve of him coming back here!

Elisa held her breath and glared out the window at the sight of Maxim skiing through the blinding snow toward the cabin. How could he possibly think this was okay?

It was morning . . . *morning!*

Ugh!

Stomping her feet, Elisa threw the curtain shut. She wasn't going to look at him. She'd pretend he wasn't there.

But . . . *ohhhh!* Where did he get off?

No strings or commitments between them did not mean that Maxim could stick his dick in whomever he pleased, whenever he pleased, then come home to her!

Her teeth gnashed together, she peeked out the curtain. Damn him. His back laden with a full pack, extra bags in his arms, he unfastened his skis, and stomped off his boots on the concrete pad at the kitchen door.

Tears threatened her and she forced them back. She fingered the shirt she'd been folding, the final item to go in her suitcase. It didn't matter. She was leaving.

She slammed the lid shut, jerked the zipper, and dragged it behind her as she walked down the hall.

After spending the night packing and crying, crying and packing, and packing and crying, her mind was made up. Today was the day. She'd load up her sled and head into town this afternoon to spend one last night with Lizzy. Come Monday, she was leaving Aspen. Joining the Peace Corps was no longer negotiable. She needed to do it, for her sanity alone.

Speaking of sanity . . .

His shadow at the back door made her pulse skip. Oh God! Leaving or not, she didn't have it in her to face him. She just . . . couldn't.

Dropping her suitcase, she raced to lock him out.

Her hand barely made contact with the knob as he pushed the door open. No, damn it! *No, no, no!*

Elisa threw her body weight against the wood, shoving the door shut. "Get lost, Maxim!"

"What?" With all his might, he pushed back, preventing her from shutting him out. "What's your problem?"

"You!" Was that really her screaming? Not loud enough! She let loose a piercing wail. "You no-good, cheating, lying, bullshitting slut!"

The door rammed in response. "Let me in! Elisa, I want to talk to you."

"No! I don't want to talk to you." Sobs became trapped in her chest as she fought to keep him out, feeling more and more helpless by the second. "Go away!"

"Elisa!" His boot wedged in the door. "I know you woke up and I was gone, but it's not what you think!"

Oh, puh-lease!

"Ha!" Who did he think he was fooling? She wasn't one of his dingbat dates. "It's what I know! I *saw* you with those girls, Maxim."

"Having dinner?" His voice lowered and he stopped pushing. "At Joe's?"

"Yes!"

"You followed me?"

"No! Well . . . yes." Elisa rested against the door, fighting a breakdown. Why did she suddenly feel like such a jerk? It was him who'd cheated! He was the one who'd betrayed her trust! So she'd followed him. So what? "Who can blame me even if I did?"

He laughed, low and deep, thoroughly grating her nerves.

"Well, it wasn't what you thought."

"Bull. One woman will never be enough for you, Maxim Cox." A lone tear slid from her right eye and she quickly wiped it away. She wouldn't shed tears over him. Angry, she rammed into the door, smashing his pinned foot. "*I'll* never be enough for you. So let's stop pretending."

"Ow!" He cried. "I was with Lizzy. Those were her friends. And damn it, that hurt!"

Rendered speechless, she stood there, letting the truth sink in. He'd been with Lizzy? Those had been Lizzy's friends?

He hadn't been cheating?

Oh God. Unwelcome drops of liquid fell from her eyes. A waterfall of emotion poured from her.

"Why?" she hiccupped.

"Why what?"

"Why were you with Lizzy?"

"I was gaining her friendship." His fingers wrapped around the door, his words, around her heart. "I didn't want your sister to hate me."

"Then where was she? I didn't see her."

"She was in the bathroom, for a long time, while her friends flirted with me."

"*What?*"

"She was testing me. I passed."

"But you didn't come home last night," she protested weakly, her walls falling faster than rain in a hurricane.

None of this made sense! She'd been so sure . . . so wrong.

"It was late and the snowstorm stopped me."

Damn Mother Nature!

Damn her spying!

"Why didn't you leave a note? Call?"

"I wanted to surprise you and I did try to call. Several times, not to mention the numerous messages I left. You didn't answer."

Because she'd been in Aspen and so angry when she'd arrived home, she'd shut off the answering machine without listening to her messages.

God. She felt like a jerk . . . but a relieved jerk. He wasn't a man-slut. And she didn't have to hate him. She stepped back and let the door swing open. Maxim fell, pack and all, through the sudden opening, landing at her feet in a *thump!*

"Oh my!" she squeaked as he groaned and rolled side to side, his body arched by the pack.

"Ow! My shoulder. Again. Ow." He moaned and shrugged the bag off, scooting down to lie flat on his back.

She couldn't contain her giggle.

"It's not funny," he grunted.

She raised a brow. "Serves you right. You scared me to death, not telling me where you were going."

"Elisa, listen to me."

"No. It doesn't matter." She swallowed, her anger fading, but reality as clear as ever. Whether he'd been with other women or not, she had to end this game with him. It was the right thing to do. "None of this does. I'm leaving. I'm joining the Corps. Now."

"You can't." He scurried to his knees, digging through his pack. "Just hold up a minute, okay?"

"I can't. I have to go." She stepped back, chewing at her lower lip. "I'm sorry, Maxim, but we aren't right. We can't be right."

Maxim tossed miscellaneous items from the pack—underwear, chocolates, keys, a CD with roses on the front—searching like a madman. "Elisa, listen to me. When I was in town, I called my mother. She's pissed, well, that's to say the least. But you see, I have to get married within a week or I'm disinherited." He jerked out a small, velvet covered box out and held it up. "That put the idea in my mind and—"

A . . . a . . . a ring box? Wait a sec! Was he . . . ?

No!

Suddenly trembling and cold, Elisa stepped back. "You're proposing?"

"Well, yes." He reached for her. "Come here, baby. Let me finish."

This was the worst thing to ever happen to her. Chilled, she stared at him, scared by how disappointed and insulted she was. "You want me to marry you so you won't get disinherited?" She stepped back again. "No."

Fear sparked in his gaze and he reached for her. "Elisa, that's not it at all. If you'd let me finish—"

She jerked away and grabbed her suitcase. "This is good-bye, Maxim."

"No." His voice was firm.

Who did he think he was talking to? His dog?

"No?" she ground out through her teeth. "*No?*"

"No." Maxim caught her by the waist and threw her over his shoulder. "No, no, no."

His hand swatted her bottom in quick succession, making her cry out. Struggling against him, she roared, "I'm not playing, Maxim! Get off me!"

"Not a chance."

Elisa kicked and twisted against his hold, but he'd be damned if he was letting her go now. Not from his hold, not from his life.

She was going to hear him out. Let him propose the right way. If the answer was still no, then the answer was still no. But he wasn't going to lose her without a fight and especially not to a silly misunderstanding.

Squeezing her upper legs tight, he stalked to the bedroom. He tossed her on the bed and fought her clothes off her. Once she was stripped naked, he pointed at her. "Don't move."

She bounded up like a rabbit leaping from its hole. "Yeah, right." In a second she was on her feet and trying to dart past him. He caught her arm and threw her back down.

"We can do this the easy way." He crawled on the bed and pinned her with his legs. "Or the hard way." Their gazes locked in a silent battle. "But we will do this."

"Maxim—"

"All I want is for you to listen to me."

She rammed against him. "And all I want is to leave!"

"Forget it." Unzipping his coat, he undid the buckle of his belt and yanked it free from his pants. He forced her hands together.

"What are doing?" She fought against his hold. "Maxim!"

Why did she have to fight him like this? Why did she have to insist upon leaving him? Of thinking so terribly of him? Of joining the Peace Corps?

He couldn't stomach the thought. He just couldn't.

He knew Elisa felt the same way about him that he did her. But she refused to admit it. Refused to love him.

She had to see . . . to understand . . .

Even if it took all night long.

"You're mine, Elisa. I won't lose you." With quick movements, he wrapped the leather strap tight around her wrists and threaded it through the buckle. He yanked it tight.

Bending down, he rested his cheek against hers and whispered roughly, "Let's try this again. Don't move. Or else."

"Bastard."

"I will catch you if you run. Don't move."

Crawling off her, Maxim stood and crossed the room. He threw open her closet, sifting through layers of clothes. He found two scarves and a robe tie. Perfect.

It was one thing if Elisa truly didn't want to be with him—it was another for her to run from something very real between them. Apparently, he hadn't quite proven himself yet.

But he would.

All night long.

He'd do *whatever* it took.

He turned to her, threading the ties through his hand. "You will hear me out, Elisa. I'm just sorry it has to be this way. I'd planned something more romantic."

He saw her swallow deeply. "Maxim, this is insane. Stop it. Please."

"Nope." Maxim returned to the bedside and seized her left leg. He tied the scarf around her ankle and then secured it to the bedpost. "I'm afraid I can't do that."

Elisa squealed in frustration and jerked her leg against his ties, but he ignored her and applied the same treatment to the opposite foot. Taking the robe tie, he used it to fasten her hands to the headboard.

"There." Straightening, he examined his handiwork. "Ready to hear me out?"

"No!"

But she had to. Elisa could no longer move, except for pathetic, tiny twists of her torso as she cursed him.

Maxim stripped off his clothes and retrieved a condom for the nightstand. Tearing the foil wrapper open, he slipped it on. "Now, about what I asked you—"

"I'm not marrying you, Maxim, I don't care how much money you offer me. I'm leaving, the moment you untie me, so you might as well give this up."

What? She thought this was only about *money*?

Not even close. She was about to learn that.

"I'm afraid I can't let you go." He climbed onto the mattress and sat on his knees between her spread legs. He drank in the sight of her pussy. She was dripping wet . . . as turned on by being tied up as he'd known she would be.

Gently caressing her, he opened her folds wide. He pressed his thumb to her clit. "I love you, Elisa."

She turned her head to the side, speaking through her teeth. "That's ridiculous. You love your money."

She pressed her eyes shut, obviously trying to ignore him.

"I don't give a damn about the money. I only want you." Maxim wanted her attention and he intended to get it. One way or the other. He placed his mouth to her cunt and slowly licked her creamy desire. "My mother may have put the idea in my mind, but you put the love in my heart."

"What a sweet line." Refusing to look at him, she arched and groaned. "You're full of them—of it—aren't you?"

He suckled her clit, pulling it between his teeth then releasing; pulling, then releasing. "Why do you think I went into town?" he asked, blowing his words into the depths of her slit. "Without telling you?"

She groaned again, jerking as if she could escape the bonds tying her to the bed. "To get laid?" Her words, though ripe with sarcasm, wavered.

Ah. He was getting to her.

He just needed to press more. To make her see. To make her admit what she wanted to refuse.

"No, Elisa." He drove three fingers into her tight sheath, forcing her to welcome him. Rotating the digits deep inside her, he returned his mouth to her clit. "I wanted to make this night special—flowers, wine, the whole bit—because I was going to ask you to take our relationship to the next level." As he spoke, he took tiny nibbles and licks of her. She bucked against him, futilely trying to resist. "But now that I think on it, that's not enough. I demand to have you as my wife."

She whimpered as he sat up, abandoning her hungry pussy. "Maxim, we'd never be compatible."

He pulled the ring box from his pocket and opened it, showing her the simple ring he'd chosen. "We are perfectly compatible. A glove cannot fit a glove, it must fit a hand. Sure, we're different, because you are my hand."

She eyed the box, and him, curiously, but said nothing.

Taking the ring, he swept the cold metal and jewels gently long her wet folds, making her moan for mercy. "Maxim. I can't . . . you can't . . . stop this . . ."

"You see this ring?" He lifted it into her sight. "I was going to buy something bigger. But that isn't you, Elisa. I know that now. So instead . . ." He trailed the ring over the curls covering her mons and up her belly, leaving a path of her silky desire wherever the diamond touched. "I purchased a smaller ring and donated what I would have spent to the Peace Corps. In your name."

She trembled in response.

"No . . ." She gulped as he brought the ring to her mouth, allowing it to gently brush against her lips.

Lowering the ring, he laid it on her chest.

"Taste how you feel for me," he told her, his lips hovering over hers. "Taste it." When she didn't obey, he seized her in a tongue-swiping kiss, forcing her to taste the desire on her lips and his tongue.

By the time they broke apart, she was panting. And crying. "Damn . . ." She swallowed again, clearly struggling with her resistance. "That was so sweet."

He kissed the salty droplets running down her cheeks. "You are sweet."

"No, I mean that you donated money. But Maxim, I don't want to be like my mother, plenty of money to throw around, but no time. *I* want to save the rainforests. To make the world a better place."

He smiled. He was finally winning! "Maybe you can't save the rainforests in Egypt, but you can do plenty of good." He kissed her forehead gently. "Think about the children whose lives you could make better. What you could teach them. About life, about the environment, the forests . . ."

"I don't know . . ."

"If my donation doesn't prove to you that I'd be right by your side, what would?"

"Actions speak louder than words. Money too."

"Without money, there would be no Peace Corps. Your mother did more for the rainforests than ten people working hands-on ever could."

"Maybe that's true . . ." For the first time during their conversation, she looked directly in his eyes. "I never thought of it that way. She changed Lizzy's life too."

"Your sister?"

"She's adopted. She was living on the streets . . ." Elisa bit her lower lip. "I could teach children about saving the rainforests . . . and so much else. I thought about doing that in the Peace Corps."

"See? So many children in Cairo are in desperate situations. They need you. I need you." He drank up her deep blues, staring straight into her soul, and knowing he'd be lost without her. "Please, Elisa. Please. Just say yes."

"I . . . can't."

"If you can't say yes, at least say you love me," he asked, never more desperate.

The tensest second of his life slid slowly past.

Finally, she nodded. "I do. I love you."

He unfastened the belt restraining her arms and enveloped her hands in his. "Then we'll make it work, don't you see, Elisa? With love comes respect. Appreciation. I would never take you away from what means the most to you." He slipped the ring on her finger and tenderly kissed her hand. "I would only ask the same from you."

She looked at the ring, then him. "I'll marry you, Maxim." A smile broadened on her face. "I will."

Never more elated, he drove into her with one full thrust, sealing the deal.

Elisa clenched his shoulders, feeling more complete than ever. Their bodies rocked in steady rhythm, united as their souls. The smile on her face spread and happiness bloomed from deep within her. If there was one thing in life she'd learned, it was that life throws you curves. The unexpected becomes the expected. And when it came to matters of the heart . . . only the heart can truly decide what's right.

Maybe Maxim wasn't her dream man—once upon a time he was her worst nightmare—but after all was said and done, he was a dream come true. She was ready. She loved him with all of her being.

No dildo could replace that.

epilogue

"I can't believe how spoiled I'm getting." Stretching on Maxim's plush bed of silk and pillows, Elisa opened her mouth to accept the grapes he fed her. She chewed the fruit slowly, enjoying every succulent bite. "I'm turning into you."

The funny thing was, she'd grown up rich, but until Maxim, she'd never enjoyed having money. While she'd taught him that life was more than parties and girls, he'd helped her to see that sometimes it was necessary to be . . . unnecessary.

"Mmmm . . ." Maxim kissed along the rim of her lips, licking miniscule little splatters of grape juice. "It's your honeymoon. You deserve to be spoiled."

He fed her another grape and she drew the juice from it, though she wished it was something else she was sucking on. They'd made love too many times to count, but soon, they'd have to join the real world and she wanted to enjoy him while she could.

"The work will start soon enough," she moaned in fake despair, thinking of all she had to do to get their life organized and their charity up and running. "Spoil away."

He chuckled and trailed a finger along her jaw. "Tomorrow, actually. Mother is quite excited about beginning work for Helen's Haven. She was so flattered that you named our youth shelter after her."

It was her turn to laugh. Since they'd arrived in Egypt, Helen had been one step away from driving her over the brink. Her new mother-in-law was a constant flurry of demands and excitement. "So much for disinheriting you. I think she's even more enthused about using me as a birthing cow."

"The promise of grandchildren can smooth over the worst of disagreements." Maxim kissed along her jawbone, planting fluttery love bites all over her face. "Don't you want babies?"

Curling her toes, Elisa closed her eyes and savored the attention. A smile spread across her face as she fantasized about her future with Maxim, filled with midnight feedings and diaper changes. At least he was used to being up late and getting little sleep.

"Six, at the minimum," she dared him, knowing having so many kids with a man like him was a long shot. "But I want a few of our children to be adopted, like Lizzy."

"Ah . . ." He pulled back and stared deep into her eyes. "Angel, believe it or not, I love kids. So you can adopt as many children as you want, as long as I can make as many as I want . . ."

"Hey! I don't think so!" She smacked his upper arm then snuggled against him. "We complement each other very well, you know that? I never would have figured, given we're such total opposites, but—"

"We finish each other. You, Elisa—" He cupped her bottom and squeezed her ass firmly, drawing her against his hard cock. "You fill the empty spot in my soul. You make me who I should be, who I want to be."

"I can't believe I'm saying this, but you do the same for me."

"How?"

"You make me less serious. More fun. Bad."

"Oh, so now I have a bad girl?" His hand patted her ass in sensuous threat.

"Who just might need a spanking . . ."

He swept her lips into an embrace, kissing her deeply, passionately. His tongue danced with hers, tangling and tangoing, withdrawing and plunging.

Relaxing, she welcomed more of him, loving the way their mouths united.

Maxim broke away, resting his nose against hers. "I love you, Elisa Cox."

"I love you too, Maxim."

He kissed along her shoulder to her collarbone, his hands roaming over her bottom. In automatic reflex, her lower half thrust toward his hand, loving the intimate feeling of him touching her.

"Ah, Elisa," he murmured, answering her movement by gripping the fleshy cheeks. "You are the most delicious creature and—"

The ringing of the telephone blasted through the room.

"Damn it! I thought I took the phone off the hook!" Maxim's hands fell away. "Pleeeasse, don't answer it."

She chuckled and climbed over Maxim's inert body. Hopefully this was a call worth abandoning him.

"I have to answer." She sighed. Elisa hopped to her feet and crossed the room. "It might be my dad. Since he didn't make it to our quickie wedding, he said he'd call yesterday or today, but he hasn't yet. Now that I'm on his good side again, I'd like to stay that way. Anyway, he said he would make a large donation to Helen's Haven."

"Fine," Maxim groaned in exaggerated manner. "Ditch me for another man."

Rolling her eyes, Elisa picked up the phone. "Hello?"

"You're contagious," Lizzy blurted, her loud statement blasting across the line.

Her eardrum ringing, Elisa held the receiver away from her face. "What?"

"You gave me the love bug," Lizzy wailed. "Or, just the craving for fun sex. But either way . . ."

Elisa's jaw dropped to the floor. "Uh, double what?"

Lizzy in love? She'd hadn't heard anything this good since Maxim had told her that her ex had been finally arrested—for selling porn to minors. She hoped the slimeball rotted in jail.

"I'm sleeping with someone," Lizzy blurted. "A lot."

"That's fantastic!"

"Uh, not really, but do me a fave?"

"Anything!"

"Kick Maxim." Lizzy's voice hardened into steel. "If that bastard can turn good, it's got me thinking even the worst of the worst can. I'm terrified."

Elisa eyed her lover, who waited impatiently on the bed. "I don't know about kicking him. We were right in the middle of—"

"Okay. Ew."

"Call back later, and we'll chat."

"Can't." Lizzy sighed, acting as if the world were about to end. "I'll be on a date, but I'll call and let you know all the awful details. Bye!"

"Bye, sweetie, and have fun!"

Elisa hung up, unable to stop her laughter. Good thing it wasn't a blind date! Whoever Lizzy was seeing, he had to be tough. And weird.

"Lizzy?" Maxim raised a brow, hungry for details.

Elisa dropped back into bed, snuggling against him. "You know, I'm not the only one you're good for. Can you believe she's dating?"

"I've always had a way with women." He enveloped her in his arms, his hands sliding directly to her ass. "Wouldn't you say?"

"Just this woman, now."

"Just this woman, *forever*."

Printed in the United States
by Baker & Taylor Publisher Services